THE
HALO
CONSPIRACY

LUCAS NASH SERIES

MICHAEL MURPHY

The Halo Conspiracy is dedicated to my wife Jennie who passed away from the effects of Coronavirus, and to everyone whose lives have been impacted by this terrible pandemic.

1

Within minutes, Homicide Detective Lucas Nash realized the crime scene had it all: sex, booze, some sap face down in a pool of blood, and a homicide partner with a chip on his shoulder. If that wasn't enough, a robot flashing a red light wheeled around the room aimlessly, threatening to contaminate the evidence.

Lucas held up one hand. "Stop. Shut down. Will someone shut off this piece of garbage?"

His partner, Freddy Gannon, paused his interview with the homeowner, Maria Alvarez, a real looker, and shouted across the room. "Deactivate!"

The robot instantly shut down.

Lucas rubbed the back of his neck. He and technology weren't the best of friends.

Freddy laughed and turned back to his witness. She was dressed to the nines if the nines meant jeans, sneakers, and a gray Cal Bears sweatshirt. She'd applied just the right amount of makeup if she spent a night on the town.

Light danced off a flashy diamond on the third finger of her left hand. She grabbed a tissue, dabbed at a tear hanging on her bottom lid, and took a quick glance at Lucas.

The kitchen was as clean and tidy as a hospital cafeteria, cluttered only by a bottle of bourbon and an empty clear glass with melting ice. Near the back door lay the poor sap, a man in a military uniform. Unlike the woman's, the soldier's ring finger was bare, and there was no white showing to indicate he might have slipped off a wedding band earlier.

Lucas considered examining the body, but the dead soldier wasn't going anywhere. He headed down the hall instead.

In the hallway hung two pictures of Maria with her husband, definitely not the soldier with the bullet holes. The first was a church wedding photo, the second an image of them on a beach at sunset, Hawaii, perhaps. A third picture showed two dozen young children and the woman holding a handmade sign that read "Best Kindergarten Teacher Ever, 2038."

A neatly made queen-sized bed sat along the wall of the master bedroom. On the dresser, a scented candle gave off the soothing fragrance of vanilla. The wick felt warm when he touched it.

A drawer was slightly ajar. When he slid it open, a black lace negligee lay on top, the kind not made for sleeping.

The crime started to clear for Lucas. A neglected wife lit a candle before entertaining the soldier. Something interfered with her plans, but she had the presence of mind to snuff out the candle before the police arrived, hoping no one would notice. In the bathroom, he searched the medicine cabinet and vanity for dope. He didn't find any and hadn't expected to. This crime wasn't about drugs.

He returned to the kitchen and watched his friend questioning the woman who snuffed out the candle. Early in his career, Freddy perfected a different style than Lucas, more sociable and charming. Lucas preferred a straightforward interrogation.

Freddy turned his back to Lucas. He still had the chip. He'd yet to get over losing out on a senior detective promotion to Lucas a week earlier. They hadn't spoken or worked together since the official announcement.

This case might prove awkward. Perhaps that's why their boss,

Lieutenant Clark, assigned both of them, so they'd work through their differences on what appeared to be a love triangle murder.

Lucas took a better look at the deceased. Someone shot the man in the back. He never saw the killer.

In addition to the coppery smell of blood, Lucas detected the aroma of cheap cologne drifting off the body. He leaned nearer. Definitely, the blue stuff like they sell from vending machines in bar restrooms, the kind he used to splash on when he was young and lonely.

Without a medical examiner present, Lucas removed an examination kit from his Green River PD jacket. With an infrared thermometer, he took the man's temperature, 95.5. A chart suggested he'd been dead less than two hours.

He slipped on a pair of latex gloves, bent down, and examined the deceased's curly matted hair where a second bullet had entered the skull. The soldier appeared to be in his late thirties, healthy-looking and fit, except for the bullet holes. The shot to his back was dead center hitting his heart, the fatal blow. The second shot was insurance.

The killing seemed like the work of a pro, not an elementary school teacher, unless Maria Alvarez was more than she seemed. Everything else about what he observed told Lucas this was a routine case of infidelity gone wrong, but intuition crawled up the back of his neck like a spider.

With a thin paper strip, he swabbed the man's lip. Thirty seconds later, the swab revealed a blood alcohol content of 1.8, officially designating him plastered. Before placing the evidence in a sealed case, Lucas took a whiff and caught the scent of gin, not bourbon from the bottle on the counter. The gin came from somewhere else.

When Freddy came over, Lucas lifted the man's shoulder, revealing the collar on the uniform. Two silver bars. "A captain."

Inside the man's jacket was an old-fashioned leather wallet, a stylus, a couple of bills, and his Army ID. "Captain William Koenig."

Lucas touched the ID with the stylus and read the data that appeared. "Interesting; he works for the Pentagon. He's been in the military for fifteen years, single, no dependents, Protestant."

"Pentagon? Captain's a long way from home."

Lucas checked the rest of Koenig's pockets and discovered all were empty except for a small bottle of breath spray. "When I arrived, I thought this might involve a dead husband."

"Same here, but the captain's not married. The hot wife tells me her husband's been out of town lately."

Near a chair by the back door, red dots stained the wall about four feet off the ground. "Blood spatter."

"Right, Sherlock. Someone shot him in the back, and he fell forward. Blood spatter from the head like the killer placed the gun close to the skull and pulled the trigger."

"Sounds like an execution."

Lucas led Freddy to the foyer. What were they dealing with? He lowered his voice to keep the woman from hearing. "You think she's capable of executing someone?"

"A husband, maybe. I mean, what wife hasn't thought of killing her husband? You know that from personal experience, but ten will get you a Tubman, she picked this guy up tonight. Execution? Doubtful. I checked her hands, no residue."

Lucas agreed. "What's your take so far?"

His partner pointed toward the back door. "The door's unlocked. No signs of forcible entry there or any of the windows. No murder weapon here or outside."

"So, she's lying. She must be doing okay to own a robot—looks pricey."

Freddy wrinkled his brow. "It's 2039, my friend. Everyone has a 'bot these days."

"I don't. I have a dog."

Freddy chuckled like old times. "I'm sorry, Bulldog. I've been a jerk since your promotion. We've been friends for what ten years?"

"I guess."

Freddy gazed into the distance with a familiar smirk. "Eleven years next month. We met at a bar on Seventh Street. You took my breath away with a yellow silk shirt and gold cufflinks."

They'd been friends since high school, and Lucas never wore cufflinks. "Shut up."

"I must be thinking of someone else." Freddy burst out laughing.

Lucas joined in the laughter.

Guarding the foyer, Officer O'Rourke shook her head and looked away.

Freddy ignored O'Rourke's look of disapproval and glanced around to make sure no one was listening. "You'll be a superstar. Though, we both know the only reason Lieutenant Clark picked you was that you slept with her."

"That was a dozen years ago when we attended the academy together, and it only happened once—technically twice. She probably doesn't even remember."

"Don't sell yourself short, stud, no pun intended."

Lucas covered a smile with one hand.

Freddy punched him in the shoulder. "I'm just messin' with you. You deserved the promotion." He shook Lucas's hand. The chip was gone.

Freddy glanced at Maria Alvarez. "Why don't I save us some time? I'm guessing the captain and the schoolteacher met at a bar, and she took him home for a game of hide the pickle. I don't understand why Clark assigned both of us. Maria must be someone important."

"She teaches Kindergarten. Could be Captain Koenig is someone significant, or the husband. Who called it in?"

Freddy thumbed toward Maria. "She did."

"Where are the shell casings? You bag them?"

Freddy stuffed both hands in his pockets. "No, I didn't find any. The lady doesn't seem savvy enough to get rid of a murder weapon and the shell casings. Claims neither she nor her husband owns any weapons, no guns, I mean."

"What are you saying, spears, knives?"

Freddy nodded. "Her old man collects knives, but they're always locked. Did I tell you about the time I got so angry at my acupuncture doctor that I stabbed him? He said, thanks, I never felt better."

Lucas tried not to laugh. Laughter only encouraged his friend. "Be sure to put that in your report. Anyone canvas the neighborhood?"

"O'Rourke spoke to the neighbor across the street. He told her he heard two gunshots around nine. I thought after you showed up, I'd interview more. I'll bring an officer with me."

Lucas gestured toward O'Rourke reading her phone by the open front door. "Take her. She could use the experience."

Freddy bit his lower lip and gazed at the young officer. "O'Rourke and I...have a history." He sighed, "Okay, I'll take her. Why don't you take a crack at interviewing Maria? You were always better with dames than me, interrogation wise, that is."

"She's not a dame; she's a schoolteacher."

Freddy rolled his eyes. "Terrific! Now that you're technically my superior, I suppose you'll throw your weight around and make me take another sensitivity class?"

"Think it would do you any good?"

Freddy held both palms up. "Hey, I'm sensitive."

At the door, their boss, the chief of homicide, Lieutenant Sylvia Clark, came in looking like General Patton landing in Sicily. She summoned Lucas and Freddy with a wave.

The two detectives joined the lieutenant outside beneath the light from a police drone hovering overhead. Despite the time, half a dozen neighbors had gathered in the street, watching and recording the activity with their phones.

The impatient lieutenant folded her arms like a drill sergeant. "Who wants to go first?"

Lucas gestured to Freddy.

His friend cleared his throat. "Maria Alvarez is a twenty-seven-year-old schoolteacher, married, husband out of town on business. She claims she never met the deceased. Said she came home alone, went into the bathroom, and changed from her school clothes. Then the back door opened and frightened her. She grabbed her cell phone to summon the police when she heard a gunshot. Before she made the call, she peeked into the family room in time to see someone in black dash out the back door; short guy, slender, nothing distinctive. Then she noticed the body and screamed and called the cops."

"The dead man is an army captain assigned to the Pentagon," Lucas added. "The perpetrator shot him dead center in the back, then at the base of the skull."

"You find the murder weapon?" the lieutenant asked.

"Not yet." Freddy glanced at Lucas. "No shell casings either."

Clark wrinkled her brow. "So, your operational theory is this savvy schoolteacher gathered the casings and got rid of them and the gun before we showed up."

"I guess so." Freddy avoided the lieutenant's gaze.

The lieutenant sighed. "Is the suspect good-looking?"

Freddy snickered. "Let's put it this way. If I had a Kindergarten teacher that fine, I might not have made it to first grade."

Clark stared at the detective in disbelief. "I'm surprised you did. What about you, Lucas?"

"Lucas thinks she's *movie star* hot, Lieutenant," Freddy said with a smile, "but I told him it's against the rules to become involved with suspects or witnesses. And, unless it's relevant to the case, even noting a suspect's appearance is objectifying women. How he missed all that sensitivity 'til now, I'll never know."

The lieutenant clamped her eyes shut for a moment. Their boss didn't enjoy Freddy's humor. "Anything you'd like to add, Lucas?"

"I believe…we believe Maria Alvarez lied about not knowing the captain. She either picked him up at a bar or met up with him on a prearranged get together here. I plan to check the route from her school to home and see what bars she might have passed."

Freddy held up a hand like he was volunteering. "I'd be happy to hit a few bars on the way home."

Lucas stifled a laugh. "I have a hunch, however. I think Ms. Alvarez told the truth about someone else coming in the back door."

"You gotta be joking." Freddy rolled his eyes. "You think a killer trailed him here and assassinated a Pentagon officer? Didn't we see a movie like that a couple of months ago?"

The lieutenant rubbed her forehead. "Why do you think this is a sexual rendezvous?"

"She lit a candle in her bedroom," Lucas answered.

"I noticed that too. According to Ms. Alvarez, scented candles help her sleep." Freddy's cynicism came through loud and clear. "Who goes to bed with a candle burning? Are women that st… gullible?"

Lucas and Freddy both stared at the lieutenant.

She sneered. "I'm not a scented candle girl. O'Rourke, front and center!"

The young officer hurried to them. "Yes, Lieutenant."

"You ever light a candle to help you sleep?"

"To sleep? No, except when the electricity is out, I only light candles when…" O'Rourke's eyes widened in embarrassment, "…entertaining a gentleman." She glared at Freddy. "Let's say it's been a while since I lit a candle." With a quick turn, the young officer went back to guarding the open door.

The lieutenant grinned at Freddy. "Ouch. That burn must sting."

Her phone rang. Clark checked the number. "I better take this." She stepped away and listened.

Through the window, Lucas saw Maria rise from her chair. She grabbed the bottle of bourbon from the kitchen counter, returned to the table, and took a long swallow.

When she ended the call, the lieutenant rejoined them. "A busy night. I need one of you to go out to Dakota Industries and check on the unexpected death of their COO."

Lucas clapped Freddy's shoulder. "He should go. Dakota's high tech, robots and artificial intelligence mumbo jumbo. I know nothing about any of that."

The lieutenant smiled. "Makes sense, but this calls for a senior homicide detective. I don't need to remind you how important Dakota Industries is to this community, so don't use the phrase mumbo jumbo. I'll help Freddy finish up here."

"Oh, excellent." Freddy's voice dripped with sarcasm. "I'm looking forward to that."

"Same here. You drew the short straw, Nash. I'll send you what little I know. The chief of security, Calvin Hawk, will be expecting you. Oh, and handle this with tact and diplomacy. I don't want the captain in my office asking why my detective offended a company whose Christmas party he attends every year. And don't make me regret your promotion."

No pressure. "Thanks for the pep talk. I'll do my best."

2

Lucas sat outside Marie Alvarez's house, struggling to figure out how to work the autopilot mode on his new GM SUV Electric. After several unsuccessful attempts, he called up the owner's manual on his phone and typed in help. A few failed tries later, he managed to set the verbal command option and spoke to the car. "Activate autopilot."

"Autopilot activated," the car responded with a hint of sarcasm.

Lucas breathed a sigh of relief. "Destination Dakota Industries."

"Navigation engaged." Lucas didn't look forward to entering the world of high tech. With the car driving through the surrounding hills, he dictated his report on the Maria Alvarez case, then reviewed the information on Dakota Industries Lieutenant Clark sent him.

At the front gate, he showed his ID to a mushroom-shaped robot with two cameras for eyes and two extendable arms with human-like hands. The machine scanned his credentials, wished him a pleasant visit in a metal voice, and opened the gate.

Lucas had gotten the hang of verbal controls. "Park in back of the Google minivan."

The car followed the circular drive in front of the main building and pulled up behind the minivan parked alongside a medical examiner vehicle.

Lucas climbed from the car and the door shut behind him. He stuffed the phone in his jacket alongside his familiar Glock.

He'd taken two steps when the buzz from two drones appeared overhead, flashing blue lights. Two guards rushed from the shadows, brandishing automatic weapons. A cold chill swept over him.

One of the guards shouted, "You have a holstered handgun. Show us your hands."

The chill turned to anger, but Lucas managed to control his emotions and place both hands on his head. "I'm a police officer. A Green River homicide detective."

Calvin Hawk hurried down the steps, his face a mask of alarm. He yelled, "He's a detective. He's a detective!"

The two guards exchanged sneers of disapproval and lowered their rifles. The drones shut off their lights and sailed off.

Hawk waited for the guards to leave before leading Lucas up the front steps. "Sorry about that, Mr. Nash. Our entrance security 'bot could use some adjustment communicating with security, but the guards are on their toes."

"The guards seemed disappointed you wouldn't let them shoot me."

Hawk smiled.

As he straightened his jacket, Lucas got a better look at the security chief. An African American, Hawk was a granite-faced, broad-shouldered brute who didn't appear to care if everyone knew it.

"Call me Lucas." He hoped the friendly approach would result in a certain amount of cooperation, despite the top-secret organization.

Hawk led him to the front steps of the building.

Inside was a modern two-story lobby with marble tile and glass and chrome furniture with white chairs, as cold and inviting as a morgue. The place was empty except for two bored-looking medical attendants watching CNN.

"You should see this place during the day." Hawk walked him to the elevators, mentioning artificial intelligence, then began talking about platforms, data entry points, and mega learning, speaking in a language Lucas couldn't possibly follow.

They got out on the fourth floor. Hawk gazed into what Lucas assumed to be a retinal scanner beside a closed metal door. A second later, the door whooshed open to reveal a modern office of glass and chrome.

At the far end was an oval desk with a white-haired man in his sixties lying on the marble tile. Beside him was a friendly face, a familiar doctor from the medical examiner's office, Dr. Nico Lee. "I take it that's Dr. Beltran on the floor."

"That's him." Hawk handed him a plastic card. "I prepared some basic info about his health and personal habits."

Lucas missed paper. He scanned the card with his phone.

Beltran was sixty-eight, in questionable health, overweight, high blood pressure, prediabetes.

Hawk stared at the dead man. "I never saw him exercise. He worked twelve-hour days, six days a week."

Lucas smiled at Hawk. "On the seventh day, he rested."

Hawk tapped his ear and nodded.

Someone was listening.

The big man spoke as if reading a script. "An alarm sounded at 10:50 when video surveillance showed Dr. Beltran collapse and fall to the floor. I arrived at 10:51, and he was dead already."

"But the call didn't come in until after midnight."

"There was considerable discussion about the proper course of action. I thought they'd send a doctor to confirm what I suspected."

"What *do* you suspect?"

"Heart attack. I wouldn't have called at all if not for the threats."

"What kind of threats?"

"We always attract our share of anti-tech nuts, but lately, religious advocates have become more vocal."

"Do you maintain a list of people or organizations that made threats against Dr. Beltran?"

"I do, but I'm not cleared to release it."

So much for cooperation. "Why don't you tap your ear and get the list released? Excuse me."

Lucas crossed the room. "Good evening, Dr. Lee."

She smiled. "Congratulations on your promotion, Senior Detective Nash."

"Thanks." He met Niko Lee in college at Cal. Over the years, their relationship evolved. Now, they enjoyed working together and were friends outside of work that often brought them together.

As she examined the body, he admired her professionalism and work ethic as he had for years.

With an electronic bioanalyzer, Dr. Lee swept a narrow beam of light over Beltran while Lucas photographed and videoed his office, particularly his desk.

Dr. Lee finished her exam. "He's all yours. I don't think you'll be working too late. This appears to be a cardiovascular event, most likely a brain aneurysm or heart-related."

"Maybe his heart stopped beating. In the case I left an hour ago, the deceased's heart stopped suddenly...after a bullet tore through it." Lucas smiled.

Lucas photographed the body from various angles. Beltran wore khaki trousers and a blue golf shirt with a gold Dakota logo. If the cause of death was a murder, then this death was far different from the one earlier, no blood or bullet wounds, no sex. If someone murdered Beltran, they would have used poison or another external factor administered under the direct view of a video.

In the man's shirt pocket, Lucas discovered a vial of small pills. The label said Nitro. The medication proved Beltran had a heart problem. He handed the vial to the medical examiner. She didn't act surprised.

A small yellow square caught Lucas's eye beside the chair. He picked up the slip of paper and read a name.

Dr. Lee peered over his shoulder. "What's that?"

"It's been a while, but I think it's something people used to call paper."

The doctor laughed. "Does that say Rachel?"

"I think so. Beltran sure lacked penmanship skills." Lucas approached Hawk and showed him the paper. "Who's Rachel?"

A moment of hesitation flickered across Hawk's face. For the first time since Lucas arrived, the big man didn't look in total control. "Dr. Beltran's intern."

An intern often knew as much about a person as a wife, sometimes more. "I need to talk to her."

"I'll see if she's available."

"Oh, and I'll need a few other things: Dr. Beltran's calendar for the day, his personnel file, Rachel's file, any video…"

Hawk stopped him. "Those items are classified."

"Classified. Who are you, the CIA?"

"Many of the government contracts require we adhere to strict classification procedures."

Enough resistance already. He pointed a finger at Hawk. "Listen…" Lieutenant Clark's admonition of Dakota's importance to the community came back to him. "I'm just trying to do my job."

"So am I, Detective." Hawk turned and left the office.

Lucas thought back to the material about Dakota he reviewed on the way over. Dr. Beltran, Calvin Hawk, and Melody Fleming were the three individuals at the top of the company food chain. From the way Hawk acted, with Beltran gone, Melody made the final decisions.

Dr. Lee tugged on his arm. She led him to the window and lowered her voice. "You get the impression someone's watching?"

Definitely. "I thought I was being paranoid."

She made a call, and, a minute later, a guard showed up along with two medical assistants with a gurney and a body bag. They wrestled Beltran into the bag and lifted him on the gurney.

Dr. Lee followed them to the door.

After they left, Hawk reentered the room. "I may have more information for you in the morning."

"I look forward to that."

Hawk glared at Lucas. "Anything else, Detective?"

"Maybe you can clarify your COO's personal life. Does he have a family?"

Hawk held out both arms. "Dakota was his life. His co-workers were family."

"My point is, who's going to shed tears over his death?"

Hawk shrugged. "Dr. Beltran will be missed by everyone who works at Dakota Industries as well as people around the world. Under his guidance, this company achieved greatness. He didn't merely lead us to momentous scientific breakthroughs, but he made sure whatever endeavor we undertook was best for humanity." He sounded like he was prepping to give a eulogy.

Lucas gazed around the office for personal items that might reveal Beltran's personality. "What did he like to do for kicks? Where did he go on vacation?"

"Kicks? He considered work fun."

"Seriously? Anyone who considers work fun should spend a shift with me."

"Don't laugh; enjoyment is in the mind of the beholder. Working for Dakota Industries is an honor and a privilege. We're a leader in the world and are on the verge of a major..." He touched his ear again. "We're always looking to meet the needs of the nation and the world."

He almost said they were about to make a major discovery.

Hawk gestured toward the door. "May I show you out?"

They rode the elevator to the lobby in silence. The door opened, and Lucas shook Hawk's hand. "I'm glad you called us. Unexpected deaths need to be investigated, especially when the death involves such a prominent member of the community."

"Let's hope our COO died of natural causes. That would be easier for both of us."

When Lucas stepped outside, the medical examiner van pulled away from the curb and sped off.

Dr. Lee reached her minivan.

Lucas hurried after her. "Wait up!"

She sighed. "Do you know what time it is?"

"What couldn't you say in there?"

She lowered her voice. "I'm not so confident that Dr. Beltran died of natural causes. Call me tomorrow for my preliminary findings." She climbed into the van and started the car. "But not too early."

Lucas sat inside his car. "Navigation."

"State destination."

With his phone linked to the dashboard monitor, he checked the address of Beltran's home. A map with the most direct route popped onto the screen. Lucas's uneventful day had turned into a long night and wasn't going to end soon.

If Beltran's death had resulted from natural causes like an aneurysm, stroke, or heart attack, he'd go home and catch a decent night's sleep. If he went home now, with everything he learned, he'd never sleep.

Lucas spoke the address and started his SUV. "Engage auto-pilot."

With the destination showing on the dashboard map, the car drove Lucas five miles through a murky, twisting two-lane road. The headlights illuminated the woods so dark it was like riding through a tunnel. His car paused, then turned onto a gravel road as fog began to descend on the surrounding area.

Fighting off fatigue, Lucas gripped the steering wheel and took over manual control of the vehicle, slowing the car. The tires crunched the gravel for a minute until he came to a hill. He gazed down at manicured grounds with illuminated halogen lights along an eight-foot wrought iron fence with a massive gate.

He stopped beside a keypad that required a code, which he didn't know. He didn't want to try for fear of triggering an alarm.

Lucas glanced in the rearview mirror and backed the car up. He drove across a thick layer of pine needles and small branches that snapped beneath the tires. He parked behind a thicket of brush that prevented the vehicle from being spotted from the road or the house and shut off the electric motor.

He reached into his glove compartment and found his night vision glasses. Lucas stuffed them into his jacket. He climbed from the car and breathed in the clean smell of pine trees that rustled in the wind. He peered through the fence toward the house below. Lights mounted to the fence illuminated the grounds every thirty yards.

The immense two-story block structure resembled an old-fashioned shopping mall more than a home, surprising for a man without a family.

The fence kept him from getting in. At least he'd yet to see drones, robots, dogs, or guards with automatic weapons appear, resembling the two jerks he encountered at Dakota.

Lucas walked softly along the perimeter, avoiding stepping on downed tree branches as he made his way along the fence, looking for a way over. This might be his best opportunity to slip inside and discover more about Dr. Beltran and the secretive Dakota organization.

Halfway around the perimeter, he gave up and retraced his steps. When he returned to the car, he took a step toward the gate, then froze when the rumble of an approaching vehicle came from the road he'd taken.

Lucas ducked behind a tree as the twenty-four-foot moving van, with no markings on the sides, pulled up to the keypad. He couldn't make out the driver or the numbers he entered, but Lucas came out of hiding as the gate swung open. The truck eased inside the property, and the gate began to swing closed.

Lucas sprinted toward the opening. With his lungs burning, he made it inside, skidding across the gravel drive as the gate clanged shut.

Hands on hips, Lucas sucked in gulps of cold air as the truck rattled toward the residence. In a crouch, he trailed after them down the winding drive. He stopped at the edge of a clearing surrounding the house as the garage door opened and the truck backed up to the open garage.

When the driver jumped out, Lucas recognized Calvin Hawk. Two other men in black exited from the passenger side; both wore holstered handguns, the same two slugs who had confronted him when he arrived at Dakota Industries. Hawk grabbed the handle of the truck's rear door. It rumbled open, and all three hopped inside the truck bed.

Lucas grabbed a pair of sound amplifiers from his jacket pocket. He slipped them in his ears and strained to hear whether Hawk and his team came to pick up or deliver. Even with the amplifiers, he couldn't hear their voices from inside the truck. A minute later, the three men climbed down and entered the house through the garage door. The halogen lights on the fence dimmed.

He slipped on his night-vision goggles and adjusted to the green glow through the lenses. For now, he'd lost the chance to find out what Dr. Beltran kept inside his home. He might learn something important from watching Hawk and his team. He'd certainly hang around long enough to determine what they were dropping off or picking up.

Lucas jumped when he felt a tap on his shoulder. He scrambled to his feet and yanked off his night-vision goggles. He pulled the sound amplifiers from his ears.

As his eyes adjusted to the dim light, Lucas faced a young woman in a navy-blue jumpsuit. She wore a Cal baseball cap and clutched a yellow duffel bag to her chest.

With only the glow of the moon and the dim lights, he could barely make out the woman's facial features.

She glanced at the house and spoke in a soft voice. "Who are you, and what are you doing here?"

He showed her his badge. "Detective Lucas Nash."

"Pleased to meet you, I think." The woman removed her cap. As if in slow motion, her blonde hair bounced to her shoulders and shimmered in the moonlight. "My name's Rachel."

3

Rachel gestured toward the tree line. "Is that your blue SUV behind the bushes?"

She had vision like an owl, and her soft green eyes weren't bad either. "Oh, now I remember where I left my car. You ought to see how often that happens in a parking lot."

Rachel cracked a smile. "Is that what folks used to call snarky?"

"I guess. What are you doing sneaking around at this time of night?"

"Waiting for Dr. Beltran. He told me to meet him here." Her eyes remained on the truck and the open garage door. "Before I made it inside, Hawk and his goons, Tom and Jerry pulled up."

"Tom and Jerry? Are those their real names?"

Rachel laughed. "No, silly. I call them that because they're cartoonish idiots." She cocked her head. "Why are *you* here?"

Lucas sighed. Breaking grim news to family and friends was the worst part of his job. "I'm sorry to tell you, but Dr. Beltran's dead."

To his surprise, she showed little emotion. "They killed him. You must be a homicide detective."

The girl was bright and intuitive. "What's in the truck?" he asked.

Before she answered, the three men returned to the garage. Hawk gestured toward the open rear of the truck; then he slipped on a pair of night vision glasses like the ones Lucas had on and pulled a handgun from his holster. He waved to the men, who grabbed automatic rifles from inside the van.

Lucas touched the Glock inside his jacket. Putting his life on the line was something he accepted years earlier, but he didn't like being outgunned. "Let's go."

Rachel crouched down and grabbed her bag. They both ran toward the locked gate. Lucas was upset he wouldn't find out why Hawk and his men brought a moving van to the house of a man who'd just died. "What are they doing here at 3 a.m.?"

"Isn't it obvious?" At the gate, Rachel stepped beside an infrared sensor Lucas hadn't noticed. She broke an invisible beam with a sensor on the other side of the gravel drive. The gate swung open. "They're removing evidence that might help you investigate Dr. Beltran's murder."

"What would they be taking?"

"How should I know? I've never been inside his house before."

Lucas wasn't convinced Rachel was telling the truth, but they had to trust each other for the moment. "You think Dr. Beltran was murdered?"

"Don't you?"

They stepped outside the perimeter, and the gate swung closed.

She glanced toward the brush. "We need to reach your car. We should assume they spotted us. That buzz is a drone."

Lucas didn't hear a buzz until they reached the car.

When the drone appeared, Rachel grabbed his hand and pulled him past the car to the cover of a thick pine tree. As Lucas backed against the tree trunk, Rachel pressed against him while the drone hovered over the car.

Rachel's body was plastered against his, uncomfortably close. He enjoyed her soft, warm body against him. Her hair smelled like a bouquet of wildflowers. Moonlight revealed just how innocent-looking she was.

She appeared as uneasy as he felt about their proximity. When the drone moved off, she pulled herself away from him and set her hat on her head. "I don't think the drone ID'd us, but I'm sure the camera took some closeup video of your car. "We better leave now."

Lucas yanked open the door, and Rachel jumped into the passenger seat and tossed her bag in the back. He hurried around the SUV and climbed into the driver's seat.

He started the car, shut off the headlights, and eased the car over the pine needles on the forest floor.

Rachel's calm surprised him. With perfect teeth and flawless skin, she looked even prettier than her file picture.

Lucas reminded himself that Rachel worked closely with the deceased. He hoped she'd be more forthcoming than Calvin Hawk, but to learn anything, he had to know more about her. "What's your full name, Rachel?"

"Rachel T. Intern."

"What?"

"Middle name is The, last name is Intern." She flashed a playful smile. "From the day I started at Dakota, everyone called me Rachel the Intern. One day at a meeting, I signed in as Rachel T. Intern. Everyone laughed."

Even in the face of danger, the young woman displayed a delicious sense of humor.

They reached the gravel road, and he engaged the driverless option. "Okay, GM, Home." He let go of the wheel and let the car drive.

Rachel thumbed toward the gate as they sped off. "How'd you make it in? Dr. Beltran only shared the gate code with a handful of people."

"I'm resourceful."

"I'll have to remember that." Rachel gazed out the passenger window. "No sign of drones."

Hawk didn't appear to Lucas like someone who would give up without a struggle. He adjusted the autopilot. "Headlights and maximum terrain speed."

Rachel glanced around the interior of the car. "You realize the artificial intelligence in this model was developed and produced by Dakota Industries?"

Lucas had never considered that his car had artificial intelligence. In the past decade, AI had become part of everyday life. Everyone accepted modern automation without questioning the ethics or morality behind the innovations.

As they zipped away, Lucas knew his primary goal was Rachel's safety. She was damned important to his investigation. In minutes, he'd seen how bright and quick-witted she was. However, if he wanted to uncover anything useful, he needed to understand the young intern, starting with finding out about her relationship with Dr. Beltran.

The car squealed tires around bends in the road, but she remained calm. She appeared to study the scenery in the darkness like she'd never see the Green River area before. "You from around here?"

"You might say that."

Every answer sounded cryptic. He wouldn't discover anything if he questioned her like a typical witness. She was too smart for that. He needed her to trust him. He glanced at the duffel bag in the back seat. "What're you carrying around?"

She flashed a wistful smile. "All my worldly possessions."

"How did you travel from Dakota to Dr. Beltran's house?"

"I walked. The hardest part was escaping Dakota."

She walked five miles at this hour? Had she fled a crime scene? "Escaping?"

"Living at Dakota sometimes feels…sometimes was like being in prison. Your every move is monitored by Calvin Hawk and his security team."

"Why live there?"

"Dakota requires employees to live on campus for most jobs."

"What did you do before Dakota Industries?"

"My intern position is the first job I ever had. Since I had no practical experience, I accepted an intern position to get my foot in the door, as they say." She peered out the back window.

Seeing Rachel's unease, Lucas kept his eyes peeled for signs of a drone. With the glow from city lights now peeking above the trees, he grabbed the steering wheel again and took over driving.

Perhaps they'd gotten away, or maybe Hawk had ID'd Lucas's SUV and decided following a cop wasn't a smart move for Dakota's security team.

She watched him drive. "Why did you take over navigation of the car?"

He flexed his fingers on the steering wheel. "Sometimes, it's best to be in charge."

"Machines are more efficient."

Lucas chuckled. "Remind me to tell you the story of John Henry, the steel drivin' man."

"Never heard of him. A friend of yours?"

Lucas laughed.

She ran a hand over the dashboard panel. "Can we listen to music?"

"Be my guest."

"Are you serious?" Rachel's eyes lit up. "Okay, GM, play Taylor Swift."

The radio came on, and Taylor Swift was singing a new hip hop song about an old boyfriend.

Rachel tapped her finger to the music. "I like her country music better than pop."

"The old stuff." Lucas was pleased to see Rachel relax and open up. "Why did you think someone murdered Dr. Beltran?"

She answered with a stare. "What's *your* favorite kind of music?"

Lucas liked all genres of music, but especially oldies rock.

"Classic Rock, Bob Seger, Bruce Springsteen. I bet you never heard of them."

"Of course, I have. One of my favorites is Seger's *Old Time Rock 'n Roll*."

Rachel continued to surprise him.

She turned and glanced at the receding road. "A man in Dr. Beltran's position has many enemies, both in the government and business rivals. Plenty of people inside the company didn't like the direction he steered the company. He's been getting threats from the outside in the past month or so."

"From religious groups?"

"Who told you that, Hawk? He'll only tell you what he's been told to say."

"By Melody Fleming?"

"That's who he reports to." She folded her arms like she realized she might have said too much. They rode in silence. When they reached the edge of the city, a liquor store, she uncrossed her arms. "Tonight, Dr. Beltran told me his life was in danger. I didn't believe him."

He still hadn't found out about Rachel's relationship with the doctor. How could he bring that up without being blunt? "What did interning for Dr. Beltran entail?"

She appeared to search her memory, or perhaps she struggled with how much to share with a homicide detective. "If you're asking about our relationship, you should come right out and ask. Dr. Beltran was many things to me, okay, boss, mentor, friend."

Time to take a chance. "Lover?"

Rachel snickered and then giggled. "I worked *with* Dr. Beltran. He was courteous and polite and treated me like the daughter he never had."

She appeared to study his face as if reading Lucas's mind. She pointed to her chest. "You think I killed him? I didn't! I couldn't! Oh, God."

She tapped the manual control and shut off the radio. She began to rock in the seat.

He waited for her to calm down. "Who then?"

"I'm not sure." She crossed her arms again.

"What direction was Dr. Beltran leading the company that caused so much trouble?"

Rachel stared straight ahead in silence like she was through talking. "I don't think I can tell you. That information is classified above top secret."

"If I'm going to find out who killed Dr. Beltran, I'll need your assistance. You want to help bring his killer to justice, don't you?"

"Of course, I do!"

She seemed to be weighing her alternatives. "I'm conflicted. Helping you is the ethical thing to do, but sometimes ethics collide with responsibility. Dr. Beltran taught me what happens inside Dakota stays inside Dakota."

He smiled. "I thought that was Las Vegas."

"What?"

"Never mind. So, what are your plans? You can't go back to Dakota, can you?"

"Not unless I want to end up like Dr. Beltran. I'll take a bus somewhere. Start a new life."

"Do you have money?"

"A little cash. I have an account, but I'm certain they'll put a hold on it."

"I doubt it. They want you to make withdrawals so they can track your location."

Cash had almost disappeared from circulation. Like most people, Lucas's financial transactions were almost completely digital. He only used cash for emergencies like tipping pizza deliveries. "I always stash a few bills in the glove compartment, not a lot, but you're welcome to them."

"Thanks, but I have enough to pay for a bus ticket."

He reached into the glove compartment, grabbed the money, and handed her a hundred bucks. "You'll need to eat."

She stuffed the cash into her pocket. "You're a kind and pleasant person."

"My ex-wife would disagree with you." Lucas grinned.

"I think the bus station is coming up soon. You should let the AI map the terminal route for you."

"I'm a cop. I've been to the bus station more than a few times." Lucas grinned. "What did you and Dr. Beltran discuss in his office earlier?"

"He told me to pack up, leave, and get away."

"Was he suggesting your life was in danger?"

"I didn't think so at the time, but now…I think so. I thought he was suggesting Dakota had slipped from his control, and I should go on my own and experience life like we sometimes talked about."

Lucas turned the corner. The bus station was a block away. "Are you sure you want me to drop you off at the bus terminal?"

Despair swept across Rachel's face. "You've done enough. I think you saved my life back there."

Lucas pulled up beside the Green River Bus Station and parked the car. "Where will you go?"

Rachel managed a smile. "People say Mexico is magnificent." She grabbed her bag from the back seat. "Thanks for the lift, and best of luck with your investigation."

She gave him a quick peck on the cheek. "I'm going to miss you, Lucas Nash." She got out, and the door closed as she headed for the terminal.

Lucas touched the side of his face where she'd kissed him. He climbed from the car and hurried after her. "Rachel." He stopped her with a touch on the arm. "The bus station is the first place I'd search if I wanted to find you."

She glanced at the busy entrance. Her plan didn't seem so definite after all. "I could hitchhike. That would be a fun way to meet people."

"Oh, come on, fun? Are you nuts?" On a bench beside the front door, a man with a thick beard and old clothes that probably hadn't been changed in several days appeared to listen to their every word.

Rachel cocked her head. "Nuts?"

Rachel wouldn't last long on the road. She was cute and naive, a modern-day Gidget, the Sandra Dee version. "Hitchhiking can be dangerous for someone as young and pretty as you are."

"You think I'm pretty? No one's ever called me that."

Once again, her naivety startled Lucas. Most women her age were aware of their looks and knew how to use their charm to their advantage.

She flipped her blonde hair like a movie star. "I don't understand why one's appearance plays a role in being in danger."

He glanced at the man on the bench. "Trust me; it does."

She laughed. "Oh, I forgot. You're a detective."

Hoping to scare him off, Lucas took a menacing step toward the man and flashed him his badge.

The man got up and disappeared inside the terminal.

Lucas led her by her arm toward his SUV. "Let's beat it. You don't have to decide now."

They drove off and came to a stop at a traffic light. A city patrol drone hovered over the intersection.

Rachel tugged the cap low over her face. When the light turned green, the car eased through the intersection, and she glanced up.

Lucas cleared his throat. He wasn't sure if helping the girl he just met was the right course of action. "There's a hotel down the street from me. I could pay for a room for you, or…"

"Or what?"

"I have a guest room." He drove toward his neighborhood. "The hotel's not much, but the rooms are clean, and the staff is well-mannered."

"You've stayed there?"

"A few times." The first was after his wife packed his things and changed the locks, and a couple of times since.

When they reached the hotel, Rachel squeezed his hand. "If the offer still stands, I'll stay with you."

4

Lucas turned into his driveway. The garage door opened, and he parked inside.

The car informed them, "You have reached your destination."

His wife's outdated sports equipment, old furniture, and empty cans of oil cluttered the garage.

Rachel carried her duffel bag toward the door leading to the house.

The door unlocked as Lucas approached it. "I hope you like dogs."

"I love pets."

In the laundry room off the kitchen, Lucas tossed his jacket on the washing machine. He held out his hand. "Would you like me to carry your bag? It looks heavy."

She gripped it like a marine clutching his rifle. "I can do this myself, thank you."

Lucas opened the kitchen door.

Beau barked at Rachel and backed up, surprising Lucas. He always took to strangers.

"Behave, Beau. This is Rachel." His dog liked everyone, and the young woman didn't appear threatening.

She held out the back of her hand and spoke in a soothing tone. "Hello, boy."

The White Collie rescued from a genetic lab stepped forward and sniffed the tips of her fingers. Slowly, the dog's tail began to wag. He gazed at Rachel and bounded down the hallway. He returned and dropped a tennis ball at her feet.

"You're a beautiful boy." She picked up the ball. "Want to fetch?"

Beau answered with a bark and raked the air with one paw.

Lucas was tired, but Beau had been home alone all day and deserved attention and playtime. "Whenever I arrive home, Beau expects either a play session out back or a w-a-l-k."

Outside, Rachel bounced the ball across the lawn.

Beau took off in hot pursuit. The game was afoot.

With a sigh, Lucas dropped onto a wooden deck swing while Rachel played with Beau. A half-hour earlier, she fled for her life; now, she was frolicking with a dog she just met.

He found himself caring for the young woman and knew he shouldn't. He couldn't let feelings interfere with the primary reason he'd invited her to stay the night, to move along his investigation into Beltran's death.

Lucas enjoyed the backyard, having a dog, and living in his modest house in a middle-income neighborhood. During the divorce five years ago, he gave up most of the cash and investments he and his wife had accumulated. He retained the house and Beau.

Before he turned in, he had to send a report to Lieutenant Clark. Most detectives would wait until morning, but Lucas wanted to record his observations while his thoughts were still fresh.

When Beau tired of fetch, Rachel sat beside Lucas. "You look like you could use some sleep."

"So do you. Let me show you the guest room."

The guest room was beside the kitchen next to a small bathroom.

On the wall in between hung a framed caricature of a bulldog. Rachel smiled at the picture. "Why do you have a drawing of a bulldog on your wall?"

"Friends on the force gave me this as a gift on my tenth anniversary. Some people consider me a bulldog."

"Because you're tough and aggressive?"

"Some consider me tenacious."

Lucas didn't like talking about himself. "Do you have a toothbrush?"

"I think I left it behind. I was in a hurry."

"I have an extra one." In the bathroom, he grabbed an unopened pink toothbrush. He glanced at the mirror and ran a hand over the stubble on his chin. His blue eyes were bloodshot, his sandy brown hair, with a few strands of gray, unkempt. He couldn't do anything about the bent nose broken in a barroom brawl his first year on the force.

In contrast, Rachel looked even better than her file photo. She took the toothbrush and entered the guestroom.

With one hand on the door, she faced him. "I don't know how to thank you for your kindness."

For a moment, the words hung in the air.

He cleared his throat. "I may be at work when you wake up. I hope you'll hang out with Beau until I come home."

She flashed a coy smile and closed the door with a slow tease. "Goodnight, Bulldog."

He should have dropped Rachel off at the hotel.

When Lucas turned around, Beau sat staring at him, sweeping the floor with his tail. "What are you looking at?"

The White Collie stood in front of his water bowl and drank, then waited in front of Rachel's door.

Lucas whistled, and Beau followed him to the master bedroom. The dog curled up on a blanket in the corner.

The clock on the nightstand read 3:09. His unmade bed looked inviting, but he wasn't one to put off work. He sat on a soft leather chair next to the bed and forced himself to reflect on the death of Dakota's COO.

Perhaps he'd died from overwork. The man had no family, few close friends, and no apparent interests outside his work.

Lucas had a sense about unexpected deaths, and his instincts told him Beltran's passing was murder. Several items led to his suspicions. Melody Fleming wasn't making herself available, and her chief of security, Calvin Hawk, had been less than helpful.

Driving a moving van with heavily armed goons in the middle of the night was more than a little odd. Hawk was covering up something, and Lucas was determined to find out what it was.

Then there was Rachel. He'd yet to get a read on the young woman. What role did she play in the company? Why did she live at the facility, and how did she evade security and make it to Dr. Beltran's house?

Lucas dictated his report of the Dakota investigation on his phone. He mentioned the need to follow up with Rachel but failed to mention she was staying in his guest room.

When he finished, the detective sent the report to Lieutenant Clark and saved the original to his computer.

"Lights off." The room darkened. Lucas settled into his pillow and closed his eyes. As was the custom, Beau waited until he thought Lucas was asleep. The dog jumped beside him and curled up at the foot of the bed before they both fell asleep.

A hot shower and shave made Lucas feel almost normal the next morning. The house was quiet, and the door to the guest room remained closed. After he fed Beau, he gave him fresh water and let the dog stay in the backyard and investigate the smells of morning.

With a quick glance at the closed guest room door, Lucas ran a hand over his chin. What had he been thinking, inviting a murder witness to spend the night in his house, and a damn attractive single one, at that? He should have paid for a hotel room and questioned her over breakfast.

Last night, it made sense to invite her to his house. In the light of morning, however, he realized he made a serious mistake, personal as well as professional. Freddy might approve, but Lieutenant Clark would shout and curse.

A clanging noise came from the garage, and Lucas went in to investigate.

In jeans and a blue T-shirt, Rachel was standing in front of the electrical charger with the panel open, holding a screwdriver. She wiped her brow with the back of her hand. "Whoever installed the electrical converter didn't calibrate the coil right when they installed the panel."

She tightened a screw, touched several buttons on the display, and closed the panel door. "There. You should achieve ten percent more charging efficiency, which will save you money on your electric bill."

"Thanks. How do you know how to do this?"

"I work for a tech company, remember?"

"My wife always assumed I was as mechanical as her father. I'm about as handy as a blind plumber."

"Is that why you got divorced?"

Lucas laughed. "It's on her list of grievances."

She handed him a round metallic device with a layer of dust and grease on the top. "I found a tracker on your vehicle."

"Damn!" He studied the device in his hand. "Someone at Dakota probably planted this on my car last night."

She pointed out the layer of dust. "Look like it's been there longer than a few hours. Someone else is interested in keeping tabs on your whereabouts."

He closed his eyes for a moment. Who would want to do that to a homicide detective? "You'd better put it back, so whoever is tracking me won't know we discovered it."

"That's logical." She took the device from his hand, squatted beside the passenger door, and slipped it beneath the car with a metallic click. She rose and wiped her hands with a clean blue paper towel.

He followed her inside to the wall next to his bedroom. Rachel pointed to a panel below the air conditioning air return. "I adjusted the filter modulator. It will definitely make the air cleaner. Last night, it didn't sound right to me."

While she explained her handiwork, he paid little attention to the details as he tried to figure out who might want to track his whereabouts. Perhaps the enemy was someone on the police force who didn't trust him.

An alarm beeped on Lucas's watch. "I need to leave. Feel free to fix anything while I'm at work."

"You're leaving for work?"

"I'm a homicide detective. Business is booming. I opened two new cases yesterday." He patted Beau on his head and handed Rachel a business card. "Call if you run into trouble. You'll be here when I return, right?"

"I promise."

"I'll bring dinner. What's your preference, Asian, Mexican, Italian?"

"I'm a vegetarian."

"Italian it is."

After Lucas left, Rachel headed for the master bedroom. Before dawn, she'd laid in the guest bed, considering her options. She got up, intending to leave before Lucas awakened, but she noticed a few items she knew how to fix.

She considered leaving, but she wanted to learn as much as possible about Lucas.

In the few hours they'd spent together, she'd formed a distinct impression. In addition to his good looks, he was a kind, empathetic man who loved his work and his dog.

As she stepped into the bedroom, her desire to learn more about Lucas overcame any guilt she felt about invading the man's privacy.

Beau pranced into the room and sat watching her. She smiled at him. "Don't judge me."

By her standards, the room was a mess, but he was a single man in his mid-thirties who answered only to himself. She ran a hand over the mahogany dresser, where a picture of two people in their mid-fifties sat in a frame. The woman wore a sundress and the man a police uniform with the Golden Gate Bridge behind them. They both had Lucas's dark hair and fair complexion. They had to be his parents.

She picked up a gray pullover sweater from a chair in the corner. She pressed the material against her face, enjoying Lucas's masculine smell. She set the sweater back the way she found it.

An old-fashioned television sat in the middle of the dresser alongside a media library tablet.

She powered up the device and discovered a list of movies Lucas had collected as well as more than three dozen digital books. She'd seen most of the movies except for *Casablanca, Gone with the Wind,* and *Psycho.* Her favorite was the rather strange sci-fi movie, *2001: A Space Odyssey.*

The books were a mixture of fiction and non-fiction. To her surprise, he had three by Isaac Asimov. She shut off the device, set it back where she found it and entered the master bathroom.

Rachel opened the medicine cabinet. No prescription drugs, just a few bottles of over the counter allergy pills.

At the sink, she opened a bottle of men's aftershave and took a whiff. She liked the outdoorsy aroma.

In a drawer beside the sink were a half dozen unopened toothbrushes in various colors. The evidence suggested she wasn't his first overnight guest who hadn't brought a toothbrush.

Rachel didn't find any signs of women's personal items or clothing, which might suggest Lucas didn't have a particular overnight companion. To her surprise, that pleased her in a way she didn't quite understand. She'd only just met the man.

Beau followed her to the family room. She searched through cabinets, and she found a dusty device labeled photo album. She tapped on the screen, and a black and white photo of a young Lucas appeared.

Rachel sat at the kitchen table and flipped through at least a hundred photos of Lucas and his family, but none were wedding photos. Maybe they were too painful to keep.

After returning the album to the cabinet, she understood the homicide detective better than when Lucas left for work.

She opened the refrigerator and grabbed a pitcher of lemonade. She poured herself a tall glass. As she sipped the soothing drink, she gazed out the kitchen window.

Next door, a neighbor in a straw hat knelt beside a rose garden. He was digging in the dirt and pulling weeds next to a rose bush with two wilted red flowers. The old man paused and wiped the sweat from his brow. He had to be hot, tired, and thirsty.

She gulped the rest of her drink, put ice in a fresh glass, and filled it with lemonade. She took the leash off a hook in the kitchen, and Beau came running.

She grabbed the glass of lemonade. "Come on, Beau."

Outside, she led the dog toward the sidewalk.

The old man tossed a handful of weeds on the drive and glanced at Rachel without speaking.

She stopped and smiled. "Hello."

He gave her the once over. "Morning."

"I'm taking Lucas's dog for a walk." She held out the glass of lemonade to him. "I brought you lemonade."

"Why would you do that?"

The curt response surprised Rachel. She set the glass in the shade beside him. "Well, in case you change your mind."

The old man pointed toward Lucas's house with a thorny twig. "I haven't seen you before. You must be a new...friend."

"I am. We met last night."

He snickered. "Figures. I might say you're prettier than most and a bit younger."

"Most? Does Lucas have a lot of female overnight guests?"

The old man yanked a weed growing beside a rose bush. "Not for me to say."

"What about you? Are you and Lucas friends?"

"Not anymore." He reached for the glass and took a long swallow. "Thanks, that was mighty kind of you, and I apologize. I was a bit rude."

"My pleasure, Mr...."

"Bernardi."

"I'm Rachel."

Beau tugged on the leash. "See you later." She hurried after the dog.

Rachel returned home and grabbed the media library from Lucas's room. She sat in a chair in the living room, facing the wall monitor. Beau curled up beside her. She stroked the dog.

Life would be so different with Lucas. She relaxed for the first time in months. She opened the media library and cast *Gone with the Wind* to the monitor. An hour later, she had a new role model, Scarlett O'Hara.

She gazed around the room. The modest home was so different from her dormitory. Life with Lucas Nash would be far different from the lies, deceit, conspiracies, and fear that dominated her existence with Project Halo. "Well, fiddle dee dee."

5

On the way to his office, Lucas thought about the ease in which Rachel had settled into his house and tinkered with technological devices he knew little about other than the benefits they provided. It was almost like she felt part of the family. Since his divorce, he valued his independence, and his "girl wants a commitment" radar flashed red.

He couldn't deny Rachel was intelligent, resourceful, and attractive, yet surprisingly naive. Lucas's feelings for the young woman were unclear. He felt protective, sure. She was a witness in a case, but his feelings went beyond protectiveness or sympathy.

Inside, cops struggled with loud and aggressive suspects being brought into the crowded lobby.

Lucas waved to a harried-looking desk sergeant, feeling sorry for the hard-working occasional drinking buddy, and headed for the elevator. Before he made it, the door opened, and Freddy Gannon came out, flashing a friendly smile.

"Lucas, old pal." Freddy checked to make sure no one was paying attention. "The lieutenant is waiting for you in the gym, and she's not thrilled you haven't updated her on the Dakota Industries case."

"When is she happy? What about you? You arrest Maria Alvarez?"

His partner gestured toward a hulk of a man sitting alone in the corner. He was focused on his phone and appeared more than a little impatient. "Maria's husband."

He looked like a rough guy who wouldn't hesitate to put a woman like Maria in her place. "Any priors?"

Freddy nodded. "He got in trouble as a juvenile. Since marrying Maria, there've been two domestic violence complaints filed…both dropped."

"He's not going to be pleased when he finds out why his wife is being questioned. What else have you found out?"

"Not much from Maria, but I discovered Koenig wasn't any old captain. He's a high-level procurement officer at the Pentagon. He's in California on a temporary assignment."

"Excellent work." The revelation was an interesting development. Lucas had barely considered the case once he arrived at Dakota Industries.

"We brought Maria to the station for questioning, but she clammed up. Say, if you have time, I'd like you to take a shot at her. I think she likes you."

Since he stepped off the elevator, Freddy was being almost frighteningly complimentary. He wanted something. "You're being nice to me. What gives?"

He patted Lucas on the shoulder. "You work too damn hard, my friend. I'll be done here after Maria is released. Why don't you stop by the sports bar near the bridge? Notre Dame is taking on Stanford. I bet a hundred bucks on the Fighting Irish."

He'd like nothing more, but Rachel was home with Beau. "I'll be tied up most of the day."

Freddy rolled his eyes. "Okay, but you met Dottie, right?"

Freddy's new girlfriend. "The stripper?"

"I like dating strippers. They put on a real show taking their clothes off. It's a learned talent like darts or laser tag."

Lucas reached around his friend and tapped the elevator up

button. He'd yet to meet Dottie, but from the way Freddy described her, Lucas had a pretty good picture in his mind.

"Her sister's in town, and I thought you two would hit it off."

Lucas let out a sigh. He didn't object to being Freddy's wingman from time to time, but most women Freddy tried to hook him up with rarely used words with more than three syllables. "Why do you think that?"

He cupped both hands in front of his chest.

"Two weeks ago, you set me up with a therapist. She worked as a masseuse in a massage parlor I busted when I was on patrol."

"I might have missed the mark on that one, but Dottie's sister is a lot like her if you get my drift."

The elevator door opened, and Lucas stepped inside. "Why are you always trying to fix me up?"

"You need to move on. Your ex has. She even has a couple of kids now."

"I'm happy for her. We're close friends."

He held the door as a shapely accounting secretary hurried toward the elevator, her heels clicking on the tile floor. She went inside and flipped her auburn hair. "Three, please, Detective Nash."

Freddy gave the backside of her snug dress the once-over before she turned and stood beside Lucas.

"This is important, Lucas. I don't recall who, maybe Shakespeare, but someone said man cannot live by bread alone." Freddy winked at the young woman.

She sneered at him. "The quote is from the Bible, Matthew 4:4. And Jesus wasn't talking about…intercourse; he was recommending becoming familiar with the word of God."

As the door closed, Freddy held both hands out wide. "So was I."

Before interviewing Maria, Lucas texted Lieutenant Clark that he'd meet her in the gym in half an hour. He walked down the familiar hallway to the interrogation rooms and found the suspect in a room.

She sat at a table with a paper cup of water and a box of tissues. She looked disheveled, tired, and more than ready to go home.

Her eyes lit up. "Did you come to let me go?" Her voice quivered. "They told me my husband is waiting. How will I ever explain all this to him?"

She'd had plenty of time to perfect her story.

Lucas sat across from her. "I'll be brief—just a couple of follow up questions."

The woman sagged back into the chair and clamped her eyes shut. "Let's go."

"How did the captain get to your place?"

"What?"

She obviously hadn't been asked the question and wasn't prepared to answer. "Monday, when I drove up to your house, your Toyota, Detective Gannon's car, and two patrol cars were parked out front. I didn't see any other vehicles in front of your house or in the drive."

"He…I guess he took an Uber."

"I looked into that. He didn't." Lucas hadn't checked. He hoped the bluff would pay off. "He's stationed out of San Francisco, but he works out of the Pentagon in Washington."

Maria stared at her hands. "I don't know anything about that."

"The easiest explanation is you picked him up and invited him home for…a drink."

Her face twisted with indignation. "That's not what happened."

Lucas didn't believe her, but if he pushed, she might lawyer up. He suspected what was bothering her. "Maria, I realize you're married. I was hitched once myself. Things happen that we're ashamed of later, but adultery isn't a crime. Murder is."

"I didn't shoot him." She squeezed his hand. "I swear."

"Tell me about the person you saw fleeing through the back door."

"Like I told the other detective, I was in the bedroom when I heard a shot. I ran out and caught a glimpse of some guy running out the back door. I hurried and locked the door in case he came back."

She heard two gunshots, and instead of hiding in the bedroom, she ran into the kitchen, toward gunfire? Her story didn't add up.

Maria reached for a tissue on the table and dabbed her eyes. "I phoned the cops right away. I was scared he'd come back."

"After you called the police, you had a drink."

She nodded.

The bottle was half empty. "Only one?"

"Maybe more. I'm not sure. I didn't realize I would be quizzed about every little detail a day later. Finding a dead man in my house kind of shook me up."

Lucas slid the chair back and rose. "I'll find out about getting you out of here."

Maria grabbed a tissue and dabbed her eyes. She mumbled as if trying to convince herself. "I'll tell him I'm not allowed to talk about what happened."

Lucas set a business card beside her. "If your husband threatens you in any way, I'll see about getting you someplace safe."

Lucas pressed his thumb on the reader, and the door to the gymnasium swung open. He entered amidst the clanging of weights and the sound of robots whirring about the room, passing out water bottles and hand towels. The sounds drowned out the overhead news network playing on 3-D screen monitors.

Lieutenant Sylvia Clark wore blue shorts and a Police Serve T-shirt, and she was in the middle of a brisk treadmill run. She stared at him with the hardened expression he'd come to know.

Lucas stopped beside the machine. "You read the Dakota report?"

She slowed the treadmill to a slow walk and wiped sweat from her face with a hand towel. "There's not a lot in it to read."

Lucas checked his watch and tried to control the sarcasm in his voice. "The investigation's not even twelve hours old."

A new guy in homicide walked by, ignoring him. "Looking buff, Lieutenant."

"Suck up," she muttered under her breath.

She slowed to a recovery walk. She accepted a fresh towel from a robot and wiped her face. "So, why the hell are you here? You should be interviewing witnesses."

"I thought you might have some questions."

"A few, and a several from the captain, an assistant with the mayor, and two reporters, none of which I could answer."

She shut off the machine, draped the towel over the back of her neck, and then led him to a deserted corner of the room. They stopped beside a stair climber. "I see you met Hawk."

Lucas leaned against a vacant weight bench and crossed both arms. "I did."

"Be alert. He can be a son-of-a-bitch."

"I can believe that."

"Level with me, Nash." She lowered her voice. "We don't need to go digging into a pile of shit if we don't have to. Is this a murder or just an old man whose time was up?"

"After this, I'm on my way to chat with Dr. Lee and find out what she learned. You'll be the first to know."

"Your gut, Lucas." She stepped on the machine and began to climb. "What do you think?"

"I think Beltran was killed, but I'll defer to Dr. Lee. He had enemies, inside and outside the company."

She wiped sweat from her brow. "A man in his position develops plenty of adversaries, like police lieutenants. How much did you learn about Dakota?"

"They're a privately-owned high-tech created and run jointly by the deceased and Melody Fleming. Dr. Beltran was the genius behind their robotics and AI programs. Fleming is the business

44

expert with plenty of contacts throughout the state and D.C. I don't expect to interview her until Dr. Lee rules the death a homicide."

She stepped off the stair climber and winced. She bent her right leg and pulled on the ankle, stretching her quads, reminding Lucas that Clark had been a high-level college basketball point guard before a dislocated kneecap ended her aspirations of a pro career. The injury didn't end her ambitions.

The lieutenant stretched the other leg then gazed out the blinds at the busy street running past the municipal building. "Forty percent of the county is employed, contracted with, or otherwise financially dependent upon Dakota Industries."

She was starting to squeeze. She wasn't usually a micromanager, and he didn't like the squeezing one bit. "Well, in that case, Boss, I'll do my best."

She glared at him for a moment before a smile interrupted her gruff expression.

A robot wheeled to a stop beside them. A tray slid out, offering a bottle of water.

His boss grabbed the bottle and took a long swallow.

The 'bot turned away from Lucas and sped off. He called after the machine. "What about me?"

"I'm suggesting you be cautious, Lucas. Dakota wasn't always secretive, but about three years ago, they went dark, indicating they were working on something new and top secret."

Something other than robotics and A.I.? He hoped Rachel would enlighten him.

Clark gulped the rest of the water and tossed the bottle into a blue recycling can. "I realize you don't have any ambition, but I do."

"I'm aware of that, *Captain.*"

Her eyes narrowed. "Smartass. Beltran's death could be nothing; then again, it might turn into the most significant case either of us has worked on. Screw this up, and you could end your career…and mine."

"I assume you assigned me to Beltran's death because you wanted this investigated the right way. If you don't think I'm up to it, the new guy who called you buff might be up to the challenge."

A flicker of a smile crossed her lips. "Be careful."

"Always."

"Now, get back to work."

"Yes, Lieutenant."

"Anything else?"

"I stopped by to chat with Maria Alvarez before I came here. She still denies it, but I'm certain she picked up the captain at a bar and invited him home for a night of fun and games."

Lucas left the municipal complex, dodging traffic as he crossed the street and entered the medical examiner building. At the front counter, he showed his badge. "Detective Lucas Nash. Is Dr. Lee available?"

The girl picked up a phone and punched in two digits. When she finished the call, she hung up. "She said to meet her in examination room two, and hurry." She bit her bottom lip.

"I know where that is."

The woman buzzed him through.

Lucas hurried down a tiled hallway and opened the second door. The room looked like it had never been used. Everything was immaculate with stainless steel tables, sinks, and counters, overhead UV lights to kill viruses, and a slight antiseptic aroma—no sign of Dr. Lee.

Dr. Lee stepped inside the doorway on unsteady legs. She wore high-tech blue personal protective equipment, including a clear face shield. As the door closed behind her, she ripped off the shield, let it drop, and sagged into a chair.

He'd never seen her so sick. "Are you alright?"

She held up a gloved hand. "Don't come any closer. Dr. Beltran died of a myocardial infarction secondary to a reaction to a nerve agent that I've yet to identify."

Nerve agent! "Holy shit."

"I closed off exam room three." She leaned forward and sucked in a gulp of air.

Fighting the instinct to help, Lucas kept his distance from her. He grabbed a wall phone and called the front desk. "Send a physician to examination room two. Dr. Lee needs assistance. Wear PPE." He hung up.

She glanced up at Lucas through bloodshot eyes. Her skin was a yellowish pale. "This is important. My report will state death by homicide. I suspect whoever did this applied the toxin through the epidermis. It would have taken hours for the agent to be absorbed by the skin into the blood system."

"How long?"

"Without knowing the agent, there's no way to be sure. If they show you a video, go back at least five hours."

Lucas wiped sweat from his brow and fought to remain calm for Niko's sake.

The door flew open, and a doctor dressed in white scrubs and a face shield rushed in. "Dr. Lee, are you alright?"

Lucas lost his temper. "Does she look alright? She's been exposed to an unknown nerve agent in examination room three."

"Nerve agent. Shit!"

Dr. Lee glanced up. "I sealed off the room."

The doctor appeared uncertain how to proceed. "What are your symptoms?"

"Shortness of breath, overall lethargy, brain fog. I need an IV stat."

Her face had grown paler by the minute. Helplessness swept over Lucas as the man struggled to make the right call. The doctor pulled a chrome sensor from his pocket and pressed the device against Dr. Lee's neck. "BP 80 over 60. Shit. Stay with me, Niko."

He glanced at Lucas. "I need to transport her to an isolation unit. I'll call so they can be prepared." The doctor grabbed the wall phone and punched in the number.

While he called, Dr. Lee struggled to her feet, holding onto the chair. "This is critical, Lucas."

"Don't overdo it, Niko."

"This is important." She struggled with the words. "My report... will state death by homicide. I suspect...whoever did this applied the toxin...through the epidermis. It would have taken hours for the agent...to be absorbed by the skin...into the...blood system."

She repeated what she said a moment earlier without realizing it. He feared for her recovery.

Dr. Lee let go of the chair. Her eyes rolled back in her head. She collapsed to the floor, held out one hand, and whispered, "Lucas."

He ran to her side.

The doctor hung up the phone. "Get away from her." He rushed to Dr. Lee's side, removed the sensor from his pocket again, and pressed it against her neck. "She's alive, for now."

A familiar feeling of dread hit Lucas in the gut when he arrived at the hospital. He waited in a hallway on a chair. He held his head with his hands, worrying about the woman he'd known almost half his life. Her husband and two children came in. They waited together, mostly in silence.

Lieutenant Clark came in at 4:00 as a doctor approached the family. He explained that the team had placed Dr. Lee in a medically-induced coma to slow the body's absorption of the nerve agent. Although the next twenty-four hours would be critical, he was optimistic she'd make a full recovery. Nevertheless, she would remain in quarantine until they knew exactly what they were dealing with.

Lucas breathed a sigh of relief, as did the family and Lieutenant Clark. Niko's husband thanked them and led the kids to the hospital cafeteria.

Clark walked with Lucas to the elevator and urged him to leave, get some rest, and focus on the investigation in the morning. "You look like shit."

Lucas agreed. He sat in the car a moment, wondering whether Rachel had delivered the nerve agent to Dr. Beltran that managed to infect Dr. Lee.

He started up the SUV and took off. He arrived at his ex-wife's favorite Italian restaurant. She was far from a vegetarian, but she loved their salads.

In a narrow waiting area, Lucas approached the front desk manned by a teenage boy in a white long-sleeved shirt and a green vest. He flashed a practiced smile. "Did you use our app?"

App? "Two dinner salads, two orders of breadsticks, two pastas with marinara sauce, please."

"I'll place the order, sir, but in the future, if you download our app, you can place and pay for your order from your car. The meal would have been ready by now. As it is, it'll be about fifteen minutes."

"I only come here every five years, so I'll pass on the app." Lucas sat on a couch.

An elderly couple came in and stepped to the front counter. They got their order right away and left. They used the app.

The familiar fragrances wafting in from the dining room behind the front desk took his mind off Dr. Lee and his two new cases. He studied the photographs of Italy and famous Italian Americans. They hadn't been changed in five years.

When the door opened, a cold chill sweep through the waiting area as Calvin Hawk came in, wearing a white jacket with the now-familiar DI logo below the collar.

The chipper teen glanced up. "May I help you, sir?"

"Nope." Hawk sat beside Lucas.

Lucas gave him a side glance. "You don't strike me as an Italian food kind of guy."

Either Dakota's chief of security had followed Lucas from the hospital or monitored his route using the tracker Dakota Industries must have placed on his SUV.

"I'm looking for Rachel."

"Did you check the bus station?"

"The first place I went."

Lucas reminded himself to tell Rachel he'd been right about the bus station. "If I meet up with her, I'll give you a call."

The teen set a bag on the counter. "Your order is ready, Mr. Nash."

Lucas didn't want Hawk to see that he ordered enough for two. "Give me a minute."

"Okay, but the breadsticks are warm."

Lucas shot the kid a glance. "I like mine cold."

"The news mentioned Dr. Lee was rushed to the hospital," Hawk said. "So sorry for your loss."

He didn't act sorry. "She's not dead yet, but thanks for the thought. If someone told you she was in the hospital, you no doubt are also aware she submitted her autopsy report and ruled Beltran's death a homicide."

Hawk looked surprised. "I hadn't heard that. You know, Detective, we should be on the same side, trying to bring Dr. Beltran's killer to justice."

"I couldn't agree more. With that in mind, what can you tell me about a Captain Koenig?"

"Never heard of her." The big man rose to leave. "Is she a police captain?"

Hawk was lying, and Dakota Industries had no interest in working together. "He, and he's Army."

7

In Lucas's backyard, Rachel sat brushing the White Collie's long hair. Beau never tired of Rachel's attention. For a moment, she pictured herself with this lifestyle in a middle-class home with Lucas and his dog.

She couldn't tell how Lucas felt about her. There had been moments when she thought he cared, but other times, she thought he suspected her in the death of Dr. Beltran.

Maybe she misinterpreted everything over the past two days. Perhaps he was acting kind and appearing to care about her, so she'd cooperate with his investigation.

Rachel paused in her reflection at the sound of an unfamiliar car turning onto the street. "Come, Beau."

She hurried inside, knelt on the couch, and parted the curtains an inch.

A Black SUV approached the house. She recognized the two men as part of Calvin Hawk's security team.

They drove past the house, made a U-turn, and parked across from Lucas's house. When they got out, she made sure to lock the front door. She dashed to the guest room.

Rachel threw everything into her duffel bag and hurried to the kitchen. She slid the wooden panel into the doggy door, preventing

Beau from following her. As the dog barked, she fled outside, closing the door behind her.

She sprinted to the fence and tossed the bag into Mr. Bernardi's backyard. She vaulted over and snatched up the bag.

Lucas's neighbor was sitting on the patio, sipping a drink. "What a lovely surprise. Can I offer you an iced tea?"

She never expected him to be outside. She glanced back toward Lucas's house as Beau continued to bark. "I need your help."

Rachel told him about the two thugs in the black van. She feared they might break into Lucas's house looking for her. She didn't explain why Hawk's creeps were searching for her, and the kind old man didn't ask.

He downed the last of his drink, then motioned her toward the back door.

His house was laid out like Lucas's with the kitchen in the back. Rachel followed him to the living room, where a wall showed a dozen or more pictures of Mr. Bernardi stream fishing. The old man peered through curtains in the front door. "They resemble the men in the *Men in Black* movies."

She rushed to the window and opened the door a crack.

The two men entered Lucas's driveway and headed for his front door.

Mr. Bernardi held up one hand. "I'll go check my mail."

He disappeared out the door.

Rachel listened as the old man shuffled toward his mailbox. "Can I help you, fellas?"

Rachel couldn't make out their reply.

He closed his mailbox. "If you're looking for Lucas Nash, he's at work. Don't expect him home anytime soon."

Rachel expected Lucas any minute.

The two men approached Bernardi, and one pulled a picture from his jacket pocket, an enlarged Dakota ID photo of Rachel. The man asked whether he'd ever seen her.

Mr. Bernardi scratched his head. "Nope, and I pay close attention to what goes on in my neighborhood. I'm retired. You'd be surprised how much vandalism and burglary happens around here, even with a cop living next door."

He took the photo and stared at the picture a moment before handing it back. "Lucas has had more than his share of lady friends over from time to time, but I'd have noticed one as fine as this one. She kill someone?" Mr. Bernardi laughed.

Rachel thought about all the unopened toothbrushes in Lucas's bathroom and tried to put the thought out of her mind.

The man with the photo stuffed it in his jacket while the other held out a business card.

Lucas's neighbor took the card. "Thanks. You fellas have a terrific day."

The two men crossed the street, climbed into their SUV, and drove off.

Mr. Bernardi waved to the men and headed for the house. He came inside with a growing smile. "I'm sure I convinced them you've never been around here."

"I appreciate your help, Mr. Bernardi. I...I don't think it would be best to tell you why those men are looking for me."

"I don't need details, young lady. I'm a decent judge of character. I don't like *them*. I like *you*. Still, I think it would be better if you waited here until Lucas comes home."

Rachel kissed his cheek. "Thanks."

"Now, about that iced tea."

With darkness falling, the streetlights blinked on as Lucas turned into his driveway and parked in his garage. He grabbed the bag of takeout, got out, and took a quick glance toward the street to make sure no one had followed him. He went inside and called out, "Rachel."

Beau greeted him with a loud bark, then ran to the back door and barked again. The board was sitting in the doggy door, preventing the dog from going out back. Lucas let him outside and removed the panel.

Where was she? Had she left for good?

To his relief, the guest room door opened, and Rachel came out wearing clothes she'd kept hidden. She was striking in a red silk blouse, black slacks, and black dress shoes. He hadn't seen her so beautiful.

"You're home." She approached him with a smile.

"With dinner." He set the takeout bag on the kitchen counter. "I thought maybe you'd left."

"No, silly."

"I have something to show you." She took Lucas's hand and led him into the dining room.

Like Rachel, the room looked gorgeous, boasting a cream-colored tablecloth, plates and silverware, and two candlesticks with red candles in them. The scene resembled one where two people were about to commence a first date. Perhaps it was time he set her straight.

She lit the candles with a lighter and sighed with a sense of satisfaction.

There would be plenty of time to talk after dinner. "You look..." he searched for the right word, "lovely."

Disappointment flickered over her face. He glanced at a table in the corner with a lace doily. His grandma's doily was lovely; Rachel was much more attractive than that. "I meant to say you look beautiful."

She smiled and sat. "Thank you."

Lucas brought the food from the kitchen and set it on the table.

The flickering candlelight made Rachel appear younger than he knew her to be and prettier than a movie star made up by a pro.

The food hadn't improved over the years. The pasta had as much flavor as a bowl of twine. Over dinner, he tried not to focus on her appearance. He told her about Dr. Lee being hospitalized after identifying that a nerve agent killed Beltran. He revealed that the doctor had determined someone had administered the toxin within five hours of his death. He didn't share the closeness of his relationship with Niko.

A sigh of relief swept from Rachel's lips. "I guess I'm in the clear."

"Not exactly. It merely means I need to determine everyone Beltran met in the five hours before he died."

"He had a busy schedule. I could find out by hacking into Dakota's system. I saw your computer and thought about helping your investigation, but I'd never touch anything of yours without your permission."

It didn't seem right, talking shop by candlelight. "How's your pasta and marinara?"

"The sauce is wonderful, and the pasta is cooked to perfection, don't you think?" She took another bite, then dabbed the corner of her mouth with a napkin. "I have something to tell you."

She took a deep breath and recounted the unexpected visit by two of Calvin Hawks' thugs. "I thought they'd break in, so I tossed my belongings into the bag, hurried out back, and climbed the fence to your neighbor's backyard."

"Bernardi's?"

"He's very sweet." Rachel told how Bernardi convinced the men that he'd never seen her.

"Hawk traced me to the restaurant. Why is he going all out to find you? He doesn't suspect you in Dr. Beltran's death. If he did, he'd be working with me."

"Isn't it obvious?"

"Not to me."

"They think I took Dakota secrets with me."

"Did you?"

She nodded toward the hallway. "Search my duffel bag if you want."

"I don't need to. I'm just glad you're safe. I guess I have to thank that crusty old geezer."

"I almost panicked." She glanced at her hands. "They got rid of Dr. Beltran, and now they can eliminate me if it suits their purposes. I'm guessing they'd make it look like you killed me."

Perhaps Rachel viewed too many cop shows, but she didn't come across as the type to frighten easily.

"Would you like another breadstick?"

"I think I've had enough."

By the time the meal ended, Rachel had grown quiet. They each snuffed out a candle.

She and Lucas cleaned up, then went to the living room, where she sat on the couch. He took a seat across from her in his favorite chair. "You may not be safe here."

Beau came through the doggy door and bounded into the room. He accepted a pat on the head from Lucas and jumped onto the couch with Rachel.

She appeared nervous as she stroked the dog's white fur.

"Is something on your mind?" Lucas asked.

She stared at her hands. "I don't know how to tell you, or if I should."

"Start with the truth."

Rachel stroked the dog under the chin. "After you left for work, I thought I'd just leave."

"Without saying goodbye? Why didn't you?"

She petted Beau as if to avoid looking at Lucas. "That's what I'm struggling with."

Would she share her knowledge about Beltran's death and reveal details about Project Halo? Like he did with suspects, he gave her time.

"You've been kind to me. You're a sweet man, and I…" She took a deep breath. "I've never cared about anyone the way I care about you."

Her admission hit Lucas like a blow to the chest. Expressing her feelings for him made no sense. They just met, yet his own feelings about Rachel had come about in record time. However, he couldn't express or even reflect upon them if she remained a person of interest in a homicide investigation of his. "We met less than twenty-four hours ago."

"It seems longer to me. After coming to Dakota, I read a poem by Roger B. Cameron. I've seen you in my dreams for years now. I'm so happy that you finally appeared now."

Lucas didn't know what to say.

She pointed to her head. "It's not logical how I feel." She touched her heart, "but feelings are held here, aren't they?"

He fought the urge to comfort Rachel, put his arms around her, and express those feelings he was reluctant to admit to himself. "Yes, they are."

For a moment, neither of them spoke. This time, she was waiting for him to go first. Lucas rose and ran a hand over his chin. "I can't think about you in that way while this investigation hangs over my head, over our heads."

Rachel cocked her head. "You don't think I killed Dr. Beltran, do you?"

"I don't." He dropped back into the chair. "But I have a job to do, and I have to see it through to the end no matter where it leads."

A shocked expression swept over her face. "Am I a suspect?"

"Not in my mind."

"Then, what am I?"

"The technical term is a person of interest. You possess information I need to locate a suspect or suspects. I need to interview you. It's why…"

"Why what?"

He knew his answer would upset her. "Why I invited you to stay with me."

Her mouth dropped open. She jumped to her feet and covered her face. "I'm such a fool."

She ran to the guest room and slammed the door.

Beau cocked his head and barked.

Lucas blew out a sigh. "I didn't handle that well, did I, boy?"

He paced the room, trying to figure a way to apologize to Rachel. He'd been insensitive and didn't understand how to make it up to her. He stared at the closed guest room door, took a deep breath, and approached the room. As he reached to knock, the door opened.

She brushed past him and headed for the dining room.

When Lucas followed, he was surprised to see a calm Rachel seated at the head of the table with her hands clasped. "Okay, ask me anything you want. I suggest, to make this official, you record the interview."

"I may have been insensitive..."

She held up one hand. "Let's get this over with. After we finish, you can arrest me or let me go."

He realized he wasn't going to win the argument. He retrieved a tripod from his room and attached the phone to it, selected video, and aimed the camera in the direction of the table using a wide-angle view.

Lucas set his tablet and a stylus on the table and prepared to take notes. He sat across from Rachel. "Are you ready?"

"Of course," she answered in a clipped tone.

She acted nervous, and some observers might even say guilty.

"Answer truthfully, but it won't help if your answers come across rehearsed or unemotional when it comes to Dr. Beltran's death."

"Is that what you think, I'm not emotional?"

"Just relax and reply to the questions like we're having a regular conversation."

"Is this advice you give everyone you interrogate?"

He ignored the question. "I'm not giving you an interrogation. This is an interview."

Rachel closed her eyes and let out a deep breath. "Okay, I'm ready."

Lucas glanced at the phone. "Record." He cited the time, place, and location of the interview. "Please, state your name."

"Rachel."

"Your last name, please."

"Smith. Rachel Smith."

Smith? Really? Was that her real name? He began to ask routine questions about her employment at Dakota, including to whom she reported.

"I worked for Project Halo, reporting to Dr. Esteban Beltran as his intern."

Despite his advice, her answer sounded rehearsed. "What was your relationship with Dr. Beltran?"

"As his intern, he was my boss, my mentor...my friend. After I came to work for Dakota, his team called him Dr. B., so I often called him Dr. B." She swallowed hard. For the first time since they met, her eyes filled with tears. A tear slid down her cheek. "He was a father to me, a father I never knew."

Lucas gave her a moment to compose herself. "When did you last see Dr. Beltran?"

Rachel closed her eyes as if replaying a painful moment. "We met in his office twenty-four hours ago."

"What was the purpose of your meeting?"

"We met almost every day. This occasion is so memorable because Dr. Beltran informed me he was halting the project he'd devoted himself to for the past three years, due to a disagreement with Melody Fleming."

"Did he share the essence of the disagreement?"

She nodded. "He did. Everyone knew Melody wanted to keep the project alive due to commitments she obtained from the government. Dr. Beltran had concluded twelve months earlier that Project Halo was doomed to failure. He informed me he was finally going to stand his ground because Project Halo wouldn't benefit Dakota Industries, the company's clients, or humanity."

"Humanity?"

Rachel glanced toward the camera as if speaking to the person viewing the interview. "Benefiting humanity was always the driving force for Dr. Beltran when it came to A.I. That created the source of the conflict with Ms. Fleming. Her focus was on profits."

"Please describe the nature of Project Halo."

She looked at Lucas. "I realize you're conducting a murder investigation, but I signed a non-disclosure agreement when I went to work for Dakota Industries. I'm afraid I can't answer that question without a court order."

"For now, how about a general question. Did Project Halo involve artificial intelligence?"

"It did."

"And you worked with Dr. Beltran on artificial intelligence."

"Yes. He taught me a great deal."

Over the next half hour, despite his probing, Rachel held her ground and shared few details about her work at Dakota and Project Halo. Her answers were clipped and to the point. Some were laced with irritation. Was she still mad at him? Of course, she was.

"Would you like a break?"

"I'm fine." Rachel smiled. "But thank you for your consideration."

"Are you familiar with any biological or nerve agents kept on the property of Dakota?"

"The work at Dakota was compartmentalized. There were many areas I was not allowed to access. I have no direct knowledge of biological or nerve agents. From time to time, gossip went around the company, but I can't be certain it was true. When you work for a tightly controlled, centralized high-tech company, there are always rumors."

"Did…"

"One time, Dr. Beltran mentioned nerve agents in passing. I didn't ask him to clarify, and he never referred to it again."

"Let's go back to the final time you were in Dr. Beltran's office. What are the last words he said to you?"

"He told me that once he shared his decision to terminate Project Halo, life would be difficult for him and the members of his team, including me. He suggested I take my belongings, leave Dakota, and never come back."

"Was he suggesting things might become dangerous for you, that your life might be at risk?"

"I didn't think so at the time, but now, I believe that's exactly what he was saying." Her voice rose, reflecting fear. "It's hard for me to understand why someone would want to kill me for being Dr. Beltran's intern."

Rachel wanting to place her fear of being killed on the record surprised Lucas. "Do you have any idea why anyone at Dakota would want you dead?"

She shook her head. "No…I guess they think Dr. Beltran shared Project Halo secrets with me."

"Did he?"

"From time to time."

"Anything else about your last meeting with Dr. Beltran?"

"He said to meet him at his house, and he'd facilitate my escape. He gave me the security code to allow access to his property. I wished him well, gave him a hug, and left. An hour later, I escaped."

"Escaped? Why couldn't you just leave?"

"Dakota is very autocratic. They're a high-tech company, but Melody runs the organization like a secret society where members are sworn to secrecy and spied on at all times with surveillance cameras and security detail."

"Did you take anything like property or documents belonging to Dakota with you?"

"Of course not."

"Did you have anything to do with the death of Dr. Beltran?"

Her voice softened a bit, with a slight tremor. "Lu…Detective Nash, you know I didn't."

"Have you ever been in possession of a nerve agent?"

"Never."

"Can you think of anything else you'd like to share that might shed light on the death of Dr. Beltran?"

Rachel leaned back in the chair and let out a sigh. Again, her eyes filled with tears. "Find out who did this to my friend, Dr. Beltran."

Lucas glanced at the camera. "End Recording."

She cocked her head. "No more questions?"

"None."

Rachel rose and headed for the guest room. She paused and glanced back at him as if waiting for him to say something, anything like suggesting she stay. When he didn't, she went inside and slammed the door behind her.

After letting Beau inside, Lucas led the dog to his room and closed the door. While Beau curled up on his corner pillow, Lucas sat in a chair and reviewed the interview on his phone. When it ended, he dictated a report to Lieutenant Clark, summarizing his questioning of Rachel. He attached the video and sent everything to her.

He reflected on his questions and Rachel's answers. She'd been forthcoming and honest, as near as he could determine. Her answers didn't appear rehearsed, and she sounded emotional at the appropriate times, but her use of sentiment bothered Lucas, though it wasn't clear why.

Overall, Rachel had shared a wealth of information, but he'd yet to learn details about Project Halo. Intuition told Lucas that Project Halo led to Dr. Beltran's death and whoever was behind administering the nerve agent.

A knock sounded at the door.

Lucas let Rachel in.

She gazed around the room. "A pleasant, manly, and surprisingly organized bedroom…exactly how I thought your room might look. Her earlier anger and embarrassment appeared to have vanished. "During the interview, I think I learned as much about you as you did about me."

"And what was that?"

"How devoted you are to discovering the truth and your dedication to your profession." She avoided his gaze a moment. "I was wrong to share my feelings about you. It couldn't have made interviewing me easy."

"Like you said, I have a job to do."

She smiled. "So, we're good?"

"We're good."

Rachel sat on the bed. "I want to help you solve the case."

"How would you do that?"

"If you loan me your computer, I could hack into the Dakota system and give you a list of who Dr. Beltran met the final five hours of his life…besides me."

"I don't think you need to go that far. Now that Dr. Lee declared Beltran's death a homicide, by law, they must cooperate. That will be the first piece of information I expect them to provide."

"But wouldn't you want to compare what they turn over with what I'm able to find out for sure from the actual records?"

Excellent point. "If anyone at Dakota found out someone hacked into their system and traced it back to my computer…"

Rachel laughed. "First, you wouldn't be the first suspect. Second, give me a little credit. I specialized in hacking for Dr. Beltran. It saved time when he wanted to borrow technology from another company."

That didn't sound legal. "You hacked into databases?"

"Among other things. Interns do what they're asked to do." She cocked her head. "Don't say it. There are plenty of backdoor techniques to protect you and your computer and me."

Lucas ran a hand over his chin. Rachel was making sense. "Okay, deal. Does that mean you're not leaving tomorrow?"

"If you let me help, I'll stick around."

"Deal." He reached out and shook her hand, holding on a bit longer than he should.

"I'll need your password."

"Beau 5. He's five years old."

Rachel laughed. "You should change your password regularly and avoid something I would have guessed in about two minutes. There are algorithms that change them for you automatically."

Lucas rolled his eyes. "The more I learn about technology, the more I realize how little I understand."

He got up from his chair. "When I return home tomorrow, we'll talk about finding a safer place for you to stay."

"That sounds like a perfect solution. We have to keep one step ahead of Calvin Hawk and his team."

Lucas held out his hand. She took it and rose from the bed, standing close enough to him for him to smell the floral scent of her shampoo.

Rachel squeezed his hand. "I'm sorry I shared my feelings with you, but I'm not sorry about how I feel."

Her face was close to his, and her eyes were soft and inviting. A rumble came from the corner where Beau was sleeping.

Rachel laughed. The spell was broken. "Is Beau snoring?"

Lucas grinned. "Oh, he's just getting started."

She cocked her head and gazed into his eyes. "Do you snore?"

For a moment, neither of them spoke. "I don't remember anyone complaining."

Rachel snickered, glanced at the bed, and headed to the door. "Goodnight, Bulldog."

8

The next morning, Lucas slipped into his terrycloth robe and made a pot of coffee. The coffee began to brew as a knock came on the front door.

Who would be knocking at 7 a.m.? The hair rose on the back of his neck.

He dashed to his bedroom and grabbed his Glock from the nightstand drawer. With Beau also on alert, the dog followed Lucas to the door as a louder knock sounded.

Through the window, Freddy was biting his nails, waiting for Lucas to answer the door. The last thing he wanted was his partner knowing Rachel spent the night. He opened the door and stood in the doorway. "Freddy, what are you doing here?"

His friend noticed the gun in Lucas's hand. "You're not a morning person, are you?"

Lucas slipped the Glock into the pocket of his robe.

Freddy checked his watch. "Seven o'clock, son, time's a-wastin'. You taking the day off or something?" He patted Beau's head and revealed a look of impatience, clearly expecting to be invited in.

"I was about to step into the shower. I'm going to drop by the hospital and check on," he peered over his shoulder, "Dr. Lee."

"If you have time, I need help on the Maria Alvarez case."

Lucas placed one hand against the door casing, holding his ground, and cast an admiring glance at Freddy's red Tesla Roadster. "What's the trouble?"

"I hit a roadblock. Maria insists she didn't bring Koenig home, and I need proof she did. Since her husband returned home, she's clammed up." He glanced over Lucas's shoulder. "Do I smell fresh coffee?"

"I'm kind of in the middle of something."

The toilet flushed in the guest bathroom.

A lascivious grin curled from the edge of Freddy's lip. "Oh, I get it."

"No, you don't."

Freddy backed up and held up both hands. "Sorry I disturbed you. Get back inside and into the middle of whatever or whoever you were doing."

As he feared, his friend got the wrong idea. "It's not what you think."

Freddy winked. He turned and bounded down the driveway like he couldn't get away fast enough. At the driver's door of his roadster, he flashed Lucas a thumbs up. "My man."

He hopped in his car and sped off.

"Who was that?" Rachel handed him a cup of coffee and took a sip from her own.

"Freddy, my partner."

"Why didn't you invite him in?"

Lucas closed the door. "I need to shower. I left the computer on the kitchen table." He reached into his pocket and gave her a phone. "I got you something. People used to refer to this as a burner phone. I entered my number. You can call or text, and it can't be tracked by GPS."

"Thanks." She set the phone beside the computer, then sat and opened the laptop. She let out a playful groan. "You tape your password next to the keyboard. What kind of security is that?"

He ignored her rebuke and sipped the coffee. "Hey, Google, turn on CNN."

The entire living room wall lit up as Lucas headed for his bathroom. He stopped when the news broadcast caught his attention.

"…Dakota Industries. The Reverend Donovan Armour voiced displeasure over the company's secrecy."

Rachel viewed the program with interest.

The image shifted to the reverend in a suit, leading a protest outside the gate of Dakota Industries. Behind him stood a woman, about Lucas's age, who appeared familiar.

"You ever meet him?" Lucas asked.

"A couple of times."

"What about the woman behind him with the red hair?"

"Her name is Chastity Moorhead."

Lucas snapped his finger. He thought he recognized her.

Rachel acted surprised. "You know her?"

"We went to high school together."

In the shower, Lucas reflected on Chastity Moorhead, the girl who had survived merciless teasing throughout high school about both names. What kind of parents would hang her with a name like Chastity? Pious fanatics, and they were all that.

Half of his senior year, Lucas dodged the innocent-looking redhead's attempts to convert him. She was cute, so he put up with her efforts and tried to convince her to break a few commandments. Nothing worked.

Looking back, he realized he'd wasted four years of high school being a jerk toward girls and people in general. It wasn't until he met his wife in college that he began to change, as she showed him respect for others.

He felt remorse over his treatment of Chastity, a girl who'd always been upfront with him. Back then, however, hormones trumped ethics.

After a handful of forgettable dates, they both gave up and drifted toward new conquests. The year after graduation, she enrolled in some religious institution on the east coast. It came as no surprise to find her connected to a national spiritual leader who showed up in her hometown preaching against technology's evils.

An hour later, Lucas hurried up the steps of the hospital. He learned Dr. Lee remained in a coma, but her condition had stabilized.

In the parking garage, he slipped into his SUV. He prepared to drive to the station when an idea occurred to him. He opened the glove compartment and pulled out the owner's manual. He flipped through the pages and found the Navigation section.

The dashboard screen came on, and Lucas spoke a one-word command. "Navigation."

A map of the city filled the screen. He gave a follow-up instruction. "Directions from Florence Henderson Elementary School to 2845 West 29th Street." Maria Alvarez's home.

The map revealed the most direct route between the two sites. "Show taverns and restaurants along the route."

Seventeen locations popped up. "Eliminate restaurants."

Only four places were left. The first one Maria Alvarez would have encountered was the Happy Camper. "Happy Camper. Go."

Fifteen minutes later, Lucas parked in the bar's lot and climbed out.

The bar didn't open for an hour. Nevertheless, he knocked. He tried again. "Police."

He'd almost given up when the door squeaked open. A tired-looking man in need of a shave stood with an impatient gaze. "Guess today's my lucky day. The other cop forget something?"

Using his phone, he held up a photo of Freddy. "Him?"

"Nah, a black guy built like a linebacker, the kind you don't say no to or ask for his name if you don't have to."

A chill shot up Lucas's spine. "This the man?" Lucas showed him a picture of Calvin Hawk.

"Yeah, but my arm's getting tired holding the door. Want to come in?"

"Sure." Lucas followed him inside to the bar, sat on a stool, and displayed his ID badge. Why was Hawk interested in information about Captain Keonig?

The man tossed a business card in front of Lucas. Nathaniel Denton, Proprietor. He walked behind the counter. "Everyone calls me Nate. Can I get you anything?"

"Coffee, black. A little early for anything else."

Nate checked the time. "Too late for me, but I'll make an exception." He poured himself a shot of Bourbon. "A couple of hours back, this cop knocked, same as you. He wanted to check if we had video from two nights ago."

"Do you?"

Nate set the coffee in front of Lucas. "I don't have fancy-schmancy high-tech stuff. It's Blue Ray from the twenties. I turned the disk over to the black guy and popped in a new one." He waved to the camera, threw back the contents of his drink, and poured himself another shot.

Damn. "Did you work two nights ago?"

"Sure." Nate wiped the counter with a damp towel from the sink. "I work every day. I own the place."

Lucas called up the case file on the shooting of Captain Koenig. He showed him a picture lifted off the man's military ID. "Ever seen this guy?"

"My memory's not so good. I see lots of guys." Nate finished wiping the counter and draped the towel over one shoulder.

"You might recall details if I take you to the station."

"Okay, that won't be necessary. I find it coming back to me. He dropped by two nights ago with another officer. I think they've both been in before, every few weeks or so. This fella chases down booze and broads."

"Anything else?"

The bar owner rubbed the back of his neck. "I've probably said too much."

Lucas could tell the man was weakening. He waited for him to continue.

"Okay, when they were talking, I found out the first guy was a captain. He referred to his buddy as colonel. Captain was throwing them down as quick as I could serve until a young looker came in and distracted him."

Lucas showed him an image of Maria Alvarez.

"Yeah, I never forget a face like that. A real beauty, don't you think? He bought her a drink and told her a couple of dirty jokes."

"How did she react?"

"She laughed at his jokes, so I assumed she was interested. Still, in my job, I can't afford to judge. I only remember because she was hot."

"Was she wearing jeans and a sweatshirt?"

The man snickered. "Hardly. She wore a tight white sweater and snug-fitting black slacks. With those pants, a guy could take her pulse without touching her wrist, if you know what I mean."

"I get the idea."

Nate took a swallow. "A lot of office girls frequent my place."

"She's a Kindergarten teacher."

He let out a long whistle. "They didn't make teachers that smokin' when I went to school. Say, how come I never saw you here before. You married or something?"

"Not anymore." Lucas took a satisfying drink of coffee. "Did you see them leave?"

"Things got busy. I took an order from a table of college girls. I came back to the bar, and Beauty and the Officer were gone, but after I went over the recording with the first cop, we watched the parking lot video. They left together. She drove. He hopped into the passenger seat like a chicken after a worm. I guess he got lucky."

Lucas climbed off the stool and slapped a five-dollar bill on the counter. "Not too lucky. The chicken's dead."

9

Lucas sat in his car and phoned the hospital to confirm that Dr. Lee's condition hadn't changed. After the call, he sent a voice to text message to Rachel. "Progress?"

A minute later, the response popped up. "Almost finished."

Lucas wanted to focus on Beltran's death, but from the owner of the Happy Camper, he learned enough to press Maria Alvarez and possibly wrap up the murder of Captain Koenig. He called Freddy and told him to meet him at her school.

Seconds after arriving in the visitor lot, Freddy pulled up and parked beside him.

Through the open window, Lucas filled him in on the meeting with the bar owner.

"Terrific work, cowboy. You want to take the lead?"

"If you insist."

When the two men stepped from their cars, Lucas pointed to the main building. "I hope they have plenty of security cameras in case any of the older kids show interest in your sweet red roadster."

Freddy's eyes widened. "You don't think...ah, you're messing with me."

Lucas chuckled. "You're right. Kids don't bother red sports cars. Come on."

They climbed the steps of the modern building. Freddy held the door open with a wistful glance back at his roadster. "Fancy school. Speaking of school, guess who's in town?"

Lucas scratched his head. "Who? Chastity Moorhead?"

Freddy blew out a burst of air. "Damn, it's hard to stay a step ahead of you."

Inside, a robot painted to resemble a Green River Police Officer greeted them. The 'bot checked their credentials and escorted them to the administrative office.

Five minutes later, they sat in a conference room where they waited for the teacher.

Freddy drummed his fingers on the table. "Whatever happened to you and Chastity? It seemed like you two were cut out for each other."

"It was never going to work out. Chastity's parents were well-to-do religious aristocrats, mine just regular folk." Lucas thought back to an awkward evening in his junior year. "The two families met one night at a school play Chastity was in. I introduced them, and they sat together, but it was like the Kennedys hanging out with redneck wrestling fans."

Freddy nudged him. "So, did you and Chastity ever...you know?"

Lucas ignored the question. "Before I forget, I need a favor. I'd like you to do some digging on Calvin Ridley Hawk, currently employed by Dakota. The database gives basic information. He was born in Springfield, Missouri, on June 10, 2001. He attended college at Stanford, graduating with honors with a degree in Biological Engineering in 2022."

"The internet is your best bet..."

"I'm talking digging, not scratching, old fashioned police work with informants. You might have to scatter a few bills around. You have cash?"

"From my poker winnings." Freddy nodded toward the door.

"Before she comes in, I was thinking my charm and good looks didn't win her over before, so maybe I need a new game plan. I'm thinking no more Mr. Nice Guy, you know, when she starts to clam up, I start throwing around furniture."

Before Lucas could reply, the door opened. Maria entered, wearing a casual gray business suit and a bright paisley scarf. Her face dropped. She closed the door and lowered her voice. "You here to arrest me?"

Lucas gestured to a chair on the other side of the table. "We think it's time for you to come clean."

Maria sat across from the detectives, crossed her fingers, and smiled as if she were about to address a class of students. "This couldn't wait until I got off work?"

Freddy's face reddened. Lucas had seen anger on his partner's face during interrogations and always marveled at how he controlled his emotions. "You can save us all time, teacher, by telling the truth. Your story changes every time you open your mouth."

"This morning, I met with the owner/bartender of the Happy Camper," Lucas said. "The video shows Captain Koenig leaving with you in your car, so it's time to tell the truth."

Maria's bravado vanished. She sagged back into the chair and clamped her eyes shut. A tear slid down her cheek. "I didn't want my husband to find out. He'll slap the shit out of me halfway to Sunday."

Lucas set a pack of tissues in front of her.

"These last few days have been a nightmare." Maria blinked away tears and glanced at the door as if someone might enter. "The truth is, we met at the bar. I invited him home for...romance, something my husband doesn't care about anymore. I didn't kill him! Why would I do that?"

From the skeptical sneer on Freddy's face, he wasn't buying her newest version of Monday night, but Lucas sensed she was finally telling the truth.

Lucas's phone buzzed with a text from Rachel. "Five hours before Dr. Beltran collapsed, he met with Calvin Hawk and Melody Fleming about Project Halo. An hour after that, he attended a meeting with Reverend Donovan Armour and Chastity Moorhead (the redhead you admired). Later, not sure how much, Hawk talked to Dr. Beltran again, just before Dr. Beltran sat with two Procurement Officers from the Pentagon, Colonel Richard Urias and Captain William (Wild Bill) Koenig. There's a strong likelihood that one of the six administered the nerve agent to Dr. Beltran. How did I do?"

Damn! Lucas almost dropped the phone. That's why Hawk went to the Happy Camper and took the video with him—because an important Dakota client had been murdered? Was that the only connection between the two murders?

Freddy returned to the table and set one hand on the back of Lucas's chair. "You alright?"

Lucas showed him Rachel's text. "Ms. Alvarez. Had you met Captain Koenig before Monday night?"

"I'd seen him at the bar. He might have bought me a drink or two before, but we never hooked up, if that's what you're getting at."

"Did you ever hear him referred to as Wild Bill?" Lucas asked.

Maria snickered. "He called himself Wild Bill, the Wild Man all the time, and so did the colonel."

"You knew the colonel?"

She shook her head no.

"Was his name Colonel Richard Urias?"

Maria bit the end of a fingernail. "I told you I didn't know him. I mean, he was at a table nearby, but I never learned his name."

Freddy folded his arms. "Did Captain Koenig talk about his work activities?"

Maria started to open up. "All he did was yak about himself, his important work, his fabulous motorcycle, exotic places he's visited. I tried to appear impressed, but he sounded like all men, blowing smoke to impress a lady."

76

Lucas asked, "Maria, did he mention Dakota Industries?"

"Yeah, he did. He said he was looking at making a huge purchase for the military that would earn him an important promotion."

Lucas led his partner to the far end of the room. He whispered. "This may not be sex murder with a love triangle angle. Colonel Urias and Captain Koenig were looking into an enormous military purchase from Dakota Industries. It had to be something involving robots, artificial intelligence, or both."

Freddy shook his head. "Weapons with artificial intelligence. What could possibly go wrong?"

Lucas had six suspects in the death of Beltran, seven counting Rachel. If the two murders were connected, Captain Koenig might have been killed by Beltran's murderer. "I bet a month's salary these two cases are connected. We just have to find out how."

"Or this might be merely a sex murder involving an abusive jealous husband and a guilty wife. Maybe she had second thoughts and told Koenig she changed her mind. Let's haul her in and work her over before she lawyers up. She's no dummy."

"I don't want to hassle her. I might need Maria's cooperation down the road with my case."

Freddy held his hands out. "What about *my* case?"

"I think they're one and the same."

Lucas returned to the table. "Tell me again about the person who fled through the back door."

"As I told your partner, Mr. Bad Cop, I was in the bedroom when a shot happened in the next room, then another. I ran out and saw a guy running out the back door. I hurried and locked the door in case he came back."

"He? Last time we talked, you said he."

Freddy checked his notes on his phone. "Monday, you told me the person was a 'short dude in a ski mask.'"

"Could it have been a woman?" Lucas asked. Three of the seven suspects were women.

"I don't think so; he moved so fast, like an athlete. Besides, most murderers are guys, aren't they?"

Freddy leaned across the table. "I'm not buying what you're selling, teacher. You heard gunshots in the next room, and instead of hiding in the bedroom, you ran into the kitchen, toward gunfire? It doesn't add up."

"I don't care anymore whether you believe me or not. It happened that way!" Maria smacked the table. "I phoned the cops right away. I was frightened the killer might come back."

The school bell rang, and instantly the din of children chatting and laughing rose in the hallway outside the door. Over the racket of excited kids came the sound of a robotic voice. "No running, no hitting, no physical display of affection."

The crestfallen woman grabbed a fresh tissue and dabbed her eyes again. "What happens now? Am I under arrest?"

Lucas thumbed toward the door. "You have a bunch of kids waiting for you."

"So, I can go?"

"For now." Freddy's scowl made The Joker look like a Sunday School Teacher.

Maria's gaze darted between the two men, her voice trembling. "What do I tell my husband, I mean about all this? Seriously?"

"You better think of something," Freddy said. "I plan to talk to him."

Lucas rose to leave. "If you tell him the truth, he'll be upset, but if he's a decent guy, it will occur to him how close you came to getting shot."

"My husband's not a decent guy."

Lucas pressed his thumb against the ID reader and entered Homicide. Before he made it to his desk, Lieutenant Clark waved from the doorway of her office.

He went in and sat across from his boss while she closed the door. She returned to her chair and tapped on her tablet. "When I came in, I had a message from the chief, and later, Captain Curtis dropped by. Both want to find out what's going on with the Dakota Industries investigation."

Being the brass's focus never worked out for Lucas. "Did you share my report and interview with Rachel?"

"They don't need details yet. I stalled them, but I don't know how long I can continue to stall."

Lucas breathed a sigh of relief. He didn't want to lose control of his investigation to a couple of bureaucrats.

A smile crept across her face. "Great work tracking down the mysterious Rachel Smith. We haven't been able to verify her identity under that name, no social security number, driver's license, Homeland Security ID."

"My guess is she's not a Smith."

Clark rolled her eyes. "You think? I don't suppose you could obtain a DNA sample from her."

Lucas thought about the pink toothbrush he'd given her. "Sure, no problem."

His boss raised an eyebrow. "Is there something you're not telling me?"

Of course, there was, but he couldn't share everything yet. "Nope."

He changed the subject. "Something I learned this morning is not in the report. Including Rachel, seven people had the opportunity to administer the nerve agent to Dr. Beltran in the five hours before his death. Calvin Hawk and Melody Fleming are on the list."

"Who else?"

"Reverend Donovan Armour and Chastity Moorhead."

The lieutenant laughed until she snorted. "Moorhead? The name must have piqued your interest."

79

"Not in the way you think. She and I knew each other in high school."

"Small world. Who are they?"

"Did you catch CNN this morning? Donovan Armour is a reverend. He lives for media coverage, always complaining about the evils of technology, among other things like alcohol, sex, and progressive politics."

"So, he's an asshole. Is he capable of murder?"

"He's a religious fanatic. They're capable of justifying anything."

"I assume you'll want to talk to them."

Lucas wasn't looking forward to seeing Chastity, but he had a job to do. "As long as they're on the list."

Clark drummed her fingers on the table. "Who else?"

The lieutenant would explode when he told her about the captain. "Two Pentagon procurement officers, Colonel Richard Urias and Captain William (Wild Bill) Koenig."

She jumped to her feet. "The dead lover at Maria Alvarez's house? Of course, it is."

Lucas smiled. He enjoyed surprising his boss.

She eased back into her chair. "So, there's a link...possible link between his death and Dakota?"

"I'd say probable link." He recounted his chat with the owner of the Happy Camper and the meeting he and Freddy had with Maria.

"Where's Freddy?"

"He wants to talk to Maria's husband. He's not convinced a link exists between the two cases. Maybe he's right."

"About Beltran's murder, I assume Calvin Hawk and the powers at Dakota will be more cooperative now that Dr. Lee ruled the death a homicide."

"I hope so. I'm on my way to Dakota as soon as I leave here."

"Then, get to work."

Lucas rose to leave.

Clark held up one hand. "Wait, what about Rachel? Is she somewhere safe?"

"I thought so. Now, I'm not so sure." Without revealing Rachel's location, Lucas told her about the two thugs snooping around.

The lieutenant rose and set both hands on her hips. "You have to make sure she's not in danger."

"I'm working on it, but Hawk knows this city well. I'll think of something."

Clark grinned. "I'd invite her to stay with me, but I don't think my wife would approve. Rachel's attractive, don't you think?"

Lucas wasn't sure if there was a correct answer. "I guess."

The lieutenant's phone rang. She picked it up and furrowed her brow. "Okay, I'll tell him."

She set the phone down. "Dr. Lee's awake. She insists on seeing you right away."

10

His heart pounding with unease, Lucas poked his head into Nico Lee's clean and antiseptic-smelling hospital room. Behind her were a UV light sanitizer and a monitor with wavy lines that danced as her heart beat. He took it as a good sign that the doctors had moved her from ICU to a private room. She waved him into the room and spoke to the automated bed control. "Raise head."

With a whir, the head of the bed elevated. She pointed to a chair next to her with an arm connected to an IV drip. "You got my message."

He sat beside the bed. "You look terrific."

"Liar." Dr. Lee snickered. She was pale and worn out, but she managed a smile. She reached out and squeezed his hand.

She took a deep breath. "They tell me I might be stuck here a few more days. I wanted to tell you what I wasn't able to say the last time I remember seeing you in case I take a turn for the worse."

"You'll be back to work in no time."

"Sure, I will." Dr. Lee reached toward the nightstand for a plastic glass with a straw in it.

Lucas gave her the glass. "If I suspected you would recover so fast, I would've sneaked you in a beer."

"That would have been awesome." She took a long swallow and

handed the glass back to him. "Before I realized the nerve agent was still active, I took readings and made some calculations. The amount administered was the perfect dose to be lethal yet produce symptoms that mimicked cardiomyopathy. If I do say so myself, most medical examiners would have missed it."

"So, you're saying whoever did this knew what they were doing."

"They either understood plenty about anatomy, perhaps a doctor or nurse, or they were expert in science, particularly nerve agents."

Only seven people came in contact with Dr. Beltran before he died. "Seven."

"Seven, what?"

Lucas told her the people with the opportunity to administer the nerve agent in the five hours before Dr. Beltran's death.

He kept Rachel on the list. She frequently demonstrated her intelligence and grasp of science beyond his capabilities. Calvin Hawk's military history and his work at Dakota no doubt familiarized him with nerve agents. Melody Fleming oversaw everything at Dakota.

Reverend Armour attended medical school before dropping out in a drug scandal, before his redemption, of course. Lucas couldn't imagine Chastity involved in a murder. She was the least likely suspect along with Rachel, but both remained on his list for now.

The two left were the military men, the late Captain Koenig and Colonel Richard Urias. Lucas had few details about them. If the two men met with Dr. Beltran, perhaps they also encountered Rachel. Maybe she could enlighten him about their background.

"The family was here earlier. It was painful seeing worry on their faces. This is the first time my job ever put me in danger. I hope you find the bastard who did this to Dr. Beltran and to me." Niko lifted her arm toward a table by the window. A bouquet of mixed flowers sat with a dozen get well cards.

"I was going to bring a card."

Her chuckle turned into a cough. "You never were good at that sort of thing."

"I didn't want you to think I turned into a softy."

Nico appeared to grow tired. She closed her eyes and muttered. "The only person knowledgeable about medicine is the reverend." She mumbled something. "My husband."

"What about your husband?"

"He's…he's a good man." She drifted off to sleep.

"Yes, he is." Lucas rose and kissed her cheek. He reached into his jacket and pulled out a card he'd purchased from the hospital gift shop. He wrote her name on the outside and placed it on the table beside the other cards.

Lucas pulled into his garage, feeling like a real heel. Like a cheating husband, he was about to sneak around in his own house, hiding his behavior from the woman who was helping him solve Dr. Beltran's murder.

At the kitchen table, Rachel glanced up. "Beau, Daddy's home."

He tried not to appear guilty. "I forgot something and also wanted to thank you for the six names you sent me."

"The person who killed Dr. Beltran is on that list."

Beau burst through the doggy door, wagging his tail. He ran up to Lucas.

"Probably." He petted the dog and sat beside Rachel. "You ever meet the reverend and Chastity Moorhead?"

"Dr. Beltran introduced me to them once. We hardly ever spoke."

"What about the two military officers?"

"I saw Koenig and Urias around about once a month. I understood they were the two most important clients Dakota had, but we never met."

"Think you can find out anything about them?"

Rachel patted his hand. "Of course."

"Thanks." Lucas got up. "Stay, Beau."

He went to his room. He grabbed a pink toothbrush, identical to the one he'd given Rachel, still in its case.

With Rachel searching on the computer and his dog next to her on a soft bed, Lucas slipped inside the guest bathroom. Her toothbrush lay on the counter beside the sink. He removed a Sharpie and a clear vial from his pocket. Using the Sharpie, he slid her toothbrush into the container without touching it. He scribbled Rachel Smith on the side, then replaced her toothbrush with the new one.

Lucas tried to shake off guilt about sneaking around in his own house, but he had to provide Lieutenant Clark what she needed.

Lucas went into the kitchen. "Can I get you anything?"

Beau sat up and barked.

"Not you."

Without looking up from the monitor, Rachel shook her head. "No, thanks."

"Okay, I have to head back to work." He patted his dog on the head. "And Rachel, I appreciate all your help with the investigation."

She gazed at him and smiled. "Thanks for believing in me."

Lucas drove back to the station, still unable to lose his guilt. Telling himself he had a job to do offered little comfort.

He hurried into the building and entered Homicide. He stepped into the lieutenant's office without knocking and set the vial with the toothbrush on her desk.

She picked it up. "A toothbrush. It'll have fingerprints and DNA. I can obtain preliminary results in a day or two. Nice work."

"Just part of the job."

"A toothbrush." The lieutenant drummed her fingers on the desk. "Should I ask how you obtained this?"

"I know where she's staying; that's all."

The chair squeaked when she leaned back. "I think Rachel's staying at your house?"

No sense lying now. "She is. But it's not what you think."

11

As Lucas approached the entrance to Dakota Industries, he slowed his SUV as he passed at least fifty protesters. Many held handmade signs containing scripture while listening to a speaker. He recognized the leader of the group as Reverend Armour. Behind him stood Chastity in a prim yellow dress with her distinctive red hair stirring in a gentle breeze.

Chastity appeared to recognize him as he drove past. He stopped at the front gate alongside the now familiar robot. "Lucas Nash to see Calvin Hawk."

Lucas glanced back at the reverend, whose baritone voice boomed. "…Genesis says God created man in his own image. Dakota Industries is creating robots in their corporate image."

Beside him, the robot chirped, then spoke. "I'm sorry, Mr. Nash, but Mr. Hawk is not available."

Lucas lost patience with the 'bot. "Tell him *Detective* Nash is here and needs to meet with him now."

"Yes, Sir." A moment later, the robot chirped again. "Mr. Hawk is in a meeting and can't be disturbed. Would you care to wait until he's out?"

He checked his rearview mirror again. The reverend's speech ended, and he and Chastity were talking. "I'll wait."

Lucas backed up and parked on the grass alongside the fence. He climbed out and approached his former high school girlfriend.

A familiar bright smile swept across her face. She held out her hand. "Lucas Nash, I thought I recognized you, small world."

He shook her hand. "Chastity. You haven't changed since high school."

"You're wrong about that." She introduced him to the reverend.

The man shook Lucas's hand with a firm, steady grip. His voice was an octave higher than baritone. "A pleasure, Mr. Nash. How do you know Chastity?"

Chastity answered for him. "We were friends when we were kids."

The reverend's brow furrowed. "Are you associated with Dakota Industries?"

"No, I'm not. I'm a homicide detective."

Chastity smiled. "I thought you would get into police work like your father, but I thought you might become a motorcycle officer."

"I was."

The reverend let out a mournful sigh that sounded as sincere as one of his infomercial pitches for contributions. "Oh, yes, the unfortunate death of Dr. Beltran. I almost canceled the protests, but God's work doesn't wait. Let us not become weary in doing good work, for, at the proper time, we will reap a harvest if we do not give up. Galatians 6:9."

How pompous. Lucas considered quoting George Carlin. "If you say so. Did you know Dr. Beltran?"

The reverend issued an uncomfortable cough. "We only met a few times when I asked him about rumors of a secret project he was working on."

"What did he say?"

Before he could answer, the reverend's phone rang. He held up one finger. "Sorry, I need to take this. Perhaps we can speak more before I leave your city."

You can count on it.

The reverend answered the call and stepped away.

With a subtle touch on his arm, Chastity led Lucas further from the phone conversation. The sun shimmered off her hair. Time had been more than kind to her. In high school, she was thin, but her legs were long and shapely. He tried not to stare. She'd filled out nicely.

The robot chirped and called from the gate. "You may go in now, Detective Nash."

Lucas held up one hand. "Tell Mr. Hawk to wait."

Chastity raised an eyebrow. "We only met once, but I don't think Calvin Hawk is used to people telling him to wait."

"Perhaps he should get used to waiting."

Chastity's green eyes sparkled. She held his gaze. "I'm staying at the Regency Hotel, downtown."

Why mention this?

She cocked her head and smiled as if reading his mind. "I thought we might get together for a drink before we leave."

Alcohol? Hooch, booze, liquid courage? He would've been less shocked if she'd told him she worked her way through college as a topless dancer. "You drink?"

Chasity grinned. "I've changed *somewhat* since high school."

"So have I."

She smirked. "I doubt it."

The robot called again. "Detective Nash."

"I'll be right there." He held out one hand to shake Chastity's hand.

She ignored the gesture and slipped both arms around his neck and gave him a hug and a kiss on the cheek.

For a moment, he relived their first kiss at a football game. "I'll call you."

"I hope so." With another flick of her hair, she turned and headed for Reverend Armour.

Lucas wasn't sure, but he apparently just got to first base with Chastity Moorhead.

Lucas stepped inside the lobby, trying to concentrate on the task at hand instead of reflecting on an old flame with red hair he hadn't thought about in a dozen years. Now he found himself juggling thoughts between an old girlfriend and a girl he met only a few days before.

Hawk's expression when he came out of the elevator took Lucas's mind off romance. The man's gruff appearance and furrowed brow seemed ready for conflict. "You think you can just show up here without an appointment?"

"Standard procedure in homicide. I'm here to meet with Melody Fleming."

Calvin stared at him like a prizefighter in the center of the ring before a bout. "She's busy."

Lucas held his ground and was ready to kick some butt if it came to that. "Dakota's COO didn't die of natural causes. I expect your and Ms. Fleming's cooperation while I investigate." Lucas took a step closer. "You do want to help find who killed Dr. Beltran, don't you?"

Hawk's eyes narrowed. "Of course, I do."

A robot whirred toward Lucas and spoke. "The subject is armed, Mr. Hawk. Shall I subdue him?"

Hawk held up one hand. "I'll take care of this myself. Standby."

"Yeah, stand by, R2; you might need to clean up Mr. Hawk's injuries."

Lucas had grown to dislike the chief of security, especially his dogged pursuit of Rachel. He took another step forward. "Run along and tell Ms. Fleming I'd appreciate chatting with her, or I'll ask the district attorney to issue a subpoena. Won't that be terrific on CNN?"

Hawk stepped closer to Lucas. The two men stood two feet apart.

A woman in a blue suit and red silk scarf appeared on the balcony above them. She looked to be in her late forties or early fifties, with shoulder-length hair the color of pewter that might have shined if she worked at it.

"You boys going to face the wall and find out which one can piss farthest?"

Lucas made a slight bow. "Melody Fleming, I presume."

"You must be Lucas Nash, homicide detective."

Hawk held up one hand. "I'll take care of him, Ms. Fleming."

"That won't be necessary. I'll see you now, Detective Nash. Mr. Hawk will show you the way." She turned and disappeared.

He followed Hawk to the elevator. "What a delightful woman."

The two men rode the elevator to the top floor in uncomfortable silence. The door opened, revealing a lobby with a couch and a table.

Inside, the office appeared to be a penthouse suite with marble tile, plate glass windows, and leather furniture. Robots stood on each side of the doors. The tall one shaped like a coffee pot followed Lucas while the other resembled a round footstool and didn't appear operational.

Standing on the balcony less than twenty feet away, Melody Fleming appeared younger than she had from a distance. She stepped into the room and gestured toward the two leather chairs on the other side of the desk. "Won't you sit down?"

Melody sat in a white leather chair behind a desk made of smoked glass and stainless steel. Behind her was a wall of security monitors that blinked off as he sat. She had the steely eyes of a four-star general and the welcoming eyes of a friendly aunt.

Lucas squeezed the arms of the comfortable chair. What did they use, cow udders? "Thank you for seeing me, Ms. Fleming. I realize this must be a difficult time professionally and personally."

"Aren't you a charmer, Detective? I thought you wanted to interrogate me." Her tone had as much sincerity as a used robot salesperson.

The meeting wasn't off to the start Lucas had hoped. "An interrogation, no. I was hoping for an informal conversation."

She glared at Hawk. "Perhaps I was misinformed."

Lucas nodded toward the huge window overlooking the entrance to Dakota. Most of the protesters had left. "When I arrived, I encountered a kind of protest."

She sighed. "Sign of the times, the old conflict between technology and religion. I believe I can reason with them. I think you'll find me reasonable, Detective."

"I hope so, Ms. Fleming."

"Call me Melody, please. She leaned back in her chair and smiled. "Since we're having an informal conversation, perhaps we could start by telling me whether you know Rachel's whereabouts."

"Rachel Smith?"

She chuckled like she'd rehearsed all day but didn't quite sell it. "Okay."

"I don't understand your company's position. Perhaps this Rachel person merely quit. It happens, especially with young people."

Beside him, Hawk scoffed.

"After years working for her boss and mentor, she disappears shortly after he is found dead." Melody shook her head. "We don't think she quit. We believe she left and made off with proprietary secrets."

"What kind of secrets?"

"They involve a project Dr. Beltran was in charge of."

"A highly classified project. How much do you know about it?"

"Just a few details, I probably wouldn't understand them without an owner's manual. I struggle every time I get a new model of phone."

Melody chuckled.

He held up one hand. "But about Rachel, I don't consider someone who left their job a police matter. Perhaps you should hire a private detective."

Hawk cleared his throat. "We don't think that's necessary. I'm leading the recovery efforts."

Lucas stared at the big man. "Oh, yes, you made that clear when I was picking up my dinner. Have you considered filing a police report?"

"I reported her disappearance to you." Hawk held up both palms. "You're the police."

Lucas lifted his jacket and displayed the homicide ID on his belt to Hawk. "I'm homicide. You might try Missing Persons, Bub."

"Bub!" He jumped to his feet. "Why'd you call me Bub?"

"There's a lady present, so I won't call you what I'm thinking."

Melody's hand erased a smile from her face. "Mr. Hawk, take a seat, or leave."

"Yes, ma'am." Hawk eased back in his chair, never taking his eyes off Lucas.

Lucas went into his aw-shucks mode. "If you'll forgive me, Ms. Fleming, I'm just a small-city cop attempting to do my job the best way I can. I make mistakes from time to time, but it's not from lack of trying."

Melody folded her hands in front of her. "Detective, Rachel is a sweet young woman, though she's more than a little naive. I'm fond of her, but she was the last one to see Dr. Beltran alive. If this indeed was a murder, I'm guessing you could characterize her as a suspect or a person of interest."

"The investigation hasn't progressed to the extent we consider anyone a person of interest."

She flashed the plastic smile he was becoming familiar with. "Let's get on with the purpose of your visit. Ask what you came to ask."

Lucas skipped the did you murder your business partner question. "I understand conflict existed between you and Dr. Beltran."

She flipped a dismissive hand. "We had disagreements from time to time, as many executives do who work together for as long as we did."

"But lately."

She gazed out the window. "In the past six months, we disagreed about the direction of the company. I prefer an approach that meets the needs of our customers."

Obviously, Dr. Beltran had been the brains behind the technical side of the company. Ms. Fleming, no doubt brilliant in her field, was the money person.

"Like the Pentagon, police agencies, and security firms. Apparently, Project Halo involves something truly extraordinary."

"Two years ago, Mr. Nash, Dakota Industries rolled out an AI platform that allows artificial intelligence to address customer service complaints, replacing call centers companies used to send offshore."

"Artificial intelligence still sounds like science fiction to me."

She smiled. "Let me give you a demonstration. Hazel."

As the round robot lit up, Melody handed Lucas a business card. "Call the number on the bottom."

Hazel, the robot, stopped beside Lucas.

He took out his phone and spoke the number.

Hazel answered in a cheerful female voice. "Dakota Industries, my name is Hazel. From the phone you're using, you must be Mr. Nash. How may I help you?"

If he weren't seeing it for himself, Lucas would have thought someone's friendly grandmother had answered the call. "Ah, my electric vehicle doesn't charge efficiently."

"Is this a new issue, or has this always been the case?"

"I guess...new."

"Sounds to me like a charging panel problem. I could contact a contractor for you and schedule an appointment."

"I'll get back to you on that. By the way, you have a pleasant voice."

"As do you, Mr. Nash. Have a wonderful day."

Although Hawk's gruff exterior remained unchanged, Melody

looked like a parent whose kid had just recited the Gettysburg address after a Thanksgiving pageant.

Lucas shut off his phone. "I must say that is truly impressive."

He patted the robot. "Excellent job, Hazel."

Melody was pleased with herself. "No need to maintain offshore call centers with AI."

"I take it you thought Dr. Beltran was more cautious with Project Halo than he needed to be."

"On the contrary, I thought Project Halo required more caution. With the potential of critical customers, only perfection will do. Dr. Beltran wanted to move into production before I thought it was prudent to do so."

Lucas didn't expect that answer. Her statement appeared as false as her eyelashes. "Conflict arose because you urged caution, and Dr. Beltran was determined to push forward to product development?"

"That's right."

Either she or Rachel was lying. Perhaps documents and videos would prove which one was telling the truth.

Lucas rubbed the stubble on his chin. "I don't suppose you care to share details about Project Halo."

"The government classifies the program as top secret. If I shared anything, I could go to jail."

"I wouldn't want that. I assume there is surveillance of Dr. Beltran's final hours."

Melody tapped on her desk, and a monitor rose from the cabinet behind her. She touched another button and a video, with no sound, came on. She turned her chair and watched along with Lucas and Hawk.

Rachel stood beside Dr. Beltran, whose furrowed brow indicated a serious discussion. When he finished, Rachel hugged the man like a daughter going off to college, then turned and left the office.

"Note the time stamp at the bottom of the recording." She sped up the video, and an hour had passed. Dr. Beltran tugged at his collar.

One hand clutched his throat. Another grabbed his chest. He stiffened and froze. A second later, his head hit the desktop, and he was in the position where Lucas saw him the night of the murder.

She stopped the video. "I'm not a medical doctor, but I think you just witnessed Dr. Beltran having a heart attack. This is much ado about nothing."

Quoting Shakespeare never endeared anyone to Lucas.

The monitor shut off.

As if she'd forgotten to express emotion, Melody let out a sigh and blinked away the tears shimmering in her eyes. Her authoritative voice trembled. "Despite our differences, I'll miss Esteban profoundly. We started working together in my garage. We struggled to acquire a foothold in the technology sector."

She blinked again. The tears vanished, and so did the sadness.

"Two items would be most helpful, Melody. A list of everyone who encountered Dr. Beltran in the five hours before his death and the video documentation."

"Mr. Hawk can obtain the list. The video might take a bit longer. We both want to find out what happened to a brilliant man and close friend of mine. I can't think of any reason for you not to have a copy." She signaled to Hawk, who rose from his chair, shot Lucas a glance, and left the office.

Melody smiled. "Let me show you something. She walked him to a sliding glass door that slid open as she drew near. She led him to a deck overlooking the grounds.

They stepped outside, where a soft breeze stirred her silver hair. She brushed a wisp from her forehead. "We're in Building A, administration, HR, testing, and security."

Melody Fleming came across as a micromanager, unlike Lieutenant Clark. He liked micromanagers about as much as IRS auditors.

She pointed to a long rectangular structure at the far end of the property near a line of trees. "Over there is Building B, where most of the artificial intelligence products and experiments take place. It's been the major source of Dakota's revenue for the past five years."

"We do develop artificial intelligence platforms for space exploration. A computer with artificial intelligence capabilities takes up less room and weighs far less than a crew of humans or even an individual."

"What's the building beside it?" The least impressive of the three, the two-story block structure had only a handful of windows.

"Project Halo."

"Why don't you tell me about Project Halo? I'll find out sooner or later. I prefer sooner."

Melody shocked Lucas when she answered right away. "Project Halo involves the next generation in robotics. Dakota Industries' bread and butter, so to speak."

"What's the building beside this one?"

"A dormitory for most of our employees. You'd be surprised how many single workers prefer to work on campus. Inside is a rec center, movie theater, food court, and an arcade."

"Does Rachel live there?"

"She did, she does." The woman led him inside and walked him to the door. "Rachel is a young, innocent woman, brilliant, inquisitive, and a hard worker, but she's incredibly naive. We want her to come home and continue to work with us on Project Halo."

"So, the project will go on?"

"Perhaps. If she contacts you, tell her we miss her and hope she'll come back after this matter is cleared up." Melody checked her watch. "I'm sorry; I'm late for an appointment. It was a pleasure meeting you, Detective."

He shook her hand. "Thank you for your time."

Her voice took on a flirtatious tone. "Hazel was right; you do have a pleasant voice."

She escorted him to the door, which opened automatically. They stepped into the lobby.

On the couch sat Reverend Armour and Chastity.

Melody greeted them. "So glad you could come."

They rose and shook her hand.

She introduced Lucas. "This is Detective Lucas Nash. Lucas, this is Reverend Donovan Armour and his lovely assistant, Chastity Moorhead."

Lucas flashed his most practiced smile. "We've met."

Melody was the type of executive who didn't like surprises. "How do you know each other?"

The reverend's baritone voice returned. "We were introduced at the protest."

Lucas smiled at Chastity, who was clearly uncomfortable. "Chastity and I go way back. Obama High, Class of '20. Go Eagles."

12

Rachel stared at the computer screen, flexing her fingers. The information she'd obtained from hacking Dakota's databases contained little about the background of the two military officers, Captain Wild Bill Koenig and Colonel Urias.

They served as liaisons to Dakota; Koenig represented the Army. Urias, while an active duty member of the military, worked for another entity, the Department of Homeland Security. Three years earlier, the Pentagon detailed him to DHS, and Koenig took his Army position.

Both Homeland Security and the Pentagon spent plenty on robotic and artificial intelligence, DHS as a liaison for many major police agencies.

She also managed to extract six emails between Melody and Calvin Hawk talking about getting rid of Dr. Beltran. Rachel couldn't wait to tell Lucas. She picked up the phone to call him.

Beside her, Beau sat patiently, his tail sweeping the floor as he smiled up at her.

Rachel ruffled the hair on the back of his neck. "You want to play? Go fetch."

Instead of grabbing the ball from the kitchen, he walked over and stared at the closed pantry door.

She rose. "Are you hungry?"

She opened the pantry door and reached for a box of dog biscuits.

Beau stood on his hind legs and snatched the leash from a hook on the inside of the door.

Rachel let out a sigh. She couldn't risk taking Beau around the block, in case Hawk and his team were watching through the dark windows of a van. She offered him a biscuit.

The dog took it in his mouth and dropped the treat next to the leash.

"Buddy, I can't."

The dog barked as if saying, yes, you can.

She grabbed the ball from beside the doggie door and bounced it. Beau didn't move.

Rachel sighed and went to the front door and peered out the window.

She saw no sign of the two men from the day before or any other strangers in the neighborhood and no drones overhead. Besides, Hawk wouldn't send security back to the same location the next day, would he?

She gazed at Mr. Bernardi's front lawn. In a straw hat, he held a hose. He was washing a dirty red pickup that was at least twenty years old. Surely, he would have alerted her if the men showed up again.

Beau deserved a walk; ten minutes tops.

She unlocked the door, poked her head out front, and looked in both directions. With some sense of assurance, she went inside, grabbed the leash, and hooked it to Beau's collar. "Let's make it quick."

She and Beau went next door and stopped beside Mr. Bernardi. "You haven't seen any strangers, have you?"

He dropped the hose in the grass. "Nope. I would've mentioned something if anyone suspicious showed up."

"That's what I told Beau."

Bernardi laughed. "Enjoy your walk."

"Come on, boy." She tugged on the leash, and they set off down the street.

They rounded the corner and almost reached the end of the street when Rachel froze. Overhead, a drone shaped like a torpedo appeared and paused above her and the dog. "We better hurry home." She turned around and ran with Beau in close pursuit. She cut through a yard, making it around the corner. Then came the familiar sound of the car engine from a day earlier. "Come on, Beau."

Rachel dropped the leash and took off running. Beau sprinted after her. She slid to a stop in front of a house with a pickup parked in the driveway with boxes and tarps in the truck bed. The gate was ajar.

She ran to the fence and shoved the gate open. It banged against the side of the house as she returned to the truck and yanked down the tailgate. She helped the excited dog climb into the bed and tugged a tarp over them both as squealing tires from the SUV turned onto the street.

Rachel kept assuring Beau they were playing kind of a game to keep him quiet. She reached for her phone and realized that, in her haste, she'd left it on the kitchen table.

The sound of hurried footsteps passed by the truck. The noise disappeared into the backyard.

Rachel threw off the tarp. She and Beau jumped down.

The two idiots had left the SUV with the engine running and doors open. She whispered, "Thanks, fellas."

As she reached the car, one of the thugs ran through the gate, holding a Taser in one hand, shouting, "Rachel, stop."

Without hesitating, she climbed behind the wheel. Beau leaped inside and stumbled over her. As the man with the Taser grabbed the door handle, Rachel hit the gas and sped off, squealing tires.

In the rearview mirror, she watched the man scramble to his feet as the second man joined him. They ran after her, then slowly disappeared as she raced away, putting distance between them. She patted Beau on the back of the neck. "Guess we lost those creeps!"

A block away, a glimpse of the earlier drone appeared from the corner of her eye. Within seconds, another arrived, a saucer-shaped police drone with a red flashing light.

Rachel took a breath. "Navigation."

The front panel lit up with a map of the local area. Accelerating, she turned right, then left. She sideswiped a trash can on the sidewalk and clipped a fence. Seconds later, she arrived at a park with a lagoon shaped like an egg. "Ready, Beau?"

She bounced up the curb, drove over the lawn, and slowed. With the vehicle moving, she reached for the passenger door handle and pushed open the door for the dog. "Come on, boy, jump."

Beau whined, hesitated, and jumped down to the grass. Rachel continued to a dock for canoes and headed for the water. Before the SUV hit the lagoon, she leaped and rolled, stopping herself by clutching a bicycle rack at the edge of the shoreline.

She scrambled to her feet, found Beau, and hid under a clump of trees with the dog as the drones arrived above the park.

With the two drones circling over the sinking SUV, Rachel and the excited dog reached the restroom fifty yards away. They disappeared inside an empty ladies' room.

Beau wagged his tail. The whole experience was an adventure. She smiled and patted his head. She leaned against the sink and caught her breath.

Rachel peeked out the open door as a patrol car and an SUV identical to the one sinking in the water arrived. Three men climbed out of their SUV and stared as the car disappeared beneath the surface of the lagoon. They began to argue as the officer stepped from his patrol car and attempted to break up the argument.

Rachel went back inside and peered into a dingy mirror and checked her face. No injuries, except for a tear on the sleeve of her right arm. She examined Beau, who appeared uninjured as well.

As the dog explored the room, she wondered how long she and Beau would have to wait. If only she'd brought her phone.

A minute later, a voice outside the restroom called, "Rachel."

She froze. When she heard her name again, she rushed to the open door and breathed a sigh of relief. "Mr. Bernardi."

He pointed to his red pickup parked along the street. "Let's beat it before they decide to search for who caused all this commotion."

Rachel grabbed the leash, and she and Beau followed Bernardi to his truck. The dog hopped inside, and Rachel sat in the passenger seat. She watched the patrol officer shake his head when one of the two security men punched the other, sending him into the lagoon with a splash.

The kindly old man climbed inside and reached into the glove compartment. He snatched a faded green cap with John Deere on it and handed it to Rachel.

She put on the cap as they drove away, leaving the park and the frustrated group of Dakota agents behind. "How did you…how did you find us?"

Bernardi smiled. "After you and Beau left, the drone came buzzing over the treetops. Thirty seconds later, those same two goons I thought I convinced to stay out of the neighborhood drove by. When they passed by, I climbed into my pickup and went after you. You did good, by the way. They're going to have some explaining to do about losing their car to a young woman on foot with a dog."

She patted his hand. "I don't know how to thank you."

He thumbed toward the lagoon. "I value my neighborhood too much to allow scum like that to dirty it up."

Lucas waved to the robot at the front gate as he drove away from Dakota. He switched to autopilot and headed home.

On the way, he reflected on Melody Fleming, a tough, strong-willed impressive woman. Along with Dr. Beltran, she'd built Dakota from a tech startup to one of the country's leading robotics and artificial intelligence companies. Although the company now belonged solely to her, with his scientific genius gone, it was hard to imagine why she'd want him dead.

She shared more than Lucas had expected to learn. She told a different story than Rachel about who urged caution about Project Halo, something a guilty person would say. Still, he was no closer to a theory of who was most motivated to kill Dr. Beltran.

He went through the other suspects on his list. He intended to find out more about the Reverend Armour through Chastity. In addition to the reverend, Lucas wanted to get more info about Wild Bill Koenig and Colonel Urias and the link between DHS, the Pentagon, and Dakota. However, Rachel hadn't texted him back since her first text about the six people who met with Dr. Beltran in his last few hours.

His SUV turned into his driveway and opened the garage door. When he climbed from his car, a sense that something was wrong swept over him. Inside, when Beau didn't bark, worry shot through him. He called Rachel's name, unlocked the back door, and called for his dog...no answer.

A knot twisted through his gut. Perhaps they'd gone for a walk. Lucas went outside and looked up and down the street. He went next door and knocked. He rang the doorbell, but Bernardi didn't answer. Where was he? "Damn."

He was headed back to his house when his phone rang. He didn't recognize the number but answered it anyway. "Lucas Nash."

Bernardi. "This is your neighbor. I'm here with Rachel and Beau."

Lucas breathed a sigh of relief and sagged into a chair next to the front door. "Are they alright?"

"I'm fine; thank you... They're okay, but we had visitors to the neighborhood this afternoon around four, so keep your eyes peeled. Can you meet us?"

"Of course, where are you?"

Over the phone, Bernardi let out a sigh. "I don't think I can say directly, in case my phone's been tapped."

"You're right."

"Do you remember where you and your wife came to my birthday a few years back?"

That was a year before the divorce. "I do."

"Think you can find it?"

Lucas checked his watch. He had to grab supplies and figure a safe place for Rachel and Beau. "I'll be there in…"

If he mentioned when he'd arrive, anyone listening could calculate a radius of where Rachel was. "I'll be there…soon."

"Got it."

Lucas went inside and hurried to his room. "And shut off your phone and take out the battery."

Bernardi chuckled. "She already told me. I'll take care of that as soon as I hang up."

"Can I talk to her?"

"Sure."

"Speaker mode." Lucas laid the phone on his dresser. He tossed an overnight case on his bed and began to pack. He threw clothes, a toothbrush, and a razor into the bag.

Rachel came on the line. "Beau and I are fine, thanks to…your caller."

Relief swept over Lucas as he heard her voice. She sounded calm and safe. "I got worried when I came home and couldn't find you or Beau…or your new friend."

"Sure, you were," Bernardi said.

"So, what happened?"

Rachel told him about taking Beau for a walk when she heard a drone approaching, followed by the two men in the SUV, and how she eluded them. She proudly recounted driving to the park and how she took care of the Dakota SUV before Bernardi came along.

"He's a good man. I owe him."

"Lucas…" She paused a moment. "I can't keep putting you, my friend here, and Beau in danger." Her voice caught. "These people are dangerous. You know that. I can make it on my own."

No, she couldn't. "Rachel, I'll figure something out."

"I'm sure you will. Did you receive the emails I sent you?"

"I did but didn't have time to check them out."

"They were talking about getting rid of Dr. Beltran."

"What? Are you sure?"

"Read them."

The information was explosive, emails that implicated both Hawk and Melody Fleming. "Excellent work. Let me speak with the man who helped you."

Bernardi came online. "I think I have a solution. We'll talk about it when you arrive."

What could that be? "Looking forward to hearing what you have in mind. Don't let Rachel do anything until I get there."

"Then, you better hurry. In case you didn't notice, she's a bit headstrong."

Lucas finished packing and began to change. He slipped into casual slacks, a long-sleeved T-shirt, and a windbreaker. "I need to thank you. You didn't have to become involved."

"I sure did. Going dark."

Lucas knew where they were, Bernardi's Pool Hall, once owned by his neighbor's brother. He hurried into the guest room and grabbed Rachel's duffel bag.

After loading the bags into the SUV, he plugged the SUV into the wall charger. He found a box half full of divorce papers and dumped them out. He rushed inside and packed the container with enough food and dog food for a day or two.

He had no idea where to take Rachel, but if he could find a quiet motel someplace, he wouldn't want to eat at restaurants. Lucas set the box in the back of the car and added a case of bottled water.

Lucas made one last inspection of the house and grabbed Rachel's toothbrush. Had DNA revealed her identity yet?

His electric vehicle was only 75 percent charged, but it would have to do. He reached beneath the car, snatched the tracking device, and stuffed it in his jacket pocket.

He sat behind the wheel and backed out. After closing the garage door, he sped toward the hotel a block away. He wanted to get to Rachel as soon as he could, but he still had one task to take care of.

Lucas parked in the lot and stood next to a bus stop bench where a half dozen people waited. He took the tracker from his pocket and bumped into a man in a loose-fitting suit.

The man turned. "Hey, knock it off it, buddy. You drunk?"

Lucas slipped the tracker into the man's suit coat pocket. "Very possibly." He staggered away and sat on the curb.

He waited until the bus arrived, and the man stepped onto the bus. The vehicle drove away. He got up and dusted off his hands.

Lucas climbed back into his SUV and powered up the car. "Autopilot mode."

The car responded. "Autopilot engaged."

"Bernardi's Pool Hall." Would Rachel still be there when he arrived?

13

Lucas made sure he hadn't picked up a tail as he headed for the pool hall. With the car on autopilot, he sent a video call request to Lieutenant Clark, who answered right away. Beside her stood her robot assistant. Lucas waved to the 'bot. "Hello, Walle."

The robot chirped. "Greetings, Detective Nash."

Clark leaned back in her chair. "What's up?"

"Hawk's men tried to kidnap Rachel this afternoon."

"Kidnap?" She muted the sound. She mouthed curse words before her voice returned. "She's your key witness, and you're only telling me now?"

"I just found out about it. There should be a police report. The incident happened about 4 p.m. at Monroe Park."

"Let me check." She silenced the sound again. Seconds later, Clark came back online. "I located a stolen vehicle incident. Someone drove an SUV into the lagoon at the park. Guess who the vehicle was registered to?"

"Dakota Industries?"

"Protecting a key witness like Rachel, you should have run this through channels. We could've found her a safe house."

"I didn't want to make her story official. The captain would know, and so would the chief. I can't say I trust them. You understand."

She cocked her head. "You trust me, don't you?

"Of course." Lucas let out a sigh, "Rachel's been staying at my house...in the guest room. It's the only way I could keep her safe."

"How's that working out, Bulldog?"

"I can't keep her stashed at my place. I'll figure something out."

"You better. Is she alright?"

"I'm on my way to pick her up. When I talked to her, she sounded fine. Did you get the DNA results yet?"

"Nope. Hopefully in a day or two."

"I'll check back with you. It would be good to know who I'm actually protecting."

Sirens wailed from a block away as Lucas parked near the entrance. The bed of his neighbor's red pickup poked out from the back of the building.

The pool hall was not in the best part of town, but the place felt safer than his neighborhood since it wasn't the type of location that would attract most employees, customers, and security staff of Dakota Industries.

A burly man in denim and a thick beard resembling a fox hanging from his chin sat in a chair by the front door, smoking a blunt. Lucas avoided eye contact as he approached the door, but when the man rose and sneered, Lucas opened his jacket, showing the police ID on his belt.

The man held up both hands and dropped back in his chair. "Go right in, sir."

"Don't mind if I do." Lucas pointed to his car. "Keep an eye on my SUV, will you, friend?"

"Yes, sir. Sweet wheels. Won't let no one mess with it."

"Much obliged." Lucas reached for the door handle. "I'm looking for an older fella, a young woman, and a dog."

The man took a hit and held out his hand. "My memory's not so good."

Lucas pulled a Tubman from his wallet and stuffed the bill in the man's hand.

He slipped the cash into the pocket of his denim shirt. "They're inside, in the back room. Knock twice; they'll let you in."

"You work here?"

The man's confidence was half pride and half arrogance. "I'm the bouncer. Welcome to Bernardi's Pool Hall."

Inside, less than half of the dozen tables were occupied by thugs and long-haired hippies. The place smelled like stale cigarettes and marijuana.

He walked to the back. He passed a counter where a clerk watched wrestling on one of the ceiling-mounted televisions while munching on a bucket of popcorn.

Lucas knocked twice on the red door, stenciled with the words "staff only."

The door opened, and a beer appeared, followed by Bernardi. "'Bout time."

Lucas went in, and Beau barked and pawed Lucas's hip, begging for attention. He petted his dog, relieved that he appeared fit and healthy.

Rachel rose from a couch and took a hesitant step toward him. Then she ran to Lucas, threw both arms around him, and kissed him. "I'm sorry I messed this up; I should never have taken Beau for a walk."

Bernardi took a long swallow of beer. "What's with this self-centered guy and nice girls?"

Lucas ignored the rebuke. He'd grown used to criticism from his neighbor over the years.

Rachel stepped back and held both of Lucas's hands. "Are you going to turn me in?"

Lucas squeezed her hands. "Of course not. My lieutenant ordered me to keep you safe. I intend to do exactly that."

"Sweet." Bernardi finished his bottle and let out a belch. "How 'bout a beer?"

"Sure." Lucas could use one. A relaxing brew might help him figure out a way to protect Rachel. "So, where's your brother?"

The old man grabbed two beers from a refrigerator and handed one to Lucas. "He died four years ago. You think I'm a son-of-a-bitch; you should have met *him*."

"Sorry for your loss," Lucas said with more than a hint of sarcasm.

Bernardi opened his beer. "So, what is it, Nash?"

What's what?"

"You and women. Rachel's as sweet as your first wife."

"First wife?" Rachel set both hands on her hips. "How many wives have you had?"

Lucas chuckled. "Just one."

Lucas opened the beer, took a sip, and relaxed ever so slightly. The lieutenant had given her blessing, but high-profile cases like this one usually involved politics. He had no way of knowing how the captain or police chief felt. When things got dicey, they hadn't always had Lucas's back.

She sat on the couch. "Where's my stuff?"

"Your duffel bag's in my car."

Rachel patted her leg, and Beau jumped on the couch beside her. She petted the dog. "Lucas, Mr. Bernardi has been wonderful to me and you too, but I can't keep putting your lives in jeopardy. I thought my problem through. I need to be on my own."

Bernardi opened his beer. "We went over this. Maybe you can talk sense into her."

Rachel rose with a determined frown. "Dakota cultivates important friends in this city, and Calvin Hawk isn't the type to give up so easily. Besides, there are drones and surveillance cameras everywhere, and don't forget the tracking device on your SUV."

"I took care of that."

"My mind's made up."

Bernardi drank half the bottle in one gulp. "I have an idea that will solve everything."

"Did she tell you why these men are after her," Lucas asked, "and why I'm involved?"

"She didn't need to. You're homicide. I guess that means she witnessed a murder...or she killed someone."

Rachel stomped her foot. "I didn't kill anyone."

Bernardi wore an apologetic frown. "I didn't think you did."

Lucas took another sip of beer and sat beside his neighbor. "What's your idea?"

"My cabin. I used to spend most summers there."

"I remember."

"I haven't been in a while, but it's in a hidden canyon and is off-grid. I put the place up for sale a couple of years back, but no one wanted a place without internet. The best thing is no one can tap into your phone, and drones couldn't track you. No cell service means you can't call out, and surveillance can't get in."

Rachel didn't look convinced, but a remote cabin sounded like a solution to Lucas. He'd brought enough food and supplies for a few days. "What kind of shape is the place in?"

"Might not have internet, but I had a new septic tank installed a couple of years ago. There's a well and propane, even a shower—and an excellent fishing stream within hiking distance. I'll draw you a map and show you how to get there. Finding the cabin in the dark might be tricky."

Lucas set his beer down and approached Rachel. "What do you think?"

"I think Mr. Bernardi's helped enough. The more involved he gets in my mess, the more danger he'll put himself in. If Hawk and his men learn I stayed at your house, they'll check the neighborhood, and someone might remember his red pickup or the two of us talking."

Lucas turned to his neighbor. "She's right, you know."

"Why don't you let me worry about that? I'm an old man. I want to help two people in love figure things out."

Rachel scoffed. "Lucas isn't in love with me, Mr. Bernardi." Her face showed the same pained expression he recalled from the night before. "Are you?"

Was he? He couldn't think about that now.

When he didn't answer, Rachel brushed past him. "I'm going. I'll get my duffel bag." She hurried out of the room.

Beau ran to the door and scratched to follow her.

Bernardi gestured with his beer. "You never told a woman you loved her when you didn't?"

"Well, sure, but…"

"She needed to hear you say it. You just going to stand there? Go after her." He picked up Lucas's bottle. "You going to drink this?"

"Beau, stay." Lucas grabbed the dog's collar and pulled him away. He slipped out the door as Rachel fled through the front.

A few customers watched as Lucas ran through the room. One whistled, "She's a fast runner." Another shouted, "I hope she's worth it!"

He pushed the door open.

Rachel was standing by Lucas's car, talking to the bouncer. She spoke to Lucas without looking at him. "The car's locked."

Lucas ran to her and caught his breath. He reached for her hands, struggling with what to say.

The man smiled with pride. "No one messed with your stuff, brother."

"Thanks. Could you give us a minute?"

The man held up both hands and backed away. "Oh, sure, Officer. I'll leave you and Rachel alone."

Rachel?

She smiled at the bouncer. "Thanks, Frank." She shook free of Lucas's hands and stood at the back of his car. "I want my duffel bag."

"Rachel, I..."

She set both hands on her hips. "What, Lucas? Why don't you want me to go?"

"Because I..."

She clamped her eyes shut.

He didn't want to share his feelings. He didn't know what they were. Despite the confusion, he wanted her safe, not to ensure the well-being of a witness, but because he needed time to figure out how he felt. "Because I care about you."

Rachel's face softened. She ran to him and threw both arms around him. "That's all you needed to say."

Lucas kissed her forehead. "Let me take you someplace safe."

Rachel let out a sigh. "Let's have Mr. Bernardi draw that map."

14

Lucas allowed himself one beer and forced himself to focus on his investigation. He knew little about Beltran. Murder victims deserve a detective focused on solving the killing, not mending broken hearts.

He didn't want to drive to the cabin in the dark. They'd be without GPS navigation, on unmarked dirt roads, and using a hand-drawn map. He thought it best to wait until morning to leave, even if the waiting gave Hawk and his men more time to find them before they slipped out of the city.

With Bernardi snoring off in a recliner with a half-full bottle of beer on a box beside him, Rachel curled up on the couch. Beau slept on a rug in the corner.

Lucas snatched a throw pillow he took from a chair in the back room. In the hall, he tried sleeping on a pool table. He found out slate wasn't the best mattress material. He grabbed the pillow and went outside, where a thick fog had enveloped the area. He managed a few winks in the back seat of his car.

When the purple glow of dawn peered through the SUV's window, Lucas climbed out of the car. With the fog thinning, he kept his eyes peeled for drones or suspicious vehicles and zipped up his windbreaker against the cool morning air. He arched his back, his bones making more cracking and popping noises than usual.

The front door of the pool hall opened. Rachel stepped out with Beau on the leash. He trotted to Lucas's side and licked his hand, then began to sniff along the pavement, searching for the perfect spot to pee.

After Beau took care of business, Lucas poured a bowl of kibble for his dog. He and Rachel sat on the chairs outside the entrance, watching the dog eat and the sun brighten.

Lucas let out a sigh. "Are you alright with spending a few days at the cabin?"

"Of course, though, I worry about Mr. Bernardi if Hawk and his team come after me again."

He worried about his neighbor too, but he didn't want Rachel to see his concern. "They don't know Bernardi helped. He'll be fine."

"I hope you're right."

Lucas was reluctant to bring up another subject. "We're not going just to hide out. I want to use the time to review the evidence and go over the list of suspects."

"I want to help."

Her answer surprised him.

"Once you solve the crime, I hope you'll stop seeing me as a witness and start treating me as…as a woman."

Before he could react, the front door creaked open. Bernardi came out, holding a gas can in one hand and the map with the other. "I found this in the shed out back. You'll need to fill it to run the generator."

The old man handed Lucas the map. "Surveillance drones do best in daylight, so I'd leave before the sun comes up."

"You're right. We'll head out when Beau finishes." Lucas shook his neighbor's hand. "I don't know how to thank you."

"Take care of Rachel. I'll keep an eye on your place and won't tell anyone where you are."

There was one person Lucas could trust. "If my homicide partner,

Freddy Gannon, drops by at my place or if he comes to you, tell him. Anybody else, call the police."

Bernardi rolled his eyes. "Freddy. I remember that guy."

Beau ate the last of the kibble and licked the bowl.

Rachel gave the old man a kiss on the cheek. "Stay safe."

"I will." He pulled the faded John Deere cap from his pocket and handed it to her. "Don't forget your lucky hat."

She smiled and slipped it on. "Thanks."

Bernardi tossed Lucas a key on a rabbit's foot key chain. "You'll need this to open the cabin."

Lucas stuffed the key chain into the front pocket of his slacks. He opened the back door of his SUV, and Beau climbed inside. He set the bowl on the floor next to a water bottle.

Rachel gave Bernardi a forlorn expression before opening the passenger door.

Lucas walked around the car, slipped behind the wheel, and started the motor.

Rachel opened the window and waved to the old man as they drove away.

They made it out of the city without seeing any drones or signs of Hawk and his men. When they reached the two-lane blacktop Bernardi had drawn, Lucas managed a sigh of relief.

An hour after they left, they began an ascent into the pine-covered mountains. She'd remained silent most of the trip. She held the John Deere hat in her hand, no doubt worrying about the man who rescued her and Beau in the park. "He'll be fine."

Rachel gazed at him as if for the first time. "I'm not upset about him. I'm worried that what I have to tell you will change the way you think about me."

"Do you think that little of me?"

"I think you're the most wonderful man I've ever met."

Lucas would never live up to Rachel's opinion of him. He also understood she was getting close to sharing whatever secret she'd kept to herself since they met.

He handed her the map and asked her to navigate. The task seemed to bring her out of her gloom. With her help, Lucas managed to find the dirt road turnoff right where Bernardi said it would be.

He worried about his neighbor but tried not to think about the old man. If all had gone well, he was back home, starting on his first beer of the day.

Rachel's eyes were focused on the passing pines, but her gaze was a thousand miles away.

He needed to change the subject. "My grandfather grew up on a farm in Kansas. Back when I was a kid, he taught me how to navigate by watching flocks of birds. Birds, especially migratory ones, are excellent navigators."

Rachel cocked her head, and a smile swept across her face. "You're making that up."

"Oh, it's true. Grandpa used to spin yarns, but this one is authentic. During migration, they use the earth's magnetic field to plot their course."

"Birds. I haven't seen any flocks of birds."

"Well, keep looking."

Rachel studied Lucas's face and let out a healthy laugh.

They rounded a bend, and Rachel pointed out the general store with the single gas pump Bernardi had explained were the last services until they reached the cabin. While she took Beau to pee in the woods, Lucas filled the one-gallon container to start the well's generator.

Tugging his cap over his brow, Lucas went inside, keeping his face hidden from the security camera behind the clerk, who was dealing a game of solitaire next to a cash register at least fifty years old.

He bought a few more groceries, sweets for Rachel, and a dog biscuit for Beau.

Lucas pulled a roll of cash from his windbreaker pocket. On the wall behind the clerk was a muted television. A FOX NEWS reporter was at Dakota Industries. The woman was interviewing Reverend Donovan Armour. Beside him stood Melody Fleming and Chastity.

The young man rang up Lucas's items and added the bill for gas. "Comes to fifty-four, nineteen."

Lucas handed him three Tubmans. "Keep the change. Mind turning that up a moment?"

The clerk pushed a button on the television, picked up the cards, and slapped a seven of diamonds below an eight of spades.

The reverend said, "After the unfortunate death of Dr. Beltran, I met with Melody Fleming. We share many beliefs. Science and technology do not have to conflict with the teachings of the New Testament. The Lord gave us free will and knowledge to use science to improve society and do God's work."

He found it hard to believe the reverend's words. Was he now in bed with Dakota Industries? Money must have changed hands.

The clerk cleared his throat. "Anything else?

"Nope." Lucas took an eight of hearts from the deck and set the card beneath a nine of clubs. He grabbed the groceries and left.

Before they took off, Lucas filled Beau's water dish. The dog drank, then jumped in the car.

As they drove away, he tried to cheer Rachel up. "Activate radio."

Rachel's eyes lit up. "Really?"

He turned the knob, searching for a station. He found mostly static but managed to come upon a classic country site from Nevada playing a Marty Robbins song about a gunfight in Agua Fria, Arizona. "What kind of music do you like?"

"Country oldies."

That was a surprise. "Seriously? I would have guessed you were a classical girl."

"Patsy Cline's my favorite. I like her songs about broken hearts."

Lucas would never have taken her for a Patsy Cline fan. "Have you ever had your heart broken?"

"Never, have you?"

"Plenty of times. The first time when I was twelve. Nellie Peterson, she acted interested just so the football quarterback would notice her."

Rachel snickered. "How awful."

Lucas clutched his heart and got her to laugh.

As if on cue, the station played Patsy's *Sweet Dreams* and Rachel's look of melancholy returned.

They encountered a handful of cars. Their progress slowed as the electric car bucked and groaned as it bounced along an ill-maintained dirt road filled with ruts and divots. They came to a fork in the old road, and Rachel pointed right. "We should arrive in another...twenty-two minutes."

The path twisted as they descended into a valley of woods and meadows. The car flashed a warning, "Internet Service Unavailable."

They lost the radio station, but Rachel's interest grew as she surveyed the ever-changing surroundings.

The old log cabin with a weathered barn behind it was nestled in a grove of trees. The place appeared as welcoming as the Bates Motel.

The cabin was one story, with a porch in front, exactly as Bernardi had described. From the outside, except for a faded coat of muddy red-colored stain, the place appeared to be in reasonably functional condition.

They climbed out of the car and gazed at the old structure. A chipmunk scurried over the porch and disappeared beneath the cabin. Lucas opened the back door. "Beau, it looks like you have some friends to play with."

Beau looked apprehensive, so Luke left the rear door open. The dog gently stepped down like he was landing on a crate of eggs.

Lucas pointed to the cabin and grinned at Beau. "You should go chase any critters away."

Rachel grabbed the gas can from the back of the SUV along with the groceries he added from the store. "Did Mr. Bernardi mention anything about the snakes?"

"He mentioned chipmunks, squirrels, and raccoons, but nothing about reptiles."

Rachel chuckled. "Maybe he thought you wouldn't come if he mentioned snakes."

"I might not have. I hate snakes, especially the ones with two legs." Lucas tossed a couple of stones under the cabin to be safe.

Something scurried beneath the front steps. Beau's ears perked up, and he took off toward the noise. He circled the old building, sniffing and marking his territory.

He carried a cooler to the porch and set it next to the gas can. "We might not see much of Beau for a few hours."

Rachel climbed the front steps and unhooked the screen door. She held it open while Lucas tried the key in the door. The tumbler turned, and the door opened with a squeaky groan.

The floor was littered with dead moths and other insects. Furniture was covered in plastic.

They returned to the car and unloaded their supplies as Beau stood with both legs on a pine tree, barking at something among the branches.

After they finished unloading, they began to clean. Lucas opened the windows to let in fresh air while Rachel used a hand sweeper to clean up the dead bugs.

They spent the morning cleaning away a couple of years of dust, cobwebs, and moths. When they were satisfied, Lucas grabbed the gas can, and Rachel followed him to the pump house.

He pulled the instructions for opening the cabin from his windbreaker pocket. He read the four pages, then handed the directions to Rachel.

She studied the pumping water information. "I spent two years in a high-tech company, and this looks really complicated. I'll read out loud; you do the hard work."

"You don't think I can figure it out?"

She smiled and patted his hand. "Of course, I do, Bulldog."

With less than certainty, he poured gasoline into the generator using a funnel and flipped the on switch. He pushed a few times on a red button.

Lucas spit on his hands, rubbed them together, and winked at Rachel. After a half dozen pulls of the rope, he was ready to give up. He gave it one more try, and the generator finally tuned over, coughing a puff of blue smoke. He opened the red valve. Water flowed to the cabin and began to fill a one-hundred-gallon tank in the attic.

With the machine running, Lucas drove the SUV to the pump house and connected the charging cable of his SUV to the generator.

While his car charged, they made their way to a white hundred-gallon tank behind the cabin. Rachel read the Propane instructions. He flipped a switch and turned a black handle, so gas flowed to the stove and hot water heater.

Inside, Lucas turned a valve beneath the stove and located the pilot light. He lit a match and moved it toward the pilot light, which lit right away. Rachel tried a burner, and they high fived each other when a burner lit.

They opened the valve to the hot water heater to allow well water to fill the hot water tank tucked inside a bathroom closet. After opening the valves to the kitchen sink, Rachel and Lucas returned to the bathroom. He knelt with a lighter and peered beneath the tank while Rachel read the instructions. Several attempts later, the water heater lit.

Lucas climbed to his feet, dusted off his clothes, and washed his hands. "Looks like everything works."

"We make a good team."

Was there a hidden message behind her comment? They weren't a team. Rachel was a witness to a murder, and he was a homicide detective. "How about lunch?"

15

With a soft breeze stirring the pines, Lucas and Rachel dined on sandwiches off paper plates on the porch while Beau explored the property.

Rachel tossed a piece of bread to a screeching blue jay who snatched up the offering and carried the treat to a tree limb and ate. She took a bite of her lettuce and tomato sandwich. "What made you want to become a cop?"

Lucas stared at his tuna salad sandwich. He enjoyed talking about feelings and emotions the way he liked speaking to his doctor about his prostate. He wanted Rachel to trust him, and sharing feelings might cause her to open up about what she seemed determined to keep from him.

"My father was a Green River Police Officer back when tough guys joined the force so they could rough someone up without getting into too much trouble. Now, people join the force when all the social work positions are filled."

Rachel smiled. "What about your mother?"

"My mother was a police dispatcher. I never thought I'd follow in their footsteps, but the Coronavirus hit during my senior year of high school, Class of '20, trying to get la...chasing girls, no plans beyond graduation."

Struggling with issues he preferred not thinking about, he took a deep breath and continued. "Then came quarantine and finishing school online, much like school is now, but at that time, the change jolted students and teachers. Instead of caps and gowns, graduation consisted of a five-minute drive through the parking lot with teachers in masks waving handmade signs to a recording of *Pomp and Circumstance*. That summer, my dad caught the disease at a political rally. Three days later, he was in the hospital on a ventilator. A month after that, he died alone.

"I'm sorry."

Lucas took a bite and went on. "After he passed away, my mother didn't seem interested in too much. Life grew serious, and the challenges almost overwhelmed me. I made decisions I now regret. A pandemic is such a random death, but murder is, by definition, premeditated, meaning someone wanted to end another's life. I accept senseless death by disease, but murder, no. There's no justification for taking a human life."

"I bet you've heard all the excuses."

Lucas chuckled. "Oh, yeah. Anyway, I wanted to become a homicide detective for the victims, families, and friends involved in an unexpected death."

For a moment, they ate in silence.

Rachel studied his face. "Family is important to you."

Lucas tossed a piece of his sandwich to Beau, who left the tree and gobbled up the food. "I never thought about the importance of family until my father passed. Maybe that's why I married too young. Neither of us was ready."

He finished his sandwich and thought back to his ex-wife. "Being a police officer is rough on a marriage. Cops struggle with issues that come up that only other cops might understand. They share things with each other they won't or can't with their spouse. As they grow close, the gap between spouses grows wider. I saw it happen to dozens of members of the force, not just me."

"Didn't you realize that might result, coming from a police family?"

"I should have, sure. My parents grew apart until Dad died. After that, Mom sat around thinking about him every hour of every day. Two years later, she swallowed a bottle of sleeping pills, ending her life."

"Oh, Lucas. I'm so sorry."

"I went away to college to leave their memories behind. I graduated in five years, but it was a struggle. I fit in at college like refried beans in a French restaurant."

Rachel smiled.

"I returned to Green River because I couldn't think of anywhere else. I didn't grieve for either one until a year after I graduated from the academy. I was involved in a shooting, and they made me attend meetings with a psychiatrist. I found out I'm an expert at avoiding issues like feelings and commitment."

Rachel sighed. "I can believe that."

"I worked through problems I had suppressed about my parents but avoided others. My ex dealt with all my troubles, but she couldn't handle one issue that ended our marriage. She wanted kids. I didn't. My wife's remarried now and happy. We're friends, actually. She and her new husband have two young kids."

Talking about his parents and his marriage wasn't what he had in mind. "What about you, your family?"

"I don't want to talk about it."

"Are you sure? I shared plenty about me. I know so little about you."

She handed the last of her sandwich to Beau. "Trust me; when we leave the cabin, you'll know everything there is to know about me."

Lucas unplugged his SUV from the generator and left the car beside the pump house. On the way back, he noticed a path leading into the woods. He hurried into the cabin and invited Rachel for a walk.

With Beau sniffing along the path, Lucas and Rachel made a game of finding different species of birds. As they went along, Beau focused on squirrels, chipmunks, and rabbits. When they returned, they spent the afternoon outside, mostly watching the dog explore. By dusk, all three were tired and hungry.

While Lucas fed Beau on the porch, Rachel searched through their collection of food. "How do guacamole salads sound?"

"Terrific." He was hungry for meat but had learned, when it came to relationships, he had to compromise.

They ate outside again in a cool breeze. When they finished, darkness closed in, and the temperature dropped. After cleaning up, they sat on the steps with Beau and watched the orange glow of sunset disappear over the pine trees.

"It's so beautiful, Bulldog." Rachel sighed. "I forgot to mention… while you were at work, I watched *Casablanca*."

"Did you like the ending?"

Rachel snorted. "I wouldn't have boarded the plane with Victor Laszlo."

"So, you would have stayed with Bogart?"

She reached over and squeezed his hand. "Of course." She gazed into his eyes then let go.

They watched the stars come out. Before long, the sky turned black with thousands of stars and a half-full moon. He'd never seen anything like the night sky. Her hair caught the moonlight, and her eyes danced. Why was life so complicated?

She petted Beau. "A quiet cabin nestled in the woods. It's almost like being on vacation."

When the cold settled in, they went inside. With flashlights taking the place of lamps, Lucas locked the door and began to close the windows. In the bedroom, a small bed presented a problem they'd yet to discuss.

He came out as she turned on a battery-powered lantern. "I think you should take the bedroom." He pointed to the narrow, uncomfortable-looking couch. "I'll sleep here."

Rachel smiled. "That's not fair. You worked hard today."

"Tell you what, you take the bed tonight, I'll sleep there tomorrow."

"Deal."

An hour later, after taking turns in the bathroom, they each took a light. After Rachel went into the bedroom, Lucas tossed a pillow and blanket on the couch. Beau jumped beside him and found room by Lucas's feet.

Lucas shut off the lamp and lay on his back under the blanket. He gazed at the moon peeking through the window. An occasional sound of an animal scurrying about reminded him how far they were from the city. He wondered if Rachel was asleep.

They'd fled to the cabin to keep her safe, as Lieutenant Clark ordered. The first day had been vacation-like, but Lucas was determined to review the evidence on Beltran's murder as he would at the police station. Rachel hinted she had more to share.

He couldn't shake the idea that Project Halo held the key to solving the case. Learning about the project would shed light on which suspect decided the only solution to their problem was to kill Dr. Beltran.

Lucas rolled over on his side without falling off and pulled the blanket up to his shoulders. In the morning, he and Rachel had to focus on the investigation. The vacation was over.

16

The next morning, Lucas woke up to a chilly cabin. Beau lay on the floor, wagging his tail. When he struggled off the couch, Lucas fell to the floor. After checking on his owner's safety, the dog ran to the door. Lucas let him out.

In the small bathroom, he shaved and changed into jeans and a sweatshirt. He lit the burner and attempted to make coffee with a device he'd only seen in movies. He set the pot on the stove and decided he needed to make a list of suspects.

Through the window, he saw Rachel on the front porch with Beau as a mist settled over the forest floor. He said good morning to Rachel. "I'm making coffee."

While the coffee percolated, Lucas removed a painting of a deer drinking from a stream from the wall across from the couch. He placed the picture on the kitchen table then retrieved a legal pad, a roll of tape, and a Sharpie from his overnight bag.

Lucas tore off a page, printed Suspects, and taped the paper high in the center of the blank wall. He yanked off six more sheets and taped them below the Suspects sheet.

Working left to right, he wrote Melody Fleming on the first paper.

Rachel and Beau came in. She poured herself some coffee. "What's this?

"An exercise to help organize my thoughts."

She took a sip and studied the six pages. "You need one more."

Rachel set her cup on the kitchen table and tore a sheet from the legal pad. She took the Sharpie from Lucas and wrote her name on the paper, then taped it to the wall next to the others. She handed the pen back to Lucas. "I'm still a suspect…until I'm not."

"Have it your way."

Rachel grabbed her cup and sat on the couch. Beau jumped up beside her. They both watched Lucas.

Beneath Melody, he printed the words power and control. "I'm looking for motives to kill Dr. Beltran or any other significant facts. Anything else?"

"Money. She stands to inherit and run a valuable company."

He wrote money on the page. "Obviously, Dakota won't be as prosperous without Beltran and Project Halo."

Rachel sipped her coffee. "Is that a rhetorical question?"

"Not necessarily."

She set down the cup. "There would be a massive loss of revenue if they canceled Project Halo, but now that Dr. Beltran's out of the way, they might try to salvage the program."

He never thought the project might be saved. Lucas tapped the second page. "What about Calvin Hawk?"

"Power."

"He's chief of security."

"He's more than that. He's Melody's top aide, number three in the company. With Beltran out of the way, his importance and influence grow. He's committed to keeping Project Halo alive."

On the third page, Lucas wrote Captain Koenig, the next Colonel Urias. "Did you find out anything about them?"

"They were both procurement specialists for the government."

"For the military."

Rachel shook her head. "Urias was around at the beginning of Project Halo, since before my time, representing the military. They wanted Dakota to develop…soldiers who were powerful, smart, and took orders without question. A year ago, the colonel transferred to Homeland Security, and the Pentagon brought in Koenig."

"A secret army? DHS hasn't had a covert force since the Trump presidency."

When Beau barked and ran to the door, Lucas let him out and left the door open, so he could keep an eye on the dog through the screen door. "Where were we?"

"Colonel Urias's clients are the biggest police forces in the country."

He thought about Lieutenant Clark's bumbling robot and couldn't imagine them helping with law enforcement. "Police departments and the military are looking for the same thing."

"Cops' mission is to serve and protect. Soldiers exist to kill the enemy."

He printed customers under both names. On the next two sheets, he wrote, Reverend Armour and Chastity Moorhead. He wrote spiritual conflict beneath their names.

Rachel scoffed. "Is that motive to murder someone?"

"Throughout history, more people were killed in the name of God than anything. If they thought Project Halo was something evil, they might think stopping it was their divine responsibility."

"Take Chastity's name down. I think she's just his mistress."

Mistress? Back in high school, she convinced him she would never engage in premarital sex, but what exactly was her role for the pious reverend?

Lucas wrote accomplice with a question mark.

Rachel twirled her blonde hair. "Maybe."

He tapped the last sheet with her name on the paper.

"I was the last one to see Dr. Beltran alive."

Lucas jotted down last person to see alive below Rachel's name.

She stared into her cup. "And I admired Dr. Beltran, cared for him like a daughter would a father."

He'd met Rachel only three days earlier, but he couldn't imagine her killing someone she cared for so much, or anyone for that matter. What kind of person would plan a murder and make sure they were the last to see the victim alive?

"Why did you go meet with him?"

"Calvin Hawk knocked on my door. I was surprised because Hawk had never come to my room before. He informed me that Dr. Beltran wanted to speak with me."

That sounded suspicious to Lucas. "Had Beltran asked to speak to you?"

She nearly spilled the coffee. "That's just it! Dr. Beltran never told Hawk he needed to talk to me at all. He told me since I was there, he wanted to tell me his plans to terminate Project Halo before I heard it from someone else."

He reached for the page to take the paper down.

"No!" Rachel jumped to her feet. "Not until you're absolutely sure."

"I'm sure."

"Absolutely?" She cocked her head. "If you were at the station with Freddy, would you keep my name up?"

"Probably."

"Then leave it." She sat back down.

Below the list of suspects, Lucas taped a blank page. He wrote Project Halo.

He stuffed the Sharpie in his pocket and poured himself a cup of coffee. He sat beside Rachel. "All seven have one thing in common, an interest in Project Halo. I think it's time you share with me what you know about Beltran's project."

"You're right."

"Melody said the project involved the next generation in robotics."

"Did she mention Biological Robotic Entity or BRE?"

He wasn't familiar with the term. "This is the next generation in robotics?"

"When Project Halo was still in the planning stage, Dr. Beltran called the products he wanted to create, Biological Robotic Entities."

"BRE."

"Right. They would be smarter, stronger, have emotions, and could physically appear human."

"You're serious."

"Five years ago, doctors created a biosynthetic skin that revolutionized the treatment of burns. Dr. Beltran figured a way to use the skin to cover the entire unit, so they would pass for human. The real breakthrough, though, was his own, in AI."

"Artificial Intelligence."

"Right."

"Did he develop any prototypes?"

She hesitated before answering. "He did."

"They were successful?"

"To varying degrees, enough to interest the Pentagon and plenty of law enforcement agencies around the country."

"Jesus! I can't believe science could produce something so extraordinary." Lucas took a gulp of coffee. "I never considered this being possible."

"Oh, you have."

"What?"

"Officially, Dakota and the military and police still refer to them as BRE's. Over time, the staff starting joking, but a new name caught on. Even Dr. Beltran, when he was alive, and Ms. Fleming stopped using the term BRE."

"What were they called?"

Rachel took a deep breath as if she'd held the knowledge inside for a long time. "Androids."

17

Lucas got up and paced. Had technology come up against fiction? "Androids."

"Androids."

He needed a drink, but he hadn't brought alcohol. "They only exist in fiction."

"Not anymore."

"Why don't you start at the beginning?"

"Dakota became a leader in artificial intelligence. The company also manufactured robotic technology for various industries. Three years ago, the two of them agreed to combine the two technologies and produce the next logical step."

"Project Halo."

"Exactly."

"When they formed the company, Melody and Dr. Beltran made an exceptional team and supported each other. She believed the effort would become the most consequential revenue stream yet for Dakota. Dr. Beltran pictured a gigantic scientific breakthrough that would change humanity for the better. She took care of the financing while he assembled a team of scientists to determine whether creating a biological robotic entity was even possible. You can see the challenges became enormous."

Lucas could only imagine.

"Japan created two next generation robots almost thirty years ago. They appeared almost human-like but would never be mistaken for you and me, and their capabilities were limited. His goal was to create an artificial entity that could pass for human. To act and behave human, he needed to incorporate not merely a powerful brain but one with the capability of learning. Ever hear the term meta-learning in college?"

"If I did, I'm sure I forgot it by the time I left the classroom."

"Meta-learning is learning to learn by observing and interacting, not just with data, but with humans."

"I thought one just downloaded data, and they'd function like a human."

"You can download data, mathematics, for example, or all the possible chess moves and counter moves. Back in the eighties, a robot beat a grandmaster. To interact with society, to solve problems, an entity must learn to learn by observing, interacting, and absorbing information, then reaching conclusions, in short, the ability to reason. Dr. Beltran's work was years ahead of anyone else's, so learning and problem solving weren't as significant problems as you might imagine."

Beau came over and nuzzled Lucas's hand. "You getting all this, boy?"

Rachel smiled. "Meta-learning also involved feelings. To function socially, an android must learn emotions and, more importantly, to control them. In the beginning, the prototype was child-like, acting out with anger, sadness, and silliness. Eventually, however, he made progress, controlling them much like a human growing up."

"This is getting good. So, androids became teenagers."

Rachel chuckled. "With the problem solved, Dakota worked to develop an entity that passed for human, was intelligent, and continued to learn. To sell in large quantities to the government, they needed androids to be at least as smart and stronger and faster than humans. Much of the technology for improved abilities was developed in the past fifteen years around artificial limbs. Still, one key element remained to be solved."

"Let me guess."

"Go right ahead."

"If androids grew as smart or smarter and stronger than humans, would they be satisfied with being service technicians, patrol officers, or infantrymen? It wouldn't take long to aspire to be generals and order humans around."

"Well done, Detective."

"How was that addressed?

"Everyone agreed, before they developed the next artificial human, they would create one with the *Do No Harm to Humans* Prime Directive programmed into the android."

"Problem solved."

"Not exactly. Melody recognized the Pentagon and police forces as their most consequential customers. The Prime Directive had to be modified. Soldiers are required to harm other humans if given a lawful order, of course."

"Of course. What about law enforcement?"

"It turns out they already had a solution for androids to become police officers. Remember meta-learning. In addition to the Prime Directive, the android learned the need to defend itself."

"If the android perceived a threat, he or she could harm a human in self-defense."

"Right."

Lucas began to comprehend the complications involved in creating artificial humans. He struggled to believe everything she said, but he didn't think she had lied about anything. "But that conflicted with the Prime Directive."

"It did. The question for the team was, how far would an android go in violating the Prime Directive to save themselves? With the prototype, they observed that learning influenced behavior as it does in humans, but they wanted to know the outcome when survival conflicted with the Prime Directive. Dr. Beltran came up with an experiment to find out. A human technician approached the android with a gun, aimed it, and prepared to fire."

"What happened?"

"The prototype didn't hesitate. He managed to take the weapon away, but in the process, injured the technician, broke his arm."

"The need to survive overcame the requirement to do no harm."

"Couldn't an artificial human learn right from wrong, the golden rule?"

"You're talking spirituality. As a last resort, Melody brought in Reverend Armour and Chastity to teach ethics to an artificial human, not necessarily religion."

"Peachy, a brilliant android, possessing super strength and intelligence combined with religious fanaticism. What could possibly go wrong?"

"Please, be serious. This is my life's work."

"Sorry. Did that fix the problem?"

Rachel sighed. "Dr. Beltran would still be alive if it had."

"What happened?"

"After weeks of learning, experiments showed the prototype always chose his own survival over the greater good. The reverend's explanation? Artificial humans lacked a soul."

That sounded like the reverend or Chastity. "After the failure to teach ethics, Dr. Beltran decide to pull the plug on the development of androids."

She nodded. "He began to suspect the longer an android existed, learning to learn would allow him to kill a human for the simplest of justifications. It goes without saying that Melody disagreed with his conclusion. Dr. Beltran, however, remained adamant."

"You think she killed him or had him killed?"

"You're the detective, but you might want to write that on her sheet of paper. Now, you have the background of Project Halo."

"What happened to the prototype?"

"They disassembled him."

Outside, Beau barked and kept it up. Lucas opened the screen door. The dog had discovered something beneath the porch.

Lucas had been inundated with information: androids, meta-learning, prime directive. He needed a break. "Let's go for a walk."

He snatched a leash from a hook in the kitchen. "I think Beau needs to chill out a while." *And so do I*, Lucas thought.

"I'll bring snacks. We missed breakfast." Her lecture on artificial humans seemed to have energized her. She opened the cooler on the counter and slipped the food into a bag. She tossed in a dog biscuit.

Rachel took the leash and hooked it to Beau's collar; Lucas put on his windbreaker and hurried to his SUV. He unlocked the glove compartment. He grabbed his Glock and stuffed the gun into his jacket in case they ran into any critters Beau couldn't handle.

He rushed to catch up to Rachel and Beau. Bernardi had told them about a stream where he fished, and they made their way toward trees in that general direction. Ten minutes later, they came to the water, a narrow brook more than a stream. Water snaked through gravel and stone and several boulders with a gentle babble.

Beau stood in the water, cooling off, and drank.

Lucas helped Rachel onto a flat boulder. They sat and gazed over the soothing water. "Bernardi said there are fish in there."

"I can see them! I've never fished before. Can we catch one?"

"If we had the gear, which we don't, what would you do with a fish? I could skin it, gut it, and fry it in butter, but you're a vegetarian."

"Well, I wouldn't eat it." Rachel laughed.

Her laughter and the serenity of the setting took Lucas's mind off his investigation and the details of Project Halo. "You ever been camping before?"

"Never. This place is so calming. I haven't thought of being kidnapped by Calvin Hawk and his men since we arrived." She threw him the bag of snacks.

He grabbed a power bar and tossed Beau the dog biscuit.

Beau caught the treat in the air, gobbled it up, and set off exploring, his nose glued to the rocks and grass.

Lucas handed the bag back to Rachel and touched her hand. He intertwined his fingers in hers.

Rachel smiled, but her face changed. "What's that noise?"

The only sounds were a few birds and the soothing babble of the flowing water. "What?"

"A helicopter."

They were out in the open. When the rumble of a helicopter appeared, he grabbed her hand. They jumped down and took cover beneath a tree.

Beau barked at the intruders until Lucas quieted him with a shouted command. With a snap of the fingers, the dog came to their feet as the chopper slowly flew over their position and disappeared beyond the tree line.

Like the first night they met at Beltran's residence, Rachel pushed against Lucas to keep from being spotted. Her blonde hair smelled of strawberries. Her softness pressed against him. For a moment, he forgot about the helicopter, androids, and prime directive and enjoyed the feel of her body against his.

As she gazed into his eyes, he thought she might be thinking the same about him. Her lips were inches from his. He kissed her. Rachel's response was soft and inviting.

For an uncomfortable moment, they stayed where they were. Rachel backed up and straightened her hair. "I don't think they saw us."

Lucas couldn't be sure. "I shouldn't have kissed you."

She touched his cheek with her hand. "I'm glad you did."

Beau ran to the other side of the boulder. He began barking at an opening between the boulder and a downed branch.

Rachel called to the dog, "Beau, get away."

When he continued to bark, Lucas's instincts took over. He drew his Glock in case he discovered something dangerous.

Lucas heard the rattle before he spotted the snake. He aimed the gun, but before he squeezed off a shot, the rattler, as if in slow motion, leaped at the dog less than six feet away.

From beside Lucas, Rachel dove. She snatched the rattlesnake out of the air, grabbing it behind the head, its dagger-like fangs inches from the dog's snout. She scrambled to her feet, still holding the snake.

Its four-inch fangs protruded, and it struggled to twist free as Rachel calmly carried the rattler across the brook. She tossed it beneath a bush.

Lucas's heart pounded and threatened to leap from his chest. He realized he still held the gun in his hand.

Rachel's reaction was much faster than his. How had she grabbed a rattlesnake in mid-strike?

She crossed the water and stopped in front of him. She took a deep breath. "I suppose now might be the time to tell you the secret I've been keeping from you."

Rachel sat on the porch chair with Beau at her feet.

Lucas preferred to stand. He leaned against the porch post and waited for her to reveal her secret she said would change how he felt about her.

She scratched the dog behind his ear and unclipped the leash.

He feared what Rachel was about to say. Despite his dread, he wanted her to speak about it. Would she say more, like confess to killing Dr. Beltran?

She avoided looking at Lucas as she held the leash. She spoke in almost a whisper. "I'm not sure where I should begin."

"From my experience, the beginning is the best place."

She gazed at him. "I already told you the beginning."

What did that mean?

For the first time since they met, Rachel raised her voice. "You saw how I saved Beau! You must know. You're a detective."

"Say it!"

She snapped the leash in two. "Lucas, I am an android."

18

Rachel was right; her secret had changed how he felt about her. Where did he go from here? He needed time to think. "I need to take a walk."

"Do you want me to come with you?" She wiped away a tear sliding down her cheek, an artificial tear rolling down artificial skin. "It could be dangerous."

"I can take care of myself."

Her comment stung, though Lucas was certain she didn't intend it that way.

He grabbed a flashlight and his Glock from the kitchen counter and zipped his windbreaker to ward off the night's cold. He stuffed the gun in his pocket. Come on, Beau."

The dog jumped off the porch. On the grass, he glanced back at Rachel, then back at Lucas.

Lucas held out his hand toward his dog. "Are you coming or not?"

To Lucas's surprise, Beau climbed the steps and laid down at Rachel's feet.

Lucas took off, sweeping the flashlight beam in a wide arc. He wandered through the trees, barely paying attention to where he was headed.

He'd met Rachel just four days earlier, but clearly, he'd developed feelings for her. Now he learned she wasn't even human; she was artificial.

As he went deeper into the woods, he couldn't wrap his mind around Rachel's secret. He came to a clearing and stopped. The moonlight glistened off a sea of grass, swaying in the soft breeze like the gentle waves of a lake.

Lucas made his way to a tree stump. He swept the light around the base of the tree in case there were any snakes. He sat and laid his Glock beside him.

Across the meadow, movement caught his attention. He grabbed his gun.

A raccoon family scurried through the grass. Lucas stuffed the pistol in his jacket. He'd accepted Bernardi's offer to come to the cabin to ensure Rachel's safety and to work on finding out who killed Dr. Beltran.

Android Rachel was stronger and more powerful than he imagined, but the threats against her were real. Now that he knew her secret, perhaps she'd be more forthcoming.

Lucas brought her to Bernardi's cabin to keep her from the clutches of Hawk and his security team. Now he understood why they were after her. Rachel was a valuable asset.

She didn't take proprietary secrets from the company. She was the secret!

If they captured her, they'd disassemble her and learn from their mistakes, so they could make a more profitable android. He would never let that happen. To save her, he had to solve Beltran's murder.

Knowing her secret placed Lucas in a difficult position. Would he need to reveal details of Project Halo to Lieutenant Clark, to Freddy? Of course, he would.

Even if she killed Beltran, though he couldn't think of a motive, could she be a suspect in a murder if she wasn't human?

Rachel could reason and experience emotion, but did she possess a conscience, principles, morality? She was an android, a machine. If she was only a machine, did she belong to Dakota, or did conscious thought and reason make her something else? Of course, it did.

What should he do besides sit on a stump in the middle of the woods?

Behind him, twigs snapped. In one motion, he turned and aimed his Glock at the tree line.

Beau emerged, wagging his tail and bounding in Lucas's direction. The dog sat at his feet, and Lucas scratched behind Beau's ears. "Decided to side with me after all, huh, buddy?"

The dog licked his hand.

"You know what I think, boy? I think if doing the right thing was easy, everyone would be doing it. Duty, honor, and integrity are going out of style."

Beau cocked his head like he understood every word, then he sniffed around the stump and explored the meadow.

"At least you listened."

The dog's ears snapped to attention, and the hair stood on his back. He spotted a raccoon. Beau froze in place.

His tail curled between his legs. He ran back to Lucas, hid behind him, and whined.

Lucas chuckled. "Coward. Let's go back, boy. There's work to do."

He led Beau into the cabin. The dog headed straight for the bowl of water and began to drink.

Rachel sat on the couch, trying to repair the leash she had snapped in two. She glanced up and set the two pieces beside her. "We need to talk."

"I think we've talked enough for one night."

She grabbed his hand. "No, Lucas, we haven't. You must have a thousand questions. If we had Wi-Fi and your computer, I'd hack into Dakota Industries again, and you could read all about me and Project Halo. I want you to understand me. I'm different from the prototype or the second Android."

Beau finished drinking and walked to the bedroom. He jumped onto the bed and curled up at the foot of the mattress.

Lucas had plenty of questions. Not all of them dealt with the investigation into Beltran's murder. He sat next to her and studied her arms. The skin seemed so real.

She offered her arm.

He ran a hand over her smooth skin and squeezed her wrist. "You'll never grow old."

"I hope I grow old, only you won't be able to tell."

Aging doesn't just manifest itself on the outside. Inside, people harden, become ill-tempered, impatient, and mean. He'd be able to tell if he lived long enough to see her age.

"If you're wondering, my skeletal system is made of Titanium."

"You eat and drink."

"They gave us digestive systems to process nutrients and keep the skin fresh, the joints lubricated, and the ability to expel what it doesn't need, just like you."

Androids poop. Could the day get any stranger?

She took his hand and pressed it in the center of her chest. "I don't have a heart. I have an energy modulator, a device that powers the body through electrical signals. It uses a fuel cell that can be recharged in case of emergency."

She held his gaze with a pleading expression.

He took his hand back. "So, you can't get a broken heart."

"Of course, I can. When Patsy Cline sang about heartbreak, she wasn't talking about the organ that pumps blood. That kind of heart is part of one's consciousness and emotions."

She pointed to her temple. "The brain is a computer with the latest AI software. I spent the last two years interacting with humans and learning from the interactions. I learned from you."

"Me? What did I teach you?"

She paused. "That you could break my heart."

For a moment, he felt guilty. "I'm just doing my job."

"Of course, you are." Rachel let out a sigh. "I know what's bothering you. I may be an artificial human, but I possess humanity. I have a consciousness, like you. I'm able to feel emotions like you. I process information and learn and make judgments. Most importantly, I can tell right from wrong."

"If I recall, you can cause harm to others, but only self-defense. Can you lie?"

"I can, but only to protect myself."

"So, everything you told me is the truth?"

"Absolutely."

"How can I be sure?"

"How can you ensure a human isn't lying to you? That's what you do as a detective, isn't it?"

She was painstakingly methodical and logical with her answers. "The prototype no longer exists. So, you're the second android?"

"I'm the third. I'm not certain who came second, but I have my suspicions."

Lucas didn't want her to keep anything from him. "If I'm going to believe what you're telling me, you can't keep secrets."

Rachel let out a sigh. "Dakota protects proprietary information like a bank protects its money. After the prototype android failure, Dr. Beltran came up with one more idea. Borrowing from the Alzheimer's breakthrough that allowed memories to be saved electronically and reintegrated into the patient, they decided to imprint a human's memories into an android."

"So, they needed a donor—a human on life support with an intact temporal lobe where memories are stored."

Rachel looked surprised.

"I went to college, you know."

"You're right. When memories are formed, they're stored in the temporal lobe, the hippocampus to be more precise, and indexed for later retrieval. Dr. Beltran retrieved the saved information from a brain before they pulled the plug and downloaded it into an android's brain. When the artificial human gained consciousness, he was able to recall the human's memories like he had experienced them himself."

"What did Beltran hope to gain?"

"Past events shape future behavior. People learn from their mistakes. He hoped the android would benefit from the human's missteps."

"Did it work?"

Rachel shrugged. "I don't know who the android is or was. I tried to find out when I hacked into the database, but that information is well guarded."

"From what Dr. Beltran told me, the memory integration was only partially successful. He thought the android could become more violent as time went on, but Melody disagreed.

"In the past month, he concluded harvesting a human's memory had a minimal long-term effect. He almost ended the program then, but Melody talked him out of it, so he tried something different when he created me. He thought the prototype's and the second android's aggression might have originated from their male programmers. Men and women process information differently and emotions as well."

"I agree. I was married once."

Behind Lucas, Beau began to snore.

He brought in a female programmer to create my database with a feminine slant. I'm the success he'd been looking for, but Melody didn't think I would make an effective soldier or police officer."

"During the two years Dr. Beltran studied me, Melody put pressure on him to produce androids on a mass scale for the military and law enforcement. He planned to send me out into society for a few years to see how I functioned, but she remained adamant that I offered zero value to Project Halo."

"But Beltran still decided to end the android program."

"But he wouldn't stop his research. He wanted me in society, so he could continue to study me. Melody said no. So, you see, I wouldn't kill Dr. Beltran. He was my only champion at Dakota. The night he died, he told me to leave Dakota and meet him at his house, and he'd help me decide where to go."

"Then, you met me."

"He would have approved of our…our interaction."

"Melody Fleming couldn't proceed with Project Halo as long as Beltran was around to stop her."

"I saw a document in a file. Melody projected revenue from Project Halo in the first two years would reach one trillion dollars."

Lucas let out a slow whistle. A trillion bucks was a ton of money, no matter how one sliced it.

Beau's snoring grew louder.

"I think we should turn in." He had plenty to think about. "I'll take the couch again."

"No, a deal's a deal." She headed for the bathroom and closed the door.

Through the door, he asked, "Are you going to sleep in your clothes?"

"I don't mind."

Lucas went into the bedroom and grabbed a fresh T-shirt from his bag. He slid the shirt under the bathroom door. "This will be more comfortable."

19

Rachel lay on her back in Lucas's T-shirt with a blanket pulled over her. After Lucas went into the bedroom, she spent the past hour thinking about the tragedy of her day. Revealing her origins and seeing the shock and disappointment on his face was the toughest challenge she ever faced.

If he shared the information in his official investigation report, her life would change forever. She threw off the blanket and tiptoed to the bedroom door.

Lucas's breathing hadn't changed. He wasn't asleep. She knocked softly. "Lucas, do you have to tell your boss I'm…an artificial human."

"I don't have a choice."

"That's what I thought."

"Why is Hawk so insistent that you return to Dakota Industries?"

"Melody doesn't want me out in society until they reveal their announcement to the world about how artificial humans would benefit the Pentagon and law enforcement. They don't want any competitors until they secure the market."

Lucas came out wearing a gray Cal Bears sweatsuit. She became self-conscious of her appearance as he gazed at the thin T-shirt that came halfway down her thighs. "Rachel, what happens after everyone learns about androids? Will you be free to go?"

"I hope, once you solve the murder, the blockbuster scientific breakthrough will be announced, and Melody can roll out the enormous marketing plan she's developing, and I won't need to hide. I'll leave and let you get on with your life if you want me to." She didn't know what he wanted or what would happen if she were free to go.

He leaned one hand on the door frame. "Other corporate entities desperate for your secret might present a danger to you. With Beltran dead, they still might learn how to construct an android by…by reverse engineering you."

She thought about the risk, but her desire to explore the world overcame her fear. "That doesn't matter. I only care that you believed me when I said I didn't kill Dr. Beltran."

"I do, Rachel, but you have to convince my boss, the captain, chief, and a host of attorneys."

"Why wouldn't they believe me? They have to accept Melody had the most to gain from Dr. Beltran's death."

"If they don't accept your innocence, the implications that an android, a non-human could commit murder is, well, it's uncharted waters. A competent defense attorney would move to dismiss any charges on the theory that an android is merely a machine."

Machine! "I hate that word."

Lucas held up one hand. "Melody Fleming is a powerful woman in this state, in the country. She'll have the best lawyers and will try to sell her innocence like she would a product to a customer. You, on the other hand, are…"

"A machine."

"Hear me out. If they charged you with murder, and I'm not saying they will, a defense attorney would argue, given the prime directive, that an android who killed was a defective machine. Dakota created the defect through improper or inadequate programming. Even if you did kill Beltran…"

"I didn't!"

"I know, but even if they thought you did, technically, legally, you can't be charged with murder any more than a vehicle could in a vehicular accident."

"As long as you or anyone thinks I killed Dr. Beltran, I *must* prove my innocence."

"A defendant doesn't need to establish their innocence; they're presumed innocent until proven guilty, but the state might make you sit in a cell for a couple of years until the case goes to trial. Hell, it would be the trial of the decade, the century, but for The People vs. Donald Trump."

Rachel thought convincing Lucas was enough to ensure her freedom. "I don't care whether your boss, your boss's boss, or a jury believes me. The only thing that matters is if *you* believe me."

Neither of them spoke until he reached for the door. "We better get to sleep and talk again in the morning."

When he closed the door, Rachel stared at it a moment. She didn't want a door or anything to stand between them. She returned to the couch, covered herself in the blanket, and forced herself asleep.

Rachel awoke as a purple glow filtered through the kitchen window. The bedroom door was still closed. She sat up. A few hours of sleep hadn't improved anything. The shock in Lucas's eyes when she revealed her identity would forever linger in her memories. The look caused a pain inside like she'd never experienced.

She liked this man, and his kiss showed that Lucas liked her, at least he did before he found out the truth about her. She'd managed to convince him of her innocence, but after the buzz from Dr. Beltran's murder went away on social media, would he want to see her?

Rachel rose and smoothed the thin T-shirt. She tiptoed to the bedroom door and went inside without waking Lucas or Beau.

Lucas's eyes were closed, and he slept on his side.

At the foot of the bed, Beau opened his eyes and wagged his tail.

She patted the dog as she walked around the far side of the bed.

She pulled back the blanket and slid behind Lucas. She draped one arm over his shoulder, enjoying something she'd never felt before, the warmth of a man's body against hers.

He mumbled something in his sleep, then raised his head and opened his eyes. Would he make her leave? He laid his head back down and didn't say a word.

Lucas reached for her hand and held it to his chest. Her heart, not her energy cell, skipped a beat.

Rachel had studied human sexuality, but she'd never experienced it for herself. Did he want her as much as she wanted him?

Beau whined and crawled between them, ending the embrace. Disappointed, Rachel sighed. She laughed as the dog licked Lucas's shoulder and settled between them with his snout on his pillow.

20

Lucas awoke the next morning with the sun peeking through the bedroom curtains. Beside him, Rachel lay on her back, her eyes closed, her breathing shallow, apparently in android sleep mode. The bottom of the T-shirt came to the top of her thighs, the material clinging to her shapely if artificial body.

He reached for his watch on the nightstand. He'd slept until 8:30.

Beau jumped down and headed for the front door. Lucas slipped out of bed, trying not to disturb Rachel.

He let his dog out of the cabin and made a pot of coffee. While he waited, he went out and sat in the chair on the porch, enjoying the soft pine-scented breeze.

After a brief exploration, Beau bounded up the steps. He stood beside Lucas, nuzzled Lucas's hand, and whined.

"What's wrong, boy?" He scratched the dog behind the ear and gazed over the mist-covered forest floor. He got up to pour a cup of coffee and noticed the fur standing up on Beau's neck.

The sound of a car came through the trees. Lucas rushed inside and grabbed his Glock. He returned just as the car emerged from the tree-lined path. Freddy's red Tesla Roadster pulled up behind his SUV.

Detective Freddy Gannon climbed out of the flashy sports car.

In jeans, a white T-shirt, and aviator sunglasses, he resembled Tom Cruise in *Top Gun*.

A sense of dread came over Lucas. "How did you find us?"

"I'm a detective, remember?" He pulled a hand-drawn map from his pocket.

Bernardi.

His friend took a handkerchief and wiped off the hood of his car. He glanced at a blue jay in a branch above where he'd parked. He gestured toward the barn. "Is that a garage?"

"A barn, but you can park in there if you want."

Freddy climbed back in his car, drove to the barn, and parked inside. He shut the barn door and returned to the porch. "Lieutenant Clark said you left to protect a witness, someone named Rachel. She hadn't heard from you, so she asked me to see if you were both alright."

"Were you followed?"

"I don't think so. Your neighbor didn't trust me until I showed him pictures of our Cabo vacation last year. He especially enjoyed the photos of the Martinez twins, Ava and Audrey." Freddy patted his leg. "Hi, Beau." He petted the dog who sat and wagged his tail.

His partner climbed the steps. "You have any coffee, water, beer?"

Lucas was reluctant to let him inside before Rachel got up from the bed they had shared. "I just brewed a pot and was going to sit out and enjoy the cool morning. Why don't you wait here?"

"I need to pee. This dump has indoor plumbing, right?"

The screen door squeaked open. Rachel stood in the doorway in Lucas's thin T-shirt that came down to mid-thigh level. She shook her blonde hair that cascaded down to her shoulders. "I thought I heard conversation. Good morning."

"I'm Freddy Gannon. You must be Rachel."

She smiled. "Nice to meet you."

Freddy stared at Rachel's legs. "The pleasure is all mine."

Rachel glanced down at her shirt. "I'd better get dressed."

She closed the door and went inside.

Freddy clapped Lucas on the shoulder. "Buddy, if I knew why you really came to this cabin in the sticks, I'd have told Clark I couldn't find you. Now, about that coffee."

"I brought Rachel here to protect her." He had to tell his partner about Rachel, but he didn't want to blurt out something so incredible and hard to believe.

"Who's protecting her from you?" Freddy went inside.

Lucas followed. "It's not what it looks like. The lieutenant practically ordered me to take her someplace safe."

"How come she never gives me those kinds of orders?" He filled a cup and handed it to Lucas, then poured himself one.

Rachel came out of the bedroom with a handful of clothes. "I'm going to take a shower."

She entered the bathroom and closed the door. A moment later, the sound of the shower came on.

As they sipped the coffee, a goofy grin crossed Freddy's face as he glanced through the open bedroom door. The sheets on the bed were rumpled with a clear outline of where two people had slept. "Do you want me to hold your cup while you slip into the shower with Rachel?"

Freddy studied the pages taped to the wall. He bent down to pick up the crumpled piece of paper and unfolded it, the one with Rachel's name. His eyes widened. He whispered. "You're doing a murder suspect? She's a hottie alright but come on!"

"She's not a suspect, at least in my mind. She's a material witness."

"Then you're sleeping with a witness. I guess I missed that chapter in the homicide manual."

This situation was going to be tough to explain. "I'm not sleeping with her."

Freddy thumbed toward the bedroom. "I can tell when two people shared one bed."

154

The shower shut off.

He took a long swallow and whispered to Lucas, "I might not be on the level of Lieutenant Clark or her go-to detective, but I can tell when two people slept in the same bed."

"Freddy…"

The bathroom door opened. Rachel entered the room wearing a tan snug-fitting jumpsuit, her blonde hair in a ponytail.

"I couldn't help overhearing. We did sleep together."

Lucas almost spit his coffee. Why would she say that?

Rachel poured a cup and smiled. Her eyes darted between the two men. "What? I was lonely on the couch."

She was making it worse. He didn't think his friend would ever believe him, but he gave it one more try. "It isn't what you think."

Freddy mumbled something before flashing a grin. "Mum's the word."

"Oh, I get it." Rachel laughed. "You think we had sex."

Lucas let out a long sigh. He needed to explain Rachel's secret by himself. "I think I want to update you on the investigation. Rachel, why don't you take Beau for a walk?"

"Come on, Beau." The dog followed Rachel to the door. "Are you going to tell him?"

Lucas shrugged. He had to come clean but wasn't sure how to break the news without Freddy overreacting like he did to most things.

When the screen door squeaked shut, Freddy set his cup down and pulled up a kitchen chair. "Tell me, and don't leave out any details."

He brought Freddy up to date on what he knew about Beltran's unexpected death, including the damaging emails between Melody and Hawk.

When he finished, Freddy leaned back in the chair. "Let me see if I have this straight. Beltran and Fleming had a dispute over the company's future, so she talked with Hawk about getting rid of Beltran in emails? Sounds more than a little sloppy for an egghead."

Lucas agreed.

Freddy continued. "Dakota is the country's biggest producer of robots and artificial intelligence for industries and government. The Pentagon is their most critical customer."

"Along with police agencies around the country."

"What was the dispute about?"

Lucas hoped Freddy would react better than he had. "Fleming wanted Dakota to proceed with the next generation of robotics and artificial intelligence, a revolutionary program, Project Halo. This was Beltran's baby for several years until he decided to pull the plug."

"What's the next generation, robots who don't spill coffee or run into walls?"

Lucas took a deep breath and plunged forward. "Biological Robotic Entity, or BRE's."

"High tech robots? What's revolutionary about that?"

"They designed Project Halo to produce…artificial humans."

"Artificial humans." Freddy smiled. "Wait…artificial humans. You mean cyborgs!"

"Androids."

Freddy burst out laughing. "Isaac Asimov. I read all his books. Did you and Rachel cook up this whole story to punk me? Where's the camera?"

"I'm serious." Lucas knew Freddy would be hard to convince.

"You're…you're on the level, aren't you?"

Freddy paced the cabin. He stopped at the wall of notes, mumbling to himself. "Let's say I believe you, and I'm not saying I do. Dakota wanted to create androids with artificial intelligence to serve as police and military personnel. It sounds like an expensive way to replace humans."

Now his friend was getting into the issues Lucas had struggled with for the past twenty-four hours. "They would be infantrymen and patrol officers."

"Well, yeah, but what happens when they want a promotion?"

"Exactly."

Freddy looked dazed. "Exactly what?"

"Beltran faced a dilemma. His creations had significant advantages over humans, strength, speed, vision, analytical ability. Over time, he felt they wouldn't be satisfied with doing whatever a human ordered them to do. He was so concerned that, in the end, he decided to pull the plug on the program. Melody Fleming disagreed."

Freddy lowered his voice. "How does Rachel fit into all this? She was the last person to see Beltran alive, but you don't think she killed this Beltran guy?"

"I don't. Dr. Lee said anyone in the final five hours of Beltran's life could have administered a lethal dose of the nerve agent."

Freddy pointed to the six pages of names on the wall. "So why is Chastity on the board? You think she could have killed Beltran with kindness?"

"She's one of six people with the opportunity to poison him."

"What about family, close friends, lovers?"

"No family, no close friends, no interests beyond his work."

His friend scanned each of the pages. "I need a piece of paper and something to write with."

Lucas handed Freddy the tablet and Sharpie. Had he thought of another suspect?

Freddy wrote a name on the page and grabbed tape. "Seems like you left a logical possibility out." He taped the paper next to the others.

Lucas stared at the name. His partner had lost it this time. "Dr. Beltran? You think he killed himself?"

"A guy like Beltran, work is his life, kind of like you. The man's life's work became a failure, and he had to terminate it. What did he have to live for? And he more than anyone would have access to the nerve agent that killed him."

Lucas wasn't buying what his partner was selling.

Freddy looked pleased with his analysis. "Do you have anything to drink, booze or weed?"

Lucas shook his head. "Sorry."

"I almost stopped at that little store a ways back to pick up a twelve-pack." He faced Lucas with a wrinkled brow. "You're holding back something important, aren't you? I can always tell."

He'd put it off long enough—time to tell him about Rachel.

"Artificial humans also possess exceptional hearing." The screen door opened. Rachel unsnapped the leash from Beau, who began to drink from a water bowl. "Dr. Beltran would never kill himself. He wouldn't have done that to me, to himself."

Freddy's face grew pale. "Wait, were you listening at the door?"

"I didn't need to." She smiled. "You see...I'm an android."

Freddy staggered back, tripped over a chair, and fell to the floor.

Lucas couldn't help but laugh as he helped his friend up.

Freddy dusted off his jeans and gazed at Rachel like she was an alien who just stepped out of a UFO. "Like the terminator?"

Rachel burst out laughing. "The terminator was a cyborg."

Freddy leaned closer to her. "But your skin, your eyes." He glanced below her waist. "Your legs." He let out a long sigh. "Damn, someone did a hell of a job."

She chuckled. "Thanks, but you don't believe me."

"Sure, I do."

Rachel gave him the once over. "Your heart rate just shot up along with your blood pressure. Your breathing is a bit shallower than before; your palms are moist. I can tell when someone's telling the truth. That would come in handy as a police officer."

"Or...or a soldier."

"Did you tell him about the Prime Directive and Meta-learning?" she asked Lucas.

"I was about to when…"

Freddy interrupted. "I've heard of meta-learning. It's an artificial intelligence term. What's the prime directive?"

Rachel explained the concept and how, over time, learning to learn could override the directive and make it useless. "The night Dr. Beltran died, he told me that without an absolute prime directive, the mass production of androids would result in the demise of the human race."

21

Lucas grabbed a bottle of water and took a long gulp as his partner studied the notes on the wall. They'd worked dozens of cases together. His friend lacked Lucas's tenacity, but he had a different way of looking at facts than most people.

Freddy folded his arms. "So, you both think Melody Fleming killed or ordered the killing of Dr. Beltran."

"She had the most to gain from Beltran's death," Lucas said. "Until I find compelling evidence against someone else, she's my leading suspect."

"That's the problem, my friend. You're making assumptions with no proof besides what you learned from her." He pointed to Rachel.

Lucas didn't like the way Freddy was treating her. "With Beltran out of the way, Melody assumes total control over Dakota and will salvage Project Halo. I suspect, however, Hawk delivered a lethal dose of the nerve agent. Knowing it wouldn't take effect for a few hours, he summoned Rachel so she would be on video as the last person to see him before he died."

Freddy smiled at Rachel. "What did Dr. Beltran say to you?"

"He told me he intended to terminate the program and destroy all the information on Project Halo. He knew how furious Ms. Fleming would be when she found out. Then, he told me to slip away from

Dakota as soon as possible and meet him at his house because my life was in danger."

"Your life?" Freddy chuckled.

Lucas didn't like his friend's cold reaction to Rachel's use of the word life, but this wasn't the first time he had wondered about her consciousness, her mortality. Did she consider herself a living being? For certain, she felt alive, but that didn't make it so.

Rachel sat back in the corner chair. "I can tell you don't think of me as a living entity. Dr. Beltran had the same attitude in the beginning. The more he worked with artificial humans, studied us, the more he concluded we are conscious entities, not machines." A forlorn expression swept across Rachel's face. "I hope when you and Lucas come to know me better, you'll feel the same as Dr. Beltran."

Lucas tried to control his anger toward his friend. "She might be artificial, but let's stop the philosophical debate. I'm as determined as ever to protect her from Calvin Hawk. If there's a trial, we're going to need her testimony."

Freddy rolled his eyes. "Testimony? She's a machine."

Lucas jumped to his feet. "Go back and tell Lieutenant Clark I'm keeping Rachel safe. Without Beltran, Dakota needs her back to keep the program running. She'll be disassembled, or her brain dissected to uncover Beltran's secrets. Then they can begin producing artificial cops and soldiers for the Pentagon and law enforcement clients."

Neither man spoke.

"I'm not sure your case against Melody Fleming is as strong as you think." Freddy gestured toward the porch.

"Anything you want to say to me, you can say in front of Rachel."

Freddy snorted with laughter. "I don't think you mean *everything* I want to say."

She went to the door. "You two need to chat…without me." She slammed the screen door on the way out.

Freddy let out a low whistle and lowered his voice. "She's a feisty machine."

"Don't call her that."

"She might be an android," Freddy held up both hands, "but whoever created Rachel did one hell of a job putting her together. She has a nice rack if I may be so crass."

"It's never stopped you before. And I might remind you, they're artificial."

His friend laughed. "Half the women I know have artificial breasts. You need to get out more, my friend."

"She can probably pick up every word we're saying." Lucas knew no matter how much he protested, his partner would believe what he wanted to.

Freddy whispered. "So, you're nailing a...a machine."

"I'm not nailing anyone."

"That's so sad."

Lucas laughed. "You talk a lot about my love life, and sometimes I listen too damn much."

"The Italians have a saying for saps like you in this situation."

Rachel threw open the door. "Helicopter."

Beau followed the two men outside.

Freddy gazed over the trees. "I don't hear anything."

Lucas nudged his friend. "I told you she has excellent hearing, remember?"

The whir of rotors sounded before Lucas could see the chopper. He pointed over the tallest pine tree on the other side of his SUV. A moment later, the helicopter appeared above the trees. They all rushed inside and stood in the open doorway out of sight. Lucas expected a team of commandoes to rappel from the chopper. He retrieved his gun and nudged Freddy aside.

The helicopter hovered over Lucas's car. A minute later, it banked and flew off.

Freddy stood beside Lucas. "What do you think?"

Lucas didn't think anyone in the chopper had spotted the three of them. "I don't think they saw us, but they got a good look at my SUV."

Freddy let out a sigh. "You sure you don't have anything to drink?"

"I think if they were Calvin Hawk's men, they would've landed." Lucas stuffed the Glock in his pocket. "I suspect they are hired investigators who snapped pictures of my car. We need to leave before Hawk does send in a retrieval team. Let's pack up."

Freddy hurried after Lucas and Rachel. "Pack plenty of food. I'm hungry."

When they finished loading the SUV, Freddy drove his roadster from the barn. He parked beside Lucas's car and climbed out. He reached into the glove compartment and handed Lucas a folded piece of paper. "I assume you didn't want this sent to your phone. Information on Calvin Hawk's background."

Lucas unfolded the paper. "Your detective skills are solid. I'll note that in your personnel file."

"You're too kind. I wrote it in code."

The writing didn't look encrypted. "Code?"

"I wrote it in cursive. I remember a case we worked where you read cursive. I had to google how to write that way on the internet." Freddy slapped Lucas on the shoulder.

"After graduation, Hawk accepted a commission in the United States Airforce and was stationed in Germany. He received a promotion to captain, and just before his accident, they promoted him to lieutenant colonel. Four years ago, on November 12, he managed to survive an airplane crash in a commercial airliner, Flight 753 out of Chicago's O'Hare Airport. He was the only survivor of a plane carrying 229 passengers. The military transported him to a Level One trauma center in Denver. Details of the injuries remain classified." Lucas folded and stuffed the paper in his jacket pocket.

The information surprised Lucas. He thought Hawk had a security background.

Freddy wiped sweat from his brow. "I didn't find Colonel Urias. You?"

"No, but don't forget. I'm a bulldog."

22

Rachel came out of the cabin, causing Beau to let out a sharp bark. With Lucas's white T-shirt stuffed into a pair of snug-fitting jeans with holes in the thighs, he barely recognized her. She'd changed her blonde hair to auburn. She stuffed her ponytail into her lucky John Deere hat she wore backward, the style in the early twenties.

She held her arms out and twirled. "I found a few clothes in a trunk in the closet. I thought I should alter my appearance."

She transformed alright.

Lucas pointed to her hair. "How'd you change your hair color?"

She took off the hat, reached in the back of her head, and made a turning motion. In an instant, her hair changed to black, then blonde, then auburn. "Didn't I mention I could do that?"

"I would have remembered."

She set the cap back on her head and put her hands on both hips. "Do I look like a boy?"

Not exactly. The baggy shirt didn't hide her curves. Lucas took off his blue windbreaker. He slipped it on her and zipped the jacket high enough to cover her artificial breasts. "You might pass."

"Wait one moment." Freddy removed a pair of dark wraparound sunglasses from his glove compartment. He climbed the steps and gently placed them on her face. "Perfect, sonny boy."

"Can I ride with you, Freddy?" Rachel adjusted her glasses. "I've never ridden in a roadster, and we can get to know each other better."

"If Lucas doesn't mind."

Lucas's laugh was louder than he intended. "Why would I care? Come on, Beau; you're riding with me."

He opened the passenger door of his SUV, and the dog hopped in. "Be careful; Freddy's a bit of a wolf."

An expression of confusion crossed Rachel's face. "A wolf?"

Freddy opened the passenger door for Rachel. "The word is slang. It means an intuitive and resourceful gentleman."

"Oh, I thought wolf might mean a lecherous male. Don't try anything. I'm stronger than you think."

Lucas chuckled. "As strong as the terminator."

Rachel climbed in the roadster and waved to Lucas as she and Freddy drove off. "Hasta la vista, baby."

Rachel asked to ride with Freddy because of his suspicions about her. She spent the first part of the trip to the general store mostly listening. Like Lucas, he'd been divorced, but, unlike his friend, he dated plenty of women.

He didn't seem as convinced as Lucas that Melody Fleming ordered the murder of Dr. Beltran, and he'd yet to accept Rachel's humanity. She hoped to win him over like she won over Lucas and Beau. She talked about her feelings toward them both.

They passed the general store and wound their way through the pine-covered mountains, the roadster taking the curves with ease. Within a minute, wi-fi lit up the roadster's panel. She glanced in the rearview mirror. Lucas was talking to his boss, no doubt.

Freddy thumbed toward Lucas's SUV. "He risked his career for you."

That wasn't fair. "I wanted to leave the city and get as far away from Green River as possible. Lucas convinced me to stay…at his house."

"You stayed at Lucas's house? I never saw that coming. My friend is as straight an arrow as they come."

"A straight arrow?"

"Yeah, he follows the rules. He's broken several to keep you safe. He also has no sense of humor. Did he tell you his favorite joke?"

"No."

"What did Roy Rogers say to his horse, Trigger?"

She grinned. "I give up."

"Why the long face?"

Rachel laughed until she snorted. "That's funny."

Freddy rolled his eyes. "You two make quite the pair."

Rachel couldn't help but smile. Freddy might not be totally convinced, but she'd made progress getting him to trust her.

Freddy cleared his throat. "It's my business only because you're a material witness, but have you and Lucas hooked up?"

"Hooked up?" She chuckled. "No. I thought we might last night, but Lucas didn't want to."

He burst out laughing until he snorted. "Didn't want to?"

Freddy's phone rang through the roadster's speaker. "Lucas, we just started talking about you. Care to listen in?"

"I called Lieutenant Clark. I couldn't say much over the phone but told her we'd meet her at the station."

"Sounds like a plan. Your car's too slow. I'll see you there." Freddy terminated the call, then shifted as they came out of a turn, and the roadster took off on a long straightaway.

With more than a little regret, Rachel turned around and watched the SUV disappear from view.

"Relax, we'll be at the station in ninety minutes. Lucas, closer to two hours."

"Why are we going there?"

"Having worked together for several years, I suspect your boyfriend wants Lieutenant Clark to get to know you."

"He's not my boyfriend."

Freddy laughed. "Lucas has it bad for you, AI, but I wasn't convinced you were on the up and up until I saw how Beau takes to you. Women fool men all the time, rarely dogs."

"Dogs are trusting and intuitive. They react well to kindness. Beau appreciates me for who I am, I guess."

Rachel turned back around. "You think Lucas likes me? I mean, *really* likes me?"

Freddy grinned. "I think so, but I'll ask him for sure at the malt shop."

When the cabin disappeared in Lucas's rearview mirror, Lucas had a sinking feeling in his gut that he'd never see the place again, at least with Rachel.

He had trouble keeping up with the red Tesla Roadster as they wound through the tree-lined road that snaked through the mountains.

After the phone call, Lucas gave up as the sports car accelerated and disappeared.

Beau whined and crawled into the back seat.

Lucas chuckled and glanced in the back. "This isn't a race, boy. We'll meet them at the station."

When the dirt road turned into a paved one, Lucas kept the SUV at the speed limit. He was glad Freddy could spend time with Rachel. Having worked together as long as they had, Lucas knew his partner wanted to interview her and come to his own conclusions.

He hoped Freddy would review the evidence objectively. His friend had nailed the biggest flaw in his case. The evidence against Melody Fleming was more theory than proof. He needed more to convince Lieutenant Clark.

Lucas wasn't the best person to analyze artificial humans and prime directives. Still, technology wasn't his greatest impediment to this case. He might have spent too much time with Rachel.

Maybe he grew too close to her in the short time they'd been together. It was more than a possibility he'd become emotionally attached, even if she was an android. He could evaluate others, not himself. Was it possible he'd overlooked her involvement in Beltran's death? He couldn't wait for Freddy's take.

As the elevation dropped, the trees turned into bushes and the mountains into hills. He made it to the top of a hill and skidded to a stop in the middle of the road.

A helicopter hovered four feet off the ground. This was different from the one earlier in the day, more modern and less noise. Through the windshield, he recognized Calvin Hawk sitting next to the pilot and a couple of others in the seat behind them.

They'd come after Rachel and thought she was in the SUV. They had no idea Freddy was at the cabin. His roadster had been parked inside the barn when the first chopper arrived.

Hawk grabbed a microphone and spoke through a loudspeaker. "By now, you probably realize Rachel is the proprietary property of Dakota Industries." He held up a piece of paper. "This is a court order from a judge granting us sole custody. Let her go, and you can be on your way."

How kind of him, Lucas thought. He doubted the validity of the document. Freddy and Rachel were perhaps thirty minutes outside of Green River. He needed to stall and buy them more time. "Beau, get down."

The dog jumped off the back seat and laid behind Lucas.

Rows of trees appeared on his right. To his left, he spotted a rolling field of bushes and boulders behind a wire fence. He had to chance it. "Hold on, boy."

Lucas hit the accelerator. He turned and crossed over the oncoming lane and bounced over the shoulder. He smashed through the wire and made it onto the grassy field. He reached back to make sure Beau was alright and weaved his way through the obstructions.

The helicopter rose and began to pursue.

Lucas didn't intend to outrun a modern chopper, but he wanted to allow Freddy and Rachel time to reach the station. "Activate text messaging."

As they made their way, he gripped the steering wheel as a question mark appeared on the screen. "To Lieutenant Clark. Being pursued by a Dakota Industries helicopter. Calvin Hawk is inside and claims they obtained a court order to release Rachel to their custody. She and Freddy are on their way to the station. End message. Send."

He glanced back at Beau as the helicopter hovered overhead. The dog remained surprisingly calm.

Lucas headed for a patch of trees and stopped between two of them, the canopy hiding him from view, though they knew exactly where he was.

The chopper flew to the other side, and two thugs, Tom and Jerry, climbed out with semiautomatic rifles. He checked the time on the dashboard. The helicopter would never stop Freddy from reaching the city.

He shut off the motor and waited. He grabbed a bottle of water and took a long swallow.

The two men stood in front of the SUV, their rifles at their side. The weapons were something Lucas had never seen before.

Hawk spoke through the loudspeaker again. "Step out with your hands up."

He reached back and patted Beau. "You stay here. I've got this."

Lucas got out and closed the door. He approached the two men. When Hawk ordered him to stop, he halted. He cupped the back of his ear like he couldn't hear over the din of the whirring chopper blades.

The helicopter landed, and the rotors began to slow. Hawk climbed from the front seat and held out his hand to someone in the back.

The woman took off her headphone and hat. Her gray hair billowed from the chopper's downdraft.

Melody and Hawk approached Lucas. She defiantly showed him the piece of paper.

The judge's order commanded the City of Green River to turn over any property belonging to Dakota Industries.

Lucas handed back the paper. "I can't do that."

She cocked her head. "Why not?"

"Rachel's not here."

She signaled to Hawk, who hurried to Lucas's SUV. When he looked inside, Beau began to bark. He turned to Melody and smiled.

She began to wheeze. When her face reddened, she grabbed an inhaler from her pocket and sucked in a deep breath. "Where's Rachel?"

"Have you checked the cabin?"

Hawk's eyes narrowed. "We will."

"Don't do any damage; I borrowed the place for a few days from a friend." Lucas pointed at the two men with automatic weapons. "Do they have permits for those things? Because I might have to arrest them."

Melody glared at Lucas like he was a staff member she'd caught stealing her sack lunch. "Save us some time. Where is she?"

He checked his watch with a sense of satisfaction. "Just about now, she's at the Green River Police Station."

Hawk looked at Melody. "He's telling the truth."

She let out a sigh. "I know Rachel can come across as a sweet innocent young girl, but she's ruthless."

"I'm sure she can be."

Melody set her hands on her hips. "You're making the biggest mistake of your career, Detective. We believe she administered the nerve agent to Dr. Beltran. I see you need more than my word."

"Why don't you meet me at the station? I'll invite the city attorney, and you can bring lawyers, and we'll hash this out. Oh, and if you have information relevant to *my* investigation, I'd appreciate you sharing whatever you have."

"Mr. Nash, Rachel's not merely a threat to you and your career; she's a danger to our way of life."

What? Rachel?

Melody handed him a business card. "This is my direct line. Call me in the morning, and I'll arrange to show you proof of Rachel's guilt." She turned and walked toward the helicopter.

Lucas headed for his SUV, reflecting on the escalation in Dakota's attempt to kidnap Rachel. He stood beside the door as the Dakota chopper flew off. Had they obtained a court order or was Melody Fleming playing a bluff?

23

Rachel remained calm as she sat across from Lieutenant Clark, who grilled her for more than an hour. She recounted everything she told Lucas and Freddy about her time at Dakota Industries.

Like her office and desk, the lieutenant's questioning was organized and to the point but felt much more like an interrogation than the chats she had with Lucas or Freddy. "That's the truth, Lieutenant; I had nothing to do with Dr. Beltran's death and didn't even know he'd been poisoned until I ran into Detective Nash Monday night."

"And you're an android."

Rachel nodded. "I prefer artificial human. Don't you believe me?"

"I think you believe you're an android."

"Lucas believes me. So does Freddy."

The one personal item in the lieutenant's office was a photograph on the credenza behind her desk. The picture showed Lieutenant Clark and another woman with blonde hair smiling. Rachel pointed to the photo. "Is that you and your wife?"

The lieutenant chuckled. "Why do you ask? She could be my sister or a best friend."

Rachel smiled.

Clark picked up the picture frame. "She *is* my wife. We were married in Mexico. Her name is Trina."

"She's lovely."

Lieutenant Clark set the frame back on the credenza. "Tell me about your relationship with Detective Nash."

"Lucas is by the book. He's professional and avoids talking about his own feelings."

Lieutenant Clark smiled. "Sounds like Lucas, but how do you feel about him?"

"I'm grateful. He may have saved my life when he helped me escape Calvin Hawk and his men outside of Dr. Beltran's house."

The lieutenant drummed her fingers on the desk. "So, you're not in love with him."

"I don't think so."

"You don't think so?"

"I'm still learning about emotions."

Before she could follow up, Lieutenant Clark glanced out her doorway. She jumped to her feet and waved to the visitor being greeted by everyone in homicide.

Dr. Lee walked with considerable caution like she was in pain. She entered the office and gave the lieutenant a hug.

Clark held the woman's hands and gave her the once over. "Niko, I'm thrilled you're looking so well."

"They told me you visited me in the hospital. That was so kind of you."

"That's what friends are for."

The doctor smiled at Rachel before letting go of the lieutenant's hand. "My physician didn't want me back at work, but with two youngsters around the house, I wasn't getting much rest."

"I'm so glad you were able to stop by."

She laughed. "With a three-year-old and a baby, I was grateful for an excuse to get out of the house."

The lieutenant gestured to the chair beside Rachel, then introduced her. "Rachel, this is Dr. Niko Lee."

Rachel hoped Dr. Lee didn't think she was responsible for the nerve agent that put her in intensive care. She wanted to make a favorable impression. "Pleased to meet you, Dr. Lee. Lucas told me you were exposed to the toxin that killed Dr. Beltran. I'm so glad you're well."

The doctor smiled. "As am I."

"I hope you don't think I had anything to do with what happened to Dr. Beltran and you," Rachel said.

Dr. Lee glanced at the lieutenant before answering. "I haven't given it any thought."

Lieutenant Clark leaned forward and clasped her hands. "I called Dr. Lee earlier and asked if she felt up to conducting a quick evaluation."

Rachel smiled. "Whatever will help with the investigation and find out who poisoned Dr. Beltran and Dr. Lee."

The doctor set her phone on the lieutenant's desk. "You told me little about Rachel."

Lieutenant Clark sighed. "Niko, this is going to be difficult to explain. She worked on a top-secret project at Dakota Industries. The project was to develop robots with artificial intelligence." She took a deep breath and let it out. "What they created went far beyond that. They developed artificial humans."

Dr. Lee studied Rachel as if seeing her for the first time. "Are you suggesting what I think you're suggesting?"

"Lucas and Freddy both say there's reason to believe Rachel is artificial, or what some call an android, but Dakota refuses to confirm it."

She slapped her knee and laughed. "You must be joking."

Rachel liked the doctor. She seemed far kinder than any physician/technician at Dakota. From her experience with Lucas, Freddy, and the lieutenant, she'd found it was best to be honest and direct.

"She is serious. I *am* an artificial being created by Dr. Beltran for Project Halo."

"That's…that's preposterous."

Lieutenant Clark locked eyes with the doctor. "It's why I wanted you to examine her, just enough to determine whether she's human or not."

"I'm used to examining dead people, so this will be a pleasant departure. You appear human. Let me see your hand."

Dr. Lee leaned closer and ran her hand over Rachel's arm as Lucas had done. "Flawless. I've seen this before, on burn victims."

Rachel ran a hand over her face. "Borrowed technology like much of the work, except for the artificial intelligence."

Dr. Lee palpated Rachel's right hand. "I count twenty-seven bones. That suggests you're human."

"They're titanium. Would you like to see?"

"Not now." Dr. Lee pulled out her phone and selected the flashlight mode. She shined the light in Rachel's eyes and gasped. "Your eyes." She glanced wide-eyed at Lieutenant Clark. "They're… artificial."

"Of course, they are," Rachel said. "They're connected to a part of my brain Dr. Beltran calls the occipital sector."

"Like the occipital lobe in humans." The doctor examined Rachel's wrist. "You have a pulse."

Rachel pointed to the center of her chest. "An energy cell provides the power."

"Let me look in your mouth."

She could see the instant the doctor began to believe she wasn't human. Rachel opened her mouth.

Dr. Lee shined the light inside. "Remarkable similarities, a human-like tongue, same number of teeth. The vocal cords are present, but I've seen those as well. The Chinese developed artificial cords for cancer victims ten years ago."

Dr. Lee sat back in her chair, held a hand over her eyes, and swayed a bit.

Rachel steadied her with one hand. "Are you alright?"

"A little flustered…that's all." She turned to the lieutenant. "I've never seen anything like it. She's…she's an artificial human."

Clark shook her head. "I'll be damned. Lucas and Freddy were right."

Rachel was pleased with the examination. "I'm so glad Lieutenant Clark found someone as kind as you to examine me. Believe me; I've had plenty of doctors who treated me like a machine."

"Where is Lucas? He's okay, isn't he?" Dr. Lee asked. "I haven't been able to reach him in the past couple of days." The concern in the doctor's voice showed Rachel she and Lucas were more than business associates. They were close friends or more.

"He's on his way," Lieutenant Clark said. "He ran into a bit of trouble on the way back to town, but he's fine. He and Rachel spent the last two days at a remote cabin. That's why you couldn't contact him."

"I worried when I couldn't reach him." There was something behind her statement, personal concern, sure, but something more.

Rachel wanted to understand the relationship between Dr. Lee and Lucas. "How long have you known Detective Nash?"

"Twelve years now. We met in college. I was pre-med. Lucas was a party animal."

The lieutenant gestured to Dr. Lee's phone. "Why don't you show Rachel my favorite picture of the two of you?"

"I haven't seen that for a long time."

Lieutenant Clark encouraged her. "Go ahead. I think Rachel would be interested."

Dr. Lee hesitated before opening a photo album on her phone and paged back several times. "This was taken nine years ago."

Rachel studied the picture of Lucas and Dr. Lee, the doctor in white, and Lucas in a tux. "You...you two were married? *You're* the ex!"

By the time he returned to Green River, Lucas realized Dr. Beltran's murder had turned into a case with national importance.

Freddy was waiting in the lobby when he led Beau into the police station. The dog pulled against the repaired leash, excited by all the commotion. Lucas was relieved to discover Melody and her team had never shown up. He shared the story of the confrontation with the Dakota helicopter.

"Sounds like Melody played a bluff and failed."

Lucas tugged on the leash, and Beau sat. "Where's Rachel?"

"She's bonding with the lieutenant in her office."

"How's that working out?"

"Rachel's consistent; I'll give her that. She told Clark what she told us both. She got on the lieutenant's good side by making a few adjustments to her robot you call Walle."

"I better go check how she's doing."

Freddy pointed to chairs along the far wall. "You have a visitor."

Chastity Moorhead.

"I never understood what that hot redhead saw in you." Freddy shook his head. "My recommendation is don't become involved with her. You're already dating an android."

Lucas handed Freddy Beau's leash and approached his former girlfriend. In a snug white dress with a hint of cleavage, she rose and kissed his cheek. She bit her lower lip. Something was bothering her. "Do you have time to talk?"

"Sure."

A shirtless man was arguing with a patrol officer. When the man grew more agitated, two more officers ran to assist, increasing the usual pandemonium in the room.

Chastity gazed around at the chaos and disorder. "I'd be more comfortable outside. Could we take a walk?"

"Of course."

Rachel couldn't believe Lucas never told her who his ex-wife was. He never mentioned Dr. Lee, only referred to his ex as the ex. "Did you love him?"

Dr. Lee appeared surprised by the question. She laughed. "I still do."

What? She didn't understand humans. Love was more complex than she ever imagined. "But...

"I still love him, but I'm not *in love* with him. I'm in love with my husband. Let me show you his picture." On her phone, she went to a photo of a blond man with a thin mustache wearing a smile in a second wedding picture. Then the doctor showed several pictures of her children.

"But you were in love with Lucas."

"The first time you fall in love is a crazy, impetuous existence where every day is a honeymoon...until it isn't." She put the phone away.

Rachel looked up, and the lieutenant was studying her.

"Do you want to tell me the truth about you and Lucas? I thought you couldn't lie."

"What I said before was true. I withheld a few details, is all." She sighed. "I care for Lucas, and I think he cares about me, but he'd never do anything to jeopardize the case."

"Have you slept with him?"

"Just once."

Dr. Lee's phone rang. She answered without talking. After a brief conversation, she hung up. "Emergency at home. The little one threw up on the dog. I think it can wait; this is getting good."

Rachel had learned from the misunderstanding with Freddy. "We slept in the same bed but didn't have sex."

Clark raised an eyebrow. "I supposed you only cuddled."

Neither woman acted like they believed her. "It's the truth. I would have, but Lucas didn't want to."

Dr. Lee laughed. "Now, I know you're lying."

Outside, Lucas and Chastity made their way down the sidewalk along the busy mid-day street. They sidestepped two officers trying to wrestle a burly, handcuffed woman out of their patrol car.

They walked half a block before she spoke. "I'm concerned about Reverend Armour. I think he's been bought off by Melody Fleming."

"How did the two of you become involved with Dakota Industries?"

"Dr. Beltran asked for our help, and the reverend's ego couldn't turn him down."

She sat on a bench outside a convenience store, and Lucas sat beside her. "I wasn't sure what our role would be until we arrived. Then they introduced us to Project Halo."

"The development of artificial humans."

Chastity brushed a wisp of hair from her eyes. "They wanted to instill values, honesty, and integrity into androids. A noble cause, right?"

"A noble cause sounds like what the Spaniards tried to do to the Aztecs."

She bit her lip. "I told him it never had a chance of success, but the reverend thought it was worth a try."

"Why didn't you think it would work?"

She cocked her head, apparently surprised that Lucas didn't understand. "An artificial human doesn't have a soul. One could *teach* right from wrong based on Judeo-Christian principles, but without a soul, androids could never accept Jesus Christ as their Lord and Savior. That's the key to goodness."

He didn't agree but didn't want a religious debate with someone who was hurting.

A man pushing a shopping cart and holding a bottle of wine stopped several feet from Chastity, giving her the once over.

She didn't appear to notice. "We spent two months trying everything. The Reverend Armour is brilliant when it comes to theology, but a few days ago, he came to view Project Halo the way I do. Then something happened."

"This was after Dr. Beltran died?"

"Two days after. Remember, the reverend perceived Project Halo as evil and dangerous. I don't refer to them as artificial humans or androids. I call them soulless artificials."

Rachel didn't have a soul. Lucas wasn't so sure humans did, for that matter, but she was kind and considerate. Anyone Beau takes to and who appreciates the pain of a Patsy Cline broken heart is inherently decent. However, he'd never convince Chastity of Rachel's inherent goodness.

"The reverend organized protests and went on cable news. Ms. Fleming asked for a meeting. He went alone and returned, explaining how satisfied he was with the direction of the company under Melody Fleming. He's appeared on the news praising Dakota, suggesting the Lord showed him the way. He's ready to return to Los Angeles and on to the next spiritual crisis."

She clutched his hands. "Lucas, this is bigger than Project Halo. If Dakota Industries isn't producing androids, someone eventually will. Without souls, they will become a force of evil."

"So, you failed to teach them the golden rule."

She squeezed his arm. "Lucas, I spent two months with two of these creatures. They can't appreciate the difference between right and wrong. They can follow orders, but at times they refused. That scared the crap out of me, pardon my language."

"If they couldn't be taught, perhaps science could program artificial humans to develop empathy, compassion, love?"

"Love? Do you realize how crazy that sounds? A machine can't love."

Lucas realized it sounded wacky better than anyone. He thought about Rachel. He'd seen her empathy and compassion, and she expressed love. And Beau loved her, that had to mean something. A soul? Religious theory was hardly his area of expertise.

The man with the shopping cart sat beside Chastity. She scooted away from him, so Lucas took her hand and led her back toward the station.

He tried to let go of her hand, but she held on and interlaced her fingers with his like they were still in high school. "What's the deal with you and the reverend? Forgive me; it's the detective in me talking. You're under no obligation to answer."

She looked so uncomfortable that he didn't expect her to reply to such a personal question. "He's a charismatic man, in case you didn't notice. After watching him preach at a service, I introduced myself. I became infatuated and flattered when he asked me to work with him. We didn't become involved right away, but when we did, he convinced me our lovemaking was a spiritual calling. I was schoolgirl stupid. Looking back, I realized I was just one in a long line of conquests. It's been over for two years, but I stick around because I believe in God and His message."

"I remember."

She smiled. "That's why *our* relationship didn't evolve."

He almost made a joke about evolution. "It didn't progress because you were a good girl."

She giggled. "And you were a bad boy."

They reached the parking lot and stopped beside a rental sedan.

Chastity unlocked the car. "I have two regrets about high school that may surprise you; one, I saved myself for marriage, and two, you and I drifted apart. Although you never came right out and said it, I suspect my first regret was responsible for the second."

"I was a self-centered jerk in high school."

She cocked her head. "And now?"

"Now, I'm divorced, no wife, no kids, but an awesome dog who thinks I can do no wrong."

She let go of his hand and handed him a business card. "I'll be leaving for Los Angeles in the morning, but maybe you could call me sometime."

He slipped the card in his pocket, though he didn't promise he'd call.

"Thanks for letting me vent and express what I've been keeping inside." She rose and slipped both arms around Lucas's neck and kissed him on the lips. When the kiss ended, her eyes glistened. "Ships passing in the night."

He'd expected a Bible verse.

She climbed into her car and drove off.

Lucas let out a sigh. As he walked to the front of the building, he grabbed his handkerchief and wiped the lipstick from his mouth. He stuffed the cloth back in his pocket.

A sense of being watched swept over him. He scanned the parking lot but saw no one. His eyes rose to the second story. Lieutenant Clark and Rachel were watching from her office window. They'd seen the kiss.

Lucas took the elevator to the second floor. He entered homicide and went to Lieutenant Clark's office. He had some explaining to do, but Rachel appeared angrier than his boss.

The lieutenant pointed to his face. "You missed a spot."

"What?"

"Lipstick."

"Oh." Lucas wiped his mouth with his handkerchief and stuffed it back in his pocket.

Lieutenant Clark pointed to the parking lot. "Unless I'm mistaken, that was Chastity Moorhead, one of the seven who had contact with Dr. Beltran in the five hours before his death. She's a suspect in a murder."

"Perhaps in the beginning, but I don't consider her a suspect."

Rachel crossed both arms. "You were holding hands!"

"She held mine." He tried to explain it to his boss. "We dated in high school. She's leaving town in the morning. It was a goodbye kiss."

Rachel's eyes narrowed with contempt. "Then she gave you her phone number."

"You have exceptional vision."

The lieutenant closed her office door. "What were you two were talking about—dating in high school?"

"A little, but we mostly talked about her concern over the work she and Reverend Armour did for Dr. Beltran."

"So, she's a witness."

"I see where this is going."

"I hoped so. You kissed a witness to a case you're investigating, Detective. This will go on your record."

"I don't suppose it'll help much to explain that she kissed me?"

"At the cabin, you kissed me!" Rachel turned her back and gazed out the window.

Lieutenant Clark glared at Lucas. "You kissed two of the seven witnesses to a murder you're investigating. I wouldn't even expect this behavior from Freddy. Do you have anything to say for yourself?"

"Nothing."

Freddy knocked and entered with Beau. The dog rushed to Lucas, wagged his tail, and nuzzled Lucas's hand.

He petted his dog. "Finally, a friendly face."

"Why so quiet?" Freddy gazed around the room. "Did I miss something?"

Lieutenant Clark sat back down. "From now on, Detective Nash, you'll have no further contact with Rachel as long as this case is active. Is that understood?"

"Yes, ma'am."

"I've arranged for her to stay at…a certain hotel that shall remain on a need to know basis. Lucas, you don't need to know. She'll share a room with a female officer, and another will be outside the room around-the-clock. Freddy, please take Rachel downstairs, where she'll meet officer Kristen O'Rourke in the lobby. She's expecting you."

Rachel glared at Lucas as she walked past him. "This is all your fault. If you hadn't kissed Chastity Moorhead… Earlier, I found out Dr. Lee is your ex, and she still loves you."

He'd never seen her so irate. "No, she doesn't."

Freddy handed the leash to Lucas. "You kissed Chastity?" He winked at Lucas. "Nice job, player."

24

After Freddy and Rachel left the office, Lieutenant Clark gestured to a vacant chair by her window.

Lucas sat and ran a hand over his face. How had he managed to stumble into this mess?

She got up and closed the door. "What I said about your involvement with a witness going on your record stands, but something else is important."

He glanced up at his boss. "What's that?"

"I wanted Rachel to think I was as pissed off as she was when we saw you holding hands and kissing Chastity." She chuckled. "You should have seen her face when she found out Dr. Lee is your ex."

"I'm glad I missed that."

"It should be obvious to anyone that while Rachel may be an artificial human, she possesses an all too human emotion, jealousy. She has the emotional temperament of a fourteen-year-old high school girl with a crush on a senior football star. I bet she could snap you in two."

Lucas had dug himself quite a hole. "I overplayed my hand. I wanted to find out whether she was capable emotionally of killing someone."

A skeptical sneer swept across the lieutenant's face. "What did you conclude?"

He'd yet to verbalize his assessment of Rachel. He was a homicide detective, not a social scientist. In his line of work, however, he learned to assess people's motivations. He was skilled at analyzing folks, at least until he met an artificial human. "As you no doubt observed, Rachel is emotional and naïve. She didn't hide her feelings from me, but I wanted to learn how she felt about Beltran. He was more than her boss. He was her mentor. More importantly, he was her creator."

"Go on."

"Also, she's been truthful. She provided a great deal of information about Project Halo that I confirmed with others, like Chastity Moorhead."

"So, you concluded she didn't kill Beltran?"

Lucas felt certain she wouldn't commit murder. "I don't think she'd kill her creator."

"You might be right. She's immature, but I don't detect homicidal tendencies, and I can't imagine what her motive to kill might have been."

Clark gazed out the window. "You have more work to do. All you have is theory, conjecture, and assessment. I want God damn facts."

The lieutenant was right. His investigation did need more evidence, documents provided by someone other than Rachel. "Melody Fleming wants me to call her in the morning. She said she would prove Rachel killed Beltran."

"Maybe she can, or perhaps she'll try to frame her." Clark folded her hands in front of her. "I like Rachel too. If she's innocent, find the proof. Oh, and take Freddy with you."

"I will and," Lucas rose, "I'll keep an open mind."

"Make sure you do."

When he got home, Lucas fed Beau and peered into the empty-looking guest room with a pang of regret. When the dog finished, Lucas let him into the backyard. He went next door and knocked.

Bernardi opened the door wearing a 49ers hat and holding a can of Amazon Stout. "I didn't expect you back so soon. You have any trouble?"

"We did encounter a rattlesnake." He didn't mention the helicopter.

"I forgot to tell you they come out this time of year."

Lucas handed him the cabin keys. "Thanks for your help. And… I apologize if I've been a crappy neighbor since Niko and I split up."

"Apology accepted." Bernardi shook Lucas's hand.

Lucas returned home, made himself a tuna sandwich, and read through the file to prepare for his meeting with Melody Fleming. What did she have on Rachel?

As he ate, he thought about Lieutenant Clark's conclusion about Rachel. She often played the role of devil's advocate on his cases, but this time felt different. Had he spent so much time with her that he'd lost his objectivity about her innocence?

He finished eating and grabbed a cold Amazon Lite. He eased into his favorite chair, determined to relax for the first time in days. He turned on soft classical music and popped the top on his beer.

His phone rang.

Freddy was on the other end. From the background noise, it sounded like he was at a bar. "I need you to join me at the Dickens Lounge at the airport."

"Now? I just opened an Amazon Lite. This better not be a scheme to hook me up with a girl."

"It's not. Leave your beer. I'll spring for one when you show up."

"I hope it's important."

"It's critical. I'm here with Colonel Urias. He's getting on a plane to Washington in…fifty-five minutes. He's ready to talk."

Lucas left the beer and grabbed his keys. "I'm on my way."

The Dickens Lounge was half-full. The place looked like most airport bars. From hidden speakers, soft music played so travelers could converse. He enjoyed actual cocktail waitresses. Automation and robots had yet to replaced them all.

The lights were dim, and the bar was decorated in red fabric and dark leather. His partner shared a corner booth in the back of the room with Colonel Urias, a middle-aged man with a crew cut wearing civilian clothes instead of a uniform. They were both nursing drinks.

Freddy introduced the two men. Lucas shook the colonel's hand.

Urias checked the time on a wall clock and spoke with a Texas drawl. "My plane leaves soon, so let's start." He downed half of his drink.

"Tell Lucas what you told me."

"I told your friend the last time Captain Koenig and I were together was at the Happy Camper, a place he discovered a few months back. I went for the booze. The captain went for the broads. He hit on ones he struck out with before, but Koenig never took no for an answer. To him, no meant, 'change my mind.' He bought this schoolteacher a drink, then another, and eventually they left. I had a flight out early the next morning and didn't know anything had happened to him until I landed in Washington. I came back and found you fellas wanted to talk to me."

A shapely waitress with a plunging neckline came to the booth, but the colonel didn't order another drink. Her perfume was exotic…similar to what Niko wore in college. She placed a cocktail napkin in front of him. "What'll it be, honey?"

Lucas pointed to Freddy. "He's buying me a beer. You pick."

Freddy held up one hand. "Just one. Lucas can't handle his liquor."

"Sure." She winked at Lucas and headed for the bar.

The colonel's story didn't sound like there was a connection between Dakota and the murder of Captain Koenig. "You met with Beltran earlier in the day."

The colonel let out a breath. "Whooee. They both bought it on the same day. Damn shame."

The waitress leaned across the table, displaying her cleavage when she set a draft beer in front of Lucas.

Urias downed the rest of his drink. "You're a lady charmer, Detective, like the late Captain Koenig."

Freddy laughed and finished his glass. "Be careful, sweetheart. I just learned today that my friend is a bit of a player."

"I can believe that." The waitress smiled. She left and walked behind the bar.

The colonel checked the time again. "The captain and I were as familiar with Project Halo as anyone this side of D.C. We became aware of problems and efforts by Beltran and Melody Fleming to fix 'em, but I suspected all along the problem with Project Halo was too complex to salvage. I recommended DHS abandon the project, but Koenig didn't want to let it go."

Lucas sipped his beer. "What kind of problems?"

"The damn androids don't follow orders and can't be controlled. I don't know too many military branches or police who would put up with that shit. They tried altering the learning, the programming, even taught 'em religion, can you believe it? Their behavior only grew more aggressive and unpredictable."

"You sure?"

"I saw it for myself. Anyway, last week, Beltran told Melody Fleming he was going to go along with her decision to end Project Halo."

What? Lucas set his glass down. "Are you saying Melody fought to end the program, and Beltran was the one determined to keep Project Halo alive?"

"That's exactly what I'm sayin'. For at least a year, she wanted Dakota to cut their losses, as she put it, while Beltran kept making excuses for the program's failure. After Melody informed us of her decision, we met with Dr. Beltran, who said he reluctantly agreed with her. The data convinced him artificial humans were inherently flawed."

Freddy appeared as surprised as he was. Rachel's story didn't jibe with the colonel's. "What was your and the captain's response to learning the program would come to an end?"

"Something that significant was above my pay grade. We told them not to make any final decision until we could run it up the chain of command at the Pentagon and DHS. They both agreed, and we made an appointment to meet today."

"Then what?"

"Koenig and I decided to drown our sorrows at the Happy Camper. I retire in eighteen months, so I wasn't as pissed off about Beltran's decision as he was. As I said, he never took no for an answer. He saw Project Halo as a way to grease the skids of his career. Failure was unthinkable."

"Did you talk about Project Halo at the Happy Camper?"

The colonel glanced around the bar, appearing to make sure no one was listening. "To be honest, the topic came up more than it should have. The project is rated top secret, and we were wrong to discuss it in public, but Koenig wouldn't let it go. Thankfully, that sexy schoolteacher came in and distracted him."

An announcement interrupted the music. Colonel Urias climbed from the booth. "My flight, gentlemen. Gotta go."

"Do you know of any link between Koenig's death and Dakota Industries?"

"None whatsoever." He grabbed his overnight bag. "I hope you fellas find out who killed Beltran and Koenig. They weren't the most likable guys, but neither deserved to die like that."

When he left the bar, Freddy stared at Lucas. "Something's wrong."

Lucas finished his beer. "Rachel said plenty of times that Melody was keeping Project Halo operational for financial reasons. Why would she lie?"

Freddy shrugged. "I thought she was programmed to tell the truth."

"Sounds like she lied about that." If she could lie about something so consequential, what else had she lied about?

He needed to talk to Rachel. "I don't suppose you want to tell me where Rachel is staying?"

Freddy looked away from Lucas and rubbed his forehead. "Don't put me in that position."

"Okay, you go ask her about what Urias told us."

"She's with O'Rourke."

"So, bring her a candle."

"I think we should meet with Melody Fleming first. See if her story backs up Rachel's, or the colonel's."

Lucas let out a sigh. "Actually, that makes sense."

The waitress came over to the booth. When she grabbed Urias's empty glass, she leaned over the table, displaying more cleavage. "Another beer, Player?"

"No, thanks." Lucas reached for his wallet.

Freddy showed her his credit on his phone.

She touched the screen with a stylus. "You guys cops?"

Lucas handed her a Tubman. "Do we look like cops?"

The waitress slipped the bill in her cleavage. "You do."

When she walked away, Lucas glared at Freddy. "Why'd you tell her I was a player?"

"I thought you might want her phone number."

"Well, I don't. Not every woman I meet is a potential conquest."

Freddy stared open-mouthed. "I hardly know you anymore."

An hour later, Lucas lay in bed, picturing the wall in the cabin. He wanted to talk to Rachel about what Urias had shared about Melody's early decision to terminate Project Halo, but that could wait.

Did Melody kill Beltran to keep Project Halo alive? Why did Rachel's story about their conflict differ from what Colonel Urias said?

Mentally, Lucas removed Captain Koenig and Colonel Urias's pages along with Reverend Armour and Chastity. Only three names remained: Hawk, Melody, and Rachel.

He read the six emails between Hawk and Melody. They'd definitely discussed getting rid of Beltran, but would they conspire to commit murder and leave an email trail? From his experience, arrogant people made stupid mistakes.

Despite what the colonel said, Lucas didn't yet disbelieve Rachel. He would have known if she were lying all this time.

The information provided by Colonel Urias cast suspicion on Rachel and Melody Fleming. Who did he believe?

In the morning, he was determined to find out the whole story about Project Halo. The truth would clarify who had the most to gain from Beltran's death. He couldn't believe it was Rachel. That left Melody and Calvin Hawk. In the morning, he intended to prove it.

25

After a sleepless night focused on the new information from Colonel Urias, Lucas grew determined to keep an open mind and hear Melody out. By the end of the day, he wanted more than two sides to the story. He wanted the truth.

He waited with Freddy in the waiting area outside of Melody Fleming's office. He'd spent all morning thinking of Rachel, androids, and creation. "Do you remember in high school when Miss Crandall assigned us Mary Shelley's *Frankenstein*?"

"No, but I read *Debbie Does the Football Team*. I think you gave me that book."

Lucas sighed. "In the book, the creature couldn't kill his creator no matter how angry at him he became."

"But *Frankenstein's* fiction, right?"

The door opened and a robot wheeled out and stopped alongside the leather couch. "You must be Detectives Nash and Gannon."

"We are." Lucas rose.

When Freddy stepped inside Melody's office, his mouth dropped, and he whispered to Lucas. "I've been in bowling alleys smaller than this."

Lucas had to agree. The office looked like a museum to modern technology, constructed of mostly chrome and glass.

Stoic Melody and Calvin Hawk sat at a conference table near a monitor that took up most of the wall. In front of the security chief were two stacks of folders, blue and green. Cups with the Dakota D logo and a coffee carafe were in the center of the table, along with a dozen gourmet doughnuts.

Lucas and Freddy sat across from them. Lucas made the introductions.

"Nice place you got here." Freddy filled a cup with coffee and added a packet of sugar. He grabbed a chocolate doughnut and a napkin. He bit into a fourth of the pastry and began to chew. "Cops liking doughnuts is a cliché, you know."

Melody ignored the quip. "Before we begin, I'd like to apologize to you, Mr. Nash, for our confrontation yesterday. We tried to apprehend Rachel, for your safety, as well as everyone else's. We thought the right thing was to appeal to a judge."

"The two thugs with long rifles were a special touch." Lucas poured himself a cup.

Melody smiled with the sincerity of a bowl of oatmeal. "We didn't bring those weapons for you. Perhaps you noticed they were high-powered rifles manufactured by Taser. We've found them effective in apprehending artificial humans who resist authority."

"Do you use them often?"

She overlooked Lucas's question. "Detective Nash, you accepted what Rachel told you, apparently for personal reasons. Nevertheless, I'm sure she didn't accurately portray her involvement in planning and executing the murder of Dr. Beltran."

Lucas didn't want to interrupt. From his experience, the more a suspect talked, the more she might incriminate herself.

"Mr. Nash, I showed you this video before, without sound, because after the system was installed, Dr. Beltran managed to disable the audio." She aimed a laser stylus at the screen, and the scene in Beltran's office lit up. Rachel was standing beside the soon to be dead COO when the video began. She listened as Beltran spoke.

The scene played out until she put both arms around Beltran and walked away.

"Rachel told me Beltran asked her to meet him at his home."

"That much is true," Melody said. "Now, let me play it with word captioning created from a lip-reading expert."

Freddy chuckled.

"I take it you don't believe the veracity of lipreading," Melody said.

"Sure, I do, but the video reminded me of something." Freddy sucked chocolate from his fingers and winked at Lucas. "Remember the lipreader at a nightclub in Vegas? Her act was risqué and incredibly funny, right, Lucas?"

Melody's eyes narrowed into two blue dots until she blinked them away. The scene rewound, and Dr. Beltran's words came on the screen. "We discussed this many times. Unfortunately, after three years and more than a billion dollars, we concluded the effort to create artificial humans has been a complete and total failure. Do you understand the implications?"

Rachel answered without hesitation or emotion. "For me, it means termination."

"I'll need you to meet me at my residence later. For now, go to your room, and I'll join you there."

"Of course, Dr. B. Thanks for everything you've done for me. I'm sorry I failed you." Then she hugged him and walked away.

The word captioning seemed legitimate to Lucas.

Hawk spoke for the first time. "We believe she administered the toxin when she hugged Dr. Beltran. An artificial human can handle a variety of skin penetrating agents because there's no blood supply to transmit the poison to the heart or brain."

"If I may." Freddy brushed doughnut crumbs from the table to his hand and sprinkled them in his coffee. "Why did Dakota Industries store a nerve agent on the premises? I thought the Federales regulated that kind of thing."

Melody chuckled like he'd just told a knee slapping Rodney Dangerfield joke. "You're correct, Detective. I didn't become aware we possessed anything like nerve agents until two days ago. In the early part of our company, Dr. Beltran worked with the Pentagon on a project I still know little about, but we found out the government granted him permission. I can show you the paperwork if you like."

"You didn't know about nerve agents?" Lucas asked. "Who else did?"

"Just Dr. Beltran."

"Not Rachel?"

"Not that I'm aware of.

Melody pointed to the frozen screen. "If you're at liberty to share, Detective Nash, what did Rachel say about her last conversation with Dr. Beltran?"

"She said he confirmed he intended to discontinue Project Halo, but you remained opposed to ending the program for financial reasons."

"Absolutely not true." She gestured to Hawk, who handed a blue folder to Lucas, Freddy, and Melody and kept one for himself.

Melody opened hers. "These are a series of communications between Dr. Beltran and me over the past twelve months. More than a year ago, I wanted to end the project. Read through all the exchanges. He was resistive while I repeatedly tried to end the project and cut our financial losses."

Lucas read through the emails with a cold stab in his gut that Rachel had lied from the beginning. Freddy's face revealed he was almost as surprised as Lucas.

"These prove," Melody said, "I concluded producing androids was a lost cause long before Dr. Beltran acknowledged it. I wanted to shut the project down once we realized the Prime Directive would eventually be overridden, but he came up with one solution after another. Don't just take my word for it."

Hawk distributed the green folders.

Melody opened hers. "These are emails from me to Captain Koenig, explaining why we had to abandon the production of artificial humans. They go back six months. You can see Dr. Beltran tried to talk me out of it until the end."

Lucas read each of the emails. Koenig and Beltran kept the program alive after Melody wanted it to end, and both were dead. There had to be a link between the two murders. Freddy's face showed he agreed.

His demeanor had changed. "Tell us about Beltran's solutions."

"First," Melody said, "he came up with the idea to harvest memories from a recently deceased subject so the artificial human would have a lifetime of recollections during which they formulated right from wrong."

"And how did that work?" Freddy said.

"At first, it worked well, but over time," she glanced at Hawk, "the artificial humans displayed resistance to authority. We conducted numerous tests about taking unlawful orders. When each attempt failed, we knew the military and police would never approve of our product. Even if they would, imagine the liability from lawsuits. Still, Dr. Beltran wasn't ready to abandon the project. He tried one more tack."

"Let me guess," Lucas said. "He brought in Reverend Armour and Chastity Moorhead to teach them a moral code."

Melody swept a strand of gray hair from her brow. "Their efforts proved futile. After that fiasco, Dr. Beltran reluctantly agreed that the program had to end."

"So, when Armour threatened to blow the lid off Project Halo, you bought him off?" Lucas suggested.

The accusation appeared to shock Melody. "I did no such thing. After Dr. Beltran's death, I met with the reverend and told him Dakota was prepared to terminate Project Halo and all existing artificial humans. After that, he began to express his support for us through the media."

Lucas let out a sigh. If Melody was being honest, Chastity's suspicions about a payoff were unfounded. "The emails are impressive, but I also read six conversations between you and your chief of security here discussing getting rid of Beltran."

She aimed the stylus at the screen and scrolled through several emails. Melody stopped at one she'd sent Hawk. She clicked on the email, so they could all read the contents. Is this one you read?"

"It is."

"When Dr. Beltran resisted my desire to end the program, we did talk about removing him. I spoke with others, as well. We had several meetings about the subject. I did want to get rid of him and would have if he hadn't agreed to cease work on Project Halo. We weren't talking about murder; we discussed buying him out."

Lucas considered her explanation, then glanced at Hawk. "Assuming you wanted to eliminate Project Halo, why haven't you terminated him?"

"Wait, what?" Freddy's eyes widened. "Seriously, this guy's an android?"

A smile spread across Melody's face. "Well done, Detective. Perhaps I underestimated you."

Hawk flashed an amused grin at Freddy. "Want me to break something with one hand or run the forty-yard dash in less than two seconds for you?"

Freddy gasped. "You ran forty in under two?"

"1.94 on a wet track. I'm sure we have a video of it."

Melody beamed like a proud parent. "A former athlete, Calvin Hawk was the human whose memories we imprinted into the brain of the next artificial human. He was created in the human's image and looks exactly like the real one. To answer your question, I thought he would prove helpful in apprehending Rachel. I was wrong."

Lucas remained unconvinced. "Why would she want to kill Beltran? He was her creator."

"We now realize survival became crucially important to Rachel.

She knew, with Project Halo being ended, she had to be terminated. She must have planned to get rid of him for months, and when he revealed his decision, she executed it."

Freddy chuckled. "No pun intended."

Melody ignored him and pointed the stylus to the screen. She called up the frame of Rachel giving her creator a final hug.

Freddy looked convinced. He leaned forward. "How does one go about terminating an android?"

"We constructed androids at this location, but Dr. Beltran programmed the artificial intelligence, at his insistence, at a laboratory in his residence. There he built a failsafe device that could remotely terminate all artificial humans regardless of their locations."

Lucas didn't buy it. "If you can deactivate remotely, why didn't you just shut Rachel down?"

Melody pointed to her chief of security.

"A few hours after Dr. Beltran died," Hawk said, "I drove a truck to his place to load up valuable equipment and discovered the device had been tampered with. It had to have been Rachel."

Lucas ran a hand over his face. "I'm not sure who to believe."

Melody sighed with frustration. "Very well, I'll show you something else I'm sure will convince you I'm telling the truth. We'll have to go to Dr. Beltran's place."

Freddy pulled out his phone. "I think we should invite Lieutenant Clark."

Lucas nodded. Rachel had been lying all along.

"Do you want me to come along?" Hawk slouched in his chair. "That place makes me uncomfortable."

Melody laid a hand on Hawk's shoulder. "You're the one who is going to convince our guests of my credibility."

Lucas didn't want to tell them he was the one to take Rachel from Beltran's home to his house. If she hadn't been honest since the day they met, as he now suspected, she'd no doubt lied about having feelings for him. Her emotions were as phony as her hair.

26

Dr. Beltran's two-story block home and well-manicured grounds looked even bigger in the daylight than it did the first time Lucas saw it. Several armed guards stood like sentinels on the property. He and Freddy sat in his SUV, waiting for the others.

Freddy was chewing on a toothpick. "What tipped you off about Hawk?"

"Oh, different things. His personality seemed to fluctuate from professional to thug, but he behaved around Melody like she was his mother."

Freddy gestured with the toothpick. "You know the thing about androids I don't get?"

"What?"

"You think they're a bunch of stiffs with no sense of humor, like Hawk, then they're telling raunchy jokes, hitting on women, and buying you drinks. Just when you think you know 'em, they turn on you."

Lieutenant Clark pulled up, and they got out of Lucas's car.

She climbed from her Green River SUV with Protect and Serve on the side. "I skipped lunch with Trina."

Lucas stepped forward. "Sorry, thanks for coming."

"You said it was important." Lieutenant Clark gazed up at the building. "Dakota must pay well."

Lucas and Freddy briefed her on their earlier meeting. When Melody drove up with Hawk in the passenger seat, Lucas introduced Clark to them.

Inside, with pots of plants and indoor trees, the marble foyer looked more like a hotel lobby than a residence. Freddy gazed at a winding staircase that led to the second level and let out a low whistle. "This would make a terrific bed and breakfast. Maybe I could low ball them 'cause the owner died."

Melody led them down a long hallway with an air of confidence as if she owned the place. Maybe she did. At the end, she pressed her hand on a palm reader, and a thick metal door swung open.

When she stepped into the room, LED lights lit up the room.

Not knowing what to expect, Lucas and the lieutenant entered, followed by the others. The B & B imagery vanished. It was a huge laboratory with electronic devices sitting on metal tables. As she led them through the room, Melody described several workstations involved in integrating artificial intelligence and artificial humans.

She opened a door on the far side of the room. "What might have been."

Melody stepped aside. Lieutenant Clark entered, followed by Lucas and Freddy.

Two dozen artificial humans with blank eyes of various colors stood in rows wearing military fatigues, and two wore police uniforms. Half appeared to be female, and they represented a variety of ethnicities.

Freddy touched the sleeve of an artificial woman officer. "Reminds me of a high-tech department store in the old days. In summer, they'll probably be wearing swimsuits."

Melody laughed before regaining her composure. "Dr. Beltran was waiting for my go-ahead to activate two dozen more androids for deployment for the armed forces and police, an approval I never gave."

They left the room, and Melody closed the door. She opened

another door to a room with a handful of chairs and a small bed along the far wall. In the center of the room sat a piece of electronic equipment the size of a tractor.

This had to be the apparatus to terminate androids.

"This is Failsafe. Let me show you what we came for." Melody opened a panel in the front. A series of lights flickered about the machine. Like a 3-D movie, two dozen lights hovered. Beside each light was a simple round button. The first light glowed red, and the third green. The second light, like the others, was a dull gray.

She pointed her stylus to the first red light, and a serial number came up. She did the same for the next two.

Hawk took a step toward the machine. "As you might have guessed, these numbers represent the three artificial humans Dakota created to date. The serial number with the red light is the prototype that we terminated before we constructed Rachel. Hers is the second. I came here two weeks ago. Her light glowed green, like mine."

"The night Dr. Beltran was murdered," Hawk continued, "I discovered Failsafe had been tampered with."

Melody sighed. "My technicians tried everything to reconnect Failsafe with Rachel. After killing Dr. Beltran, she came here and erased her connection to Failsafe. So, you see, if I selected her light and pushed the Failsafe button, it would have no effect."

The lieutenant pointed to the security cameras in each corner. "Can we view the video of her disabling the cameras and tampering with this device?"

Melody shook her head. "Unfortunately, Rachel disabled all internal security connections the minute she arrived."

"At your office," Lucas said, "you suggested you would prove you were telling the truth about terminating Project Halo."

She pointed the stylus at Hawk's green light, and another panel slid out with a gold button in the center. Melody turned to Hawk. "It's time."

"Time for what, ma'am?" Hawk's toughness faded.

"Time to terminate your existence."

Hawk paused before replying. "Are you sure?"

Lucas didn't believe she would go through with it. "Is that necessary?"

"I need to convince you it was my intention all along to end Project Halo and deactivate artificial humans. With Hawk gone, we'll only have Rachel to deactivate."

Hawk spoke in almost a whisper, "Will it hurt?"

Melody pointed to the far wall. "Lie down and put yourself in sleep mode."

"Yes, ma'am." Without hesitating, the big android walked toward the bed.

The lieutenant hung her head. "Son-of-a-bitch."

"Thank you for your two years of service," Melody said without emotion.

To Lucas, who never liked Hawk, the android displayed more feeling than she did. He held up one hand. "Wait, a damn minute! How can you do this? Don't you care about him?"

Melody wrinkled her brow. "Hawk is not a him, Detective. He's an artificial human. I regret the time and financial resources we invested in his creation, programming, and maintenance."

"Jesus!" Freddy dropped onto a metal chair. "But he's a…"

Melody's eyes narrowed. "He's a machine, a high tech, expensive one, but a damn machine, nevertheless. In college, I drove a car that saw me through all my years of study. After graduation, I traded it in on a new model. I had regret then, the same as I feel now for Hawk."

Without hesitating, Hawk climbed on the bed. "Goodbye, Ms. Fleming. Best of luck finding and terminating Rachel." His eyes closed. "Entering sleep mode."

Freddy gave Lieutenant Clark a look of desperation. When she didn't intervene, he surprised Lucas by jumping to his feet and smacking his hand against the wall. "I don't know what kind of piece of shit you drove in college, but I drive a red Tesla Roadster, and I *love* that car." He left the room, banging the door shut behind him.

Lucas had often clashed with Hawk, but he almost felt sorry for the android. Freddy barely knew him, and he was upset that Melody intended to terminate him.

She reached for the button.

Lucas couldn't imagine his reaction if Rachel were to be terminated, despite all the lies she'd told him. "Wait!"

Her hand hovered over the panel. "What?"

"Doesn't Hawk's following your order to allow himself to be terminated mean he's putting the greater good above his own existence?"

Melody looked uncertain. "It might. Most interesting. Still, I'm committed to ending Project Halo."

"You won't accomplish anything if you deactivate Hawk unless you do the same to Rachel. He has skills the rest of us lack. He could enhance our ability to apprehend her."

"I suppose he might." She cocked her head. "Why do you care?"

Lucas shrugged. "It seems like the...humane thing to do."

"Damn it!" For the first time, emotion swept across Melody's face. "I came here to convince you and the Green River Police that Rachel killed Dr. Beltran to ensure her own survival because that's what she did."

Melody turned to Lucas and threw up her hands. "And she spent the past week making a fool out of you, pretending she was capable of loving you."

He wasn't sure how to respond. Maybe pretending to care was exactly what Rachel did.

The lieutenant spoke. "Lucas is right."

Lucas took a deep breath. "It should be easy to take her down. Rachel trusts me."

Melody's eyes widened in surprise. "You know where she is?"

Lieutenant Clark raised a finger. "No, but I do."

"If everyone agrees, let's go take her down." She shot Hawk a commanding look. "We'll deal with them both at the same time."

Lucas breathed a sigh of relief.

She shut down the Failsafe machine, and the 3-D lights disappeared. She walked over to the bed and touched his shoulder. "End sleep."

"Is it…" Hawk sat up. "Is it over?"

Melody smiled. "We need your assistance to apprehend Rachel."

"That will be my pleasure." He jumped to his feet. "I won't help you just to capture her. She must be eliminated!"

Melody's face reddened. "You'll do as you're ordered, Mr. Hawk. Is that understood?"

He took a quick glance at Lucas and raised his voice. "Yes, ma'am!"

27

Lucas and Freddy drove from the Beltran residence through the twisting, hilly roads. Lucas forced himself to pay attention to his driving as he considered what he'd learned from Melody Fleming. Had his feelings for Rachel blinded his objectivity?

For several days, he'd observed and studied her. Beltran programmed androids to learn through observation and interaction with humans. Could they grasp emotions like they could master the ability to drive a car or recognize faces?

On the outskirts of Green River, Freddy cleared his throat. "Okay, GM. Switch to autopilot mode. Destination Regency Hotel."

The car responded. "Autopilot mode engaged. Destination confirmed."

His car took control, so Lucas let go of the wheel. "What's up?"

"I don't know. I guess I'd like some conversation, especially about what we just learned about the murders we're investigating."

"The two murders are connected. The two people who fought for Dakota to keep producing androids were Beltran and Captain Koenig. They're both dead."

"That's what I'm thinking." Freddy let out a sigh. "Don't tell anyone how I almost lost it back there."

Lucas chuckled. "I thought you were going to cry."

"Shut up." Freddy's grin turned into a laugh. "You're in love with a damn machine."

Could he or anyone love an artificial human? She was a doll, a dish, and liked old movies and classic country music. She was smart, athletic, and fearless. If she walked into a bar alone, three drinks would be waiting for her before she sat down. The only problem was…she wasn't real. "Rachel's more than a machine. From what I see, artificial humans can learn empathy, compassion, and kindness."

"And love?"

"Forget that for now. What if Melody, after all this time, is wrong about androids? What separates humans from animals is the degree of emotions they can show. You've seen psychotic humans who couldn't express empathy, compassion, guilt, or remorse, right?"

Freddy pulled an energy bar from his pocket and offered Lucas one.

He wasn't hungry. "No, thanks."

Freddy unwrapped the bar. "Dogs express sympathy and compassion. They're not human. Beau gets depressed when you leave, ecstatic when you return. He showers you with kisses to express his joy, for God's sake."

At a light, Lieutenant Clark's SUV pulled up behind them. Maybe the lieutenant was right, but Lucas had only told Melody she convinced him of Rachel's guilt to save Hawk from being terminated.

The emails were compelling and suggested Rachel had lied from the time he picked her up. That night, she told him she hadn't made it into the house; now, it appeared that she went there to deactivate the link to the Failsafe machine. "Rachel told me she didn't go into Beltran's house. Still…"

"Still? Jesus. There are never two sides to every story. There's only the truth, and you and I know it. Your girlfriend killed Beltran and Captain Koenig after learning he would no longer fight to keep the program alive."

Lucas gazed out the window, gathering his thoughts, and tried to make sense of it all. "Humans have the ability to reason, write poetry and music."

When the light turned green, the car lurched forward and stopped for a pedestrian crossing against a red light.

Freddy smacked the dash. "One feature I don't like about Driverless Mode is cars can't make obscene gestures."

They drove through the intersection, and Freddy took a bite of the energy bar. "I heard robots with artificial intelligence can paint, even write poetry and music. They say you can't tell their creative ability from human work."

"You're getting to my point. What is a human? Humanity must be more than blood in our veins and a heart that pumps. How far must an android progress to be considered human?"

"When they feel remorse over something they've done."

"That sounds reasonable."

"Lucas, old buddy, you're betting your career on everything Rachel has told you. Do you realize how much crap I'd be in if I believed everything women told *me*? If Melody Fleming is right, Rachel's been lying to you, to both of us all this time, and she murdered Dr. Beltran, and I suspect Captain Koenig."

Lucas drummed his fingers on the steering wheel. "You're a detective. You think she's telling the truth?"

Freddy finished the energy bar and wiped his hands with his handkerchief. "If she's telling the truth, I'm the Pope. Rachel's the best liar I've ever seen, but still, you sound like a lawyer arguing a case."

The hotel was less than a block away. "Let's say Rachel did kill Beltran. She's entitled to her day in court, instead of letting Melody Fleming flip a damn switch like she almost did to Hawk."

"You're joking! Court?"

"The law will free her."

"Then what, you're going to marry her?"

"I wouldn't do that to her."

Freddy laughed as the car turned into the hotel parking lot. "Destination reached."

The two men got out and waited as the lieutenant parked beside them. Lucas tried not to show his unease. After Rachel opened the hotel room door, she would never look at him the same way again.

Just as Lucas thought something might have gone wrong, Melody and Hawk arrived. When they got out, Hawk reached into the back seat and grabbed one of the Taser Long Rifles that Lucas had seen the day before. Melody held a traditional taser in her hand.

Lieutenant Clark stood beside her car and addressed them all. "Lucas is going to take point on this operation. Rachel trusts him. He'll knock and ask her to open up. The rest of us will be out of sight but close enough to move when she opens the door. Once the door opens, Hawk will take her down. We use the Tasers as a last resort. Any questions?"

Melody looked concerned. "Shouldn't you call for backup or something?"

Clark didn't like being second-guessed. "You and Mr. Hawk are guests. This is a police operation, and I'm in charge. I don't want anything to spook her."

"Then, let's go." Lucas headed for the entrance. Inside the lobby, Clark pushed the elevator button, and the door opened. She led the five into the elevator and spoke, "Fourth floor."

Time seemed to slow as they passed each floor. "Once we leave the elevator," Lucas said, "only use hand signals. Rachel's superior hearing might tip her off."

The lieutenant whispered. "She and O'Rourke are in room 404."

The door opened to the fourth floor.

Lucas took a deep breath, led the team down the hallway, and stopped beside room 404. While the others pressed their backs along the wall, he knocked, then knocked again. "Rachel, it's me. Lucas."

No response. Lucas glanced at Freddy, who whispered, "Something's not right,"

A cold chill swept up Lucas's neck. He knocked a third time, hoping his partner was wrong. "Officer O'Rourke, this is Detective Nash."

"She's running," Hawk said calmly.

A second later, the sound of shattered glass came from inside the room.

Hawk nudged Lucas aside and kicked in the door. Ducking through a rain of splinters, he burst into the room with his long rifle Taser.

O'Rourke lay on the bed, her hands handcuffed behind her back and a hand towel stuffed in her mouth.

Lieutenant Clark removed the gag and uncuffed the officer as Lucas and Freddy rushed to the shattered window. Rachel had reached the ground floor and ran to the parking lot. She'd jumped or climbed down four stories.

"What tipped her off?" Freddy asked.

Hawk sprinted out the shattered door and ran toward the stairs.

Knowing he'd never reach Rachel in time to stop her, Lucas stood and watched with Freddy.

Lieutenant Clark helped the young officer to her feet.

Below him, Rachel reached Lieutenant Clark's SUV and kicked in the tires with a force only an android could provide. She reached into Melody's car and yanked out the steering wheel like she was pulling a radish from a garden. In seconds, she'd disabled both vehicles.

She stopped beside Lucas's SUV, but instead of disabling his car, Rachel looked up at him and waved. She climbed into his car. With the wail of sirens approaching the hotel, she sped off, squealing smoking tires and fishtailing into traffic.

28

Lucas couldn't wait to go after Rachel. Any doubts about her guilt vanished with the shattered hotel window.

He paced while the lieutenant barked out assignments to capture Rachel and take her down. When she finished, Lucas took her aside. "I think she'll go to my neighbor's house. If you come in with a half dozen cars, she'll slip away before we get deployed. And no drones. She'd hear them before they got close enough to do any good."

"We tried it without backup, and you saw how that worked out." She entered Lucas's address on her phone and studied the surrounding area on a map. "I'll make sure the neighborhood is surrounded. You and Freddy take O'Rourke's patrol car."

She signaled to the young officer, apparently recovered from being overpowered by an android.

Freddy approached O'Rourke. "You might want to sit this one out."

"You sit this one out. I'm going after the bitch." O'Rourke tossed Lucas her key fob.

A black Dakota Industries van drove up. Melody opened the side door and began to pass out Taser long rifles. She handed one to Lucas and one to Freddy.

Hawk showed the two men how to use the weapons. "Rachel's exoskeleton is made of titanium. Bullets have minimal effect." He pointed to his head. "There's little feeling in an artificial human's skull."

Freddy chuckled. "That explains a lot, Numb Skull."

Like others before him, Hawk didn't get Freddy's humor. "An electronic charge to the head will incapacitate her." He touched the middle of his chest. "A shot dead center is a kill shot. I should go with you."

Hawk's speed and strength might come in handy. "I have no objections, but I'll need a hand Taser." Lucas didn't want to walk up to Bernardi's house with a weapon that resembled an assault rifle.

When Freddy flashed a thumbs up, Lucas added his approval. "Stay out of sight in the back seat. And you follow my orders. No more shoving me out of the way."

"If I had shoved you, you'd still be in the hotel room." Hawk pointed to the fourth floor. "I barely touched you."

Melody handed her Taser to Lucas. "Press the red button to activate, aim, and fire. Unlike the rifle, this will only disable her. It won't be fatal."

"Got it." He stuck the weapon in his jacket pocket.

He went to Lieutenant Clark. "If Rachel's not at my neighbor's house, she'll be at the bus depot."

"Ms. Fleming, Officer O'Rourke, and I will wait at the terminal." The lieutenant checked her watch. "Let's roll, Cowboys."

Lucas forced himself not to speed to his house. When he drew closer, he counted forty officers blocking off his neighborhood.

Hawk leaned forward and placed his thick hands on the back of Lucas's seat. "Melody told me you and Freddy talked her out of terminating me."

Lucas glanced in the rearview mirror. "Don't get all mushy on me. Freddy convinced her when he got all teary-eyed."

Hawk clapped Freddy on the back. "Thanks, bro."

Freddy stared at the burly android. "No one says bro anymore."

Hawk scratched the back of his head. "Human slang is so complex. Thanks, cutie pie."

Freddy thumbed toward the android and asked Lucas, "Is he messing with me?"

"I think so." Lucas snickered. "I told you he was different when he wasn't around Melody."

Hawk sat back and smiled.

Lucas turned onto his street. His SUV that Rachel stole sat in front of his house. Perhaps they'd made it in time. "Lock and load."

He turned to Hawk in the back seat. "Go wait by my garage. I don't want to spook my neighbor."

Freddy bit his lower lip. "I have a bad sensation in my gut about this."

"I keep antacids in my bathroom. That reminds me; I have a special assignment for you." He held out a key to his house. "Go inside and make sure Beau is alright and has enough water. Then put the wood slat in the doggie door, so he can't get out when this all comes down."

"You're joking. I'm a trained detective."

"Do I have to pull rank on you?"

"I don't care what you pull. Send Hawk to tend to your personal errands."

Lucas snickered. "I don't think Beau would like him."

"You're right." Freddy snatched the key. "But you owe me."

Freddy and Hawk climbed from the patrol car and crossed the yard toward Lucas's house.

He parked behind his SUV. Since Rachel might be watching, he walked to his neighbor's house like he was about to ask for a cup of sugar. He stuffed his hand in his jacket and grabbed the Taser.

He pressed the activation button and kept it in his pocket.

The curtains were drawn in all the windows of Bernardi's house. If Rachel were inside, the old man would be in danger—change in plans. He waved to Freddy and Hawk to join him.

The android arrived first. When Freddy joined him, he sucked in a gulp of air. "I ran a 4.9 forty in college."

Hawk chuckled. "But can you do this?" He reached out to a tree beside the driveway and snapped a three-inch branch in two with one hand.

If she was in the house, Lucas hoped Rachel would surrender quietly. He didn't want Hawk to kick in his neighbor's door. He gestured for him to cover the back door. Hawk disappeared around the corner and rattled the gate when he jumped over.

Before he touched the doorbell, Bernardi opened the door. The old man was holding a can of Amazon Stout. "I was expecting you."

Lucas let out a sigh of relief at seeing the old man unharmed. "Is Rachel here?"

"She was." He sipped the beer and noticed Freddy's rifle. "Would you fellas like one?"

Freddy smiled. "Sure."

Lucas glared at Freddy. "Some other time."

The gate rattled again, and Hawk appeared beside them with his rifle at his side. "I heard."

The old man took another gulp. "I gave Rachel the keys to my pickup. She said she didn't want me involved, just needed transportation to the bus stop. She's leaving the Silverado in the lot, and I'll bum a ride to pick it up tomorrow. I slipped her some cash before she left. She's a sweet girl."

Damn. He wished Bernardi were more like the recluse he remembered before Rachel showed up. "Red Silverado, right? What year?"

"'21."

Lucas tapped the collar of his jacket, activating the police radio. "Lieutenant, Rachel's driving a red Silverado pickup."

"My truck's old but dependable." Bernardi finished his beer and let out a belch. "Like my girlfriend, Lydia."

"I'll make sure you get your truck back." Lucas thanked his neighbor and hurried to O'Rourke's car with Freddy and Hawk.

29

By the time Lucas arrived at the bus station, a dozen officers and security members from Dakota Industries outnumbered arriving passengers. Red flashing lights came from two police drones circling overhead, no doubt recording the activity below.

Hawk and Freddy climbed out of O'Rourke's patrol car while Lucas sat in his SUV. He knew they were too late.

Lucas stepped over the police tape and joined Lieutenant Clark and Melody Fleming beside Bernardi's red pickup. "The damn hood's still warm," Clark said. "No one's left the scene. We're interviewing everyone, staff and passengers. I arranged to view the security footage."

Their effort was a waste of time. "Don't bother. She's a hundred miles away by now. I suspect you'll discover Rachel never went inside."

"What do you mean?" the lieutenant shouted. "Damn it; you said if she weren't at your neighbor's house, she'd be at the bus terminal."

"Rachel's not stupid. She abandoned the pickup here to throw us off the track. I'm sure you'll find a report of a stolen vehicle nearby. With so many officers playing backup, I'm certain she made it out of town."

"Son of a bitch." Clark smacked the hood of the truck. "I'll put out an APB."

Clark called O'Rourke over. "Find out if anyone's missing a car."

"Yes, Lieutenant." The officer reported to a sergeant at the front entrance.

"You might be a little vague on her hair color." He explained about android hair.

"Shit!" The lieutenant clamped her eyes shut and let out a breath. "The crackling sound you hear is my career going up in flames."

Melody gave her a wistful smile. "Don't consider this a failure, Lieutenant. This isn't the first time I've underestimated Rachel."

A news crew arrived with a satellite dish on top of their van. An attractive blonde reporter climbed out and surveyed the scene, no doubt hoping this was more than a missing person case.

Clark rolled her eyes. "Oh, goody. My favorite part of the job."

She stepped over the yellow tape and approached the reporter.

Lucas grabbed the Taser from his pocket and offered the weapon to Melody.

She held up one hand. "Keep it, Detective. You never know if you'll need it."

"Thanks."

He approached Freddy and Hawk, who weren't busy with much of anything. "Now, I get why you never managed to apprehend her, Hawk."

The android's frustration suggested he needed a branch to snap in two. "Rachel always manages to convince a man to help: Dr. Beltran, you, your neighbor, Freddy."

"Me?" Freddy asked. "How did I help her?"

Lucas tapped his chest. "I'm the one who messed up this case. I kept her away from you. Damn, I can't believe a woman...an android could manipulate me like this."

His friend clapped Lucas on the shoulder. "Women have manipulated us saps all our lives. Why would an artificial woman be any different?"

Lucas bit his lower lip. She'd made an idiot of him. No, that wasn't entirely accurate. He made a fool of himself. He had to find her and bring her in.

Freddy grabbed Lucas's shoulder. "I don't like what I see in your eye. You need to let this go. The Feds will oversee finding Rachel anyway."

Lucas shook off Freddy's grip. "She's just a machine, like the car she probably stole."

His partner glanced away. "I was wrong about her. No mere machine could outsmart two brilliant detectives like you and me."

This time, his friend's humor didn't work. Lucas walked away.

"Don't expect any help from me!" Freddy called out.

He didn't want Freddy's assistance. Lucas's career, even his life, meant little. He was prepared to abandon everything to apprehend Rachel. He wouldn't ask anyone to do the same.

He walked to the parking lot entrance, gazing up and down the street, trying to imagine where Rachel might be headed. She might have slipped away, but he wouldn't give up. If she made it out of town, he'd go after her, even if it meant leaving his job.

Hawk stood beside him. His tough-guy image of the past week had vanished. "I realize you don't consider me a living creature, but from my perspective, you saved my life."

"Freddy stood up for you as well."

The android nodded toward Freddy. "He'll help you find her if you ask him, you know."

Lucas knew.

"I don't know how Rachel became this way," Hawk said. "Sure, there's a period of adjusting to society. I went through it myself. Guess I still am, but to murder two humans is unforgivable. All future artificial humans will be compared to the evil she did."

"You underestimate yourself. I'll never forget you."

Hawk smiled. "Thanks, bro."

30

Two days after Rachel disappeared, Lucas sat across from Lieute-nant Clark in the Homicide conference room down the hall from her office. After dictating most of the final report, he summarized Rachel's complicity in the deaths of Dr. Beltran and Captain Koenig. He learned the details from interviews with Melody and Hawk the day before.

"Knowing Dr. Beltran's decision to discontinue Project Halo meant her own termination, Rachel prepared a plan. When the COO summoned her, she assumed the worst and brought with her a small sample of the nerve agent she'd learned about from Beltran. After administering the toxin with a final hug, she drove his car to the Happy Camper, which she knew Koenig and Colonel Urias frequented. She shot out two lights in the parking lot and intended to shoot them both when they left the bar, but when Koenig exited with Maria Alvarez, Rachel followed them to Alvarez's house. She went inside and shot Koenig twice while the woman got ready for a sexual encounter with the captain."

Lucas took a long swallow of water before continuing. "She took off and drove to Beltran's house and disconnected her history to the Failsafe device. She prepared to leave and begin a new life when she observed my presence outside the residence. She changed her plans and left with me in my car."

Lucas continued the report about the rest of the week, including the circumstances of becoming aware that Rachel was an artificial human. He finished the dictation. "End Report."

Lieutenant Clark gave the final instruction. "Save to hard drive with a copy to my personnel file. End recording."

Clark folded her hands in front of her. "There's one question you didn't address in your narrative. After Rachel spent the night in your guest room, you left for work the next morning. Why didn't she leave and start her life over as a human like she originally planned?"

Lucas rubbed the back of his neck. "I'm not sure."

"I think she fell in love with you."

She manipulated him from the moment they met. "Rachel's conception of love came from old movies and Patsy Cline songs."

Clark drummed her fingers on the table. "Your actions since meeting Rachel, while regrettable, are not criminal. You violated a number of regulations, and therefore, the captain approved a five-day suspension."

That's all? If he hesitated, Lucas might not go through with his decision. His life was about to change. This place and these people held many memories, mostly favorable.

Lucas placed his badge in front of the lieutenant. He set his revolver beside it. He removed an envelope from his pocket and handed Clark a four-line resignation letter.

Clark read the letter. "Damn! The mistakes you made don't justify separation. I'm not accepting your resignation. I'll give you an indefinite leave of absence."

Lucas felt grateful that the department wanted him back. "I don't know how long it'll take."

"Take as much time as you need." She set the letter next to his badge. "I need you back here."

Her words meant a lot to Lucas.

"Going after Rachel will be dangerous. She's already killed two people."

"I didn't make this decision lightly."

"Then I hope you find her. Plenty of questions remain about Dakota Industries, not just in the deaths of Dr. Beltran and Captain Koenig."

"That was all Rachel."

"I have to answer about my own role in all this. The media isn't going to give up. Imagine the circus if they found out this case involved androids."

"Any criticism you receive is unjustified. I tried to make that clear in my report."

"I appreciate your efforts, but not everyone will see my decisions in a positive light. I was in charge when Rachel slipped through our trap."

If he managed to return Rachel intact, the heat would be off Clark somewhat.

The lieutenant stood. "You have any idea where she would go?"

"A few. Rachel likes the mountains. She might go back to the cabin. She also mentioned Mexico, and of course, she speaks the language, among others."

"Mexico's a vast country, and you don't speak Spanish."

"I'll get by." Lucas stood and held out his hand to shake.

Clark ignored the hand and hugged him for the first time ever. "Be careful."

He let go and left without looking back. In the hallway, Lucas struggled to keep his emotions in check. He walked down the hall and stopped beside Freddy's desk.

Freddy handed him a tissue. "I think you're about to cry."

Lucas laughed. "Shut up."

Freddy's expression hardened. "I wish I could go with you, Bulldog."

"Just take care of Beau until I return. You're the only one I trust with him." Lucas shook his friend's hand.

"Will do." With misty eyes, his friend rose and hugged Lucas.

Lucas said goodbye to the others and left the office, perhaps for the last time.

In the lobby, Officer O'Rourke chatted with a fellow officer. She glanced his way, hurried to him, and shook his hand. "I hope you find that bitch."

He took an envelope from his jacket and handed it to her.

"What's this?" O'Rourke unfolded the paper. "A letter of recommendation?"

"Someone told me you want to be a homicide detective."

She gave the letter back. "I'm not ready."

"I think you are. I know you are."

"That means a lot, Bulldog." She kissed his cheek and stuck the recommendation in her pocket.

He headed for the door, then turned back and called, "I'll find her."

Outside, Calvin Hawk waited with an umbrella in a steady rain.

Lucas went out, and the big artificial human handed him the umbrella.

"Melody Fleming wants to meet with you." Hawk gestured toward a white limo with dark tinted windows across the street.

"I thought you'd be terminated by now."

"She has another assignment for me."

Lucas didn't want to talk to the woman, but she'd cooperated in wrapping up the details of the two murders. He crossed the street to the limousine.

Hawk opened the limo door.

Lucas climbed in and handed the umbrella back to the android. He sat across from Melody, who smiled with her usual confidence.

"You look like a man on a mission. You going after her?"

"I am."

She reached inside a leather briefcase and gave him an electronic reader. "*We* want you to find Rachel and eliminate her. I've prepared an employment agreement, so there's no misunderstanding."

Her offer didn't surprise Lucas, but he had no intention of terminating Rachel. Out of curiosity, he read the document. The money was more than he'd made over the past five years. "You're more than generous, but I'm not sure I want to report to anyone."

"The offer's not generosity, Mr. Nash. It's business. After this is over, and I terminate Hawk and Rachel, Dakota Industries will need a new chief of security."

Why the buttering up? Hawk was standing in the rain with his back to the limousine. She was treating him more like a valet than head of security. He'd never let her treat him that way. "Why would you want me? I messed up this whole thing."

"You're tenacious, something I thought Hawk would become." She glanced at her android with a surprising expression of compassion.

Melody shook off her momentary lapse into humanity. "You'll have carte blanche. The only requirement is that Rachel must be terminated, not apprehended. And this needs to be done quietly with no publicity anyone could trace back to Dakota."

That sounded like more than one condition, but he had no intention of quibbling. Lucas felt himself weaken. He planned to go after Rachel anyway. He might as well get paid for his effort.

She held up one finger. "Just one more requirement."

That better be her last one.

Melody pointed to Hawk, still standing with his back to the limo. "You're to take him with you."

"I thought he didn't follow orders well."

"He assures me that he'll observe yours."

Lucas chuckled. "And you believe him like I believed Rachel." He let out a sigh. Over the past few days, he'd grown to appreciate Hawk. "Deal."

Melody shook his hand with the grip of a sailor. "Remember, if you find her, don't hesitate. Apparently, you've struggled with your feelings for Rachel, but she's not alive. She's a machine. Construction companies sometimes have defective equipment that injures or even kills humans because of a defect; if they can't repair it, they get rid of the machine. Any questions?"

Only one. "Why didn't you give her a past like you did for Hawk?"

"That was our plan before she killed Dr. Beltran. Solving a problem by committing murder demonstrated the ultimate disregard for the Prime Directive. There's no way to rehabilitate her now."

Melody handed him a silver case the size of a purse.

Lucas opened it. "What's this?"

"The latest high-tech handgun Taser with a laser sight. It might appear undersized but packs a kick more powerful than the long rifle. It's constructed of ceramics to pass through x-ray. It should fry the circuits and terminate her…whatever part of her anatomy it hits.

"You can adjust the power with the dial on the handle. I recommend leaving it set on ten. Ten will guarantee her destruction. If you don't take her out when presented with the opportunity, you'll be risking your own life."

Melody took the reader and swiped the screen, revealing an e-contract. Lucas read through it and signed with her stylus. She stuck the device back in her briefcase. "Check your account balance. The first month's salary has already been deposited."

"You're pretty sure of yourself." He checked his phone, called up the account, and let out a whistle. "How'd you obtain my bank information without a court order?"

Melody ignored the question with a laugh. "After we confirm her termination, we'll pay you a generous bonus."

Because money is the most important item on earth. He started to get out, but Melody grabbed his wrist. "Before you go after her, remember this, the danger she presents isn't just to you or my company. Rachel is a threat to humanity."

Her words sounded like hyperbole. "I'll never underestimate her again."

The rain slowed to a drizzle as Lucas climbed out of the car with the silver case.

Hawk flashed him a smile. "You found out how hard it is to say no to Melody Fleming."

"I forgot about your excellent hearing."

"Why do you think I stood next to the limo in a downpour?" He folded the umbrella and shook it as they crossed the street. He reached into his jacket and pulled out gray handcuffs. "Titanium. They're designed to restrain androids in case you might need them."

"Thanks." Lucas stuffed the cuffs in his jacket and gestured toward his parked SUV. "You hungry?"

"I don't get hungry, but if you are, I'd consume something."

In his car, Lucas set the destination to Geraldo's, his favorite fast Mexican food joint, despite the name.

Minutes later, they got out and went to the window. "They make fabulous tacos."

"I rarely eat meat. Beef is dead cow flesh, you know."

"They don't go out back and slaughter a cow. The cows are already dead."

Hawk didn't look convinced. "Don't they have any vegetarian dishes?"

"They have fish tacos."

"Fish are living organisms too."

Lucas chuckled. "I respect vegetarians, but I think you should give it a try. It won't kill you."

After ordering the tacos, they found an isolated table. With some hesitation, the android took a bite of a taco, then another. He winced like he'd cracked a tooth. He swallowed, then took another bite and wiped his mouth with a paper napkin. He appeared to like the food.

As the meal went on, Lucas enjoyed not talking about Rachel. "You enjoying the tacos?"

Hawk smiled. "Very tasty, but I feel bad for the cow."

"Let's find a bar and talk over a plan to locate Rachel. You do drink, don't you?"

"Everything except alcoholic beverages."

Lucas rolled his eyes. He got up and tossed the trash into a receptacle shaped like a Saguaro Cactus.

When they reached his SUV, Hawk let out a belch. He covered his mouth. "I've never belched before. Beef can't be good for you!"

"Warn me if you're going to fart."

Hawk climbed into the passenger seat and shut the door.

Lucas reached for the driver's door, and his phone rang. The call came from an unknown number. He stood beside the car and answered, "Lucas Nash."

"Don't come after me." Rachel's voice.

Rachel! Could he find any clues to her location? "Why would I?"

"Because that's what you do. I'm getting rid of the phone as soon as I end the call, so don't try to track me that way."

Lucas didn't hear anything in the background that might clue him in to her location. Perhaps Hawk's hearing could. "Do you mind if I put you on speakerphone?"

"Do it, and I'll hang up."

"What do you want, Rachel?"

"I'm sorry I wasn't entirely truthful with you."

Entirely truthful? "You lied the whole time."

"Only to protect myself. I *had* to eliminate Dr. Beltran, Lucas. He left me no choice. He planned to eliminate me!"

"What about Captain Koenig?"

"Koenig was prepared to convince the Pentagon to go along with the termination of Project Halo and elimination of all artificial humans. I did what I had to, to ensure my survival."

Her weak self-defense argument—how had she fooled him so completely?

Rachel's voice quivered. "I never lied about my feelings toward you."

She was still trying to manipulate him, to play on his emotions. He pictured an artificial tear sliding down her face. "Spare me."

The call ended.

His hand trembled as Lucas shouted into the phone. "I'm coming for you, Rachel!"

31

Six months later.

In the dimly lit bar named La Cantina, just south of San Vicente, Mexico, Lucas ran a hand over the beard he'd grown in the past month. He checked the cards in his hand and slid five pretzel sticks to the center of the table.

On the other side, Hawk studied Lucas's face and called the bet. "I think you're bluffing again."

Lucas laid his cards on the table. "Heart flush."

"Estupido Americano!" Hawk tossed his cards in the middle of the table.

Lucas smiled. "I know a little Spanish."

"Three Jacks. I thought I had you. The odds of keeping three of one suit and drawing two more are…"

"I don't care what the odds are." The android's pretzels dwindled to seven. Lucas had several dozen. He handed Hawk ten of his. He shuffled the deck and dealt. "I think we're close this time."

Hawk picked up each card as Lucas dealt. "You thought we'd find her in Albuquerque, in Las Vegas, and Yuma. We have photos and video of Rachel, but she's managed to elude us. Now, all we have is the word of a fisherman in a village so tiny it isn't even on a map."

Lucas swept up his cards. Without looking at them, he tossed two pretzels to the middle of the table.

He and Hawk couldn't follow financial transactions because Rachel apparently used only cash. What little confidence they had came from Lucas's intuition. He checked his cards. Three tens!

Hawk looked at his. "I forgot the rules. Can I draw four?"

"Sure."

"I'll take four," Hawk called the bet.

It had taken Lucas at least three months to trust the android. He didn't want to be used like Rachel had used him. They weren't exactly friends, but they spent most of their time together, working, sharing meals, and Hawk listening to Lucas's old war stories.

Lucas dealt the cards. "What's Melody Fleming really like?"

Hawk picked up his cards and smiled. "She's tough, demanding, and authoritative. She likes being in charge."

"Is she happy?"

"She's rich. She doesn't have to be happy." He slid five pretzels forward.

Lucas folded and glanced at a twenty-year-old television broadcasting CNN in Spanish. A reporter was interviewing Melody Fleming in her office. He pointed out the broadcast.

The android turned around and watched.

Lucas didn't know exactly what Melody and the reporter were saying. However, the visuals stuck like a stab in the gut when a video of Hawk running the forty-yard dash came on the screen with two Spanish words that didn't need translating: Proyecto Halo.

Hawk faced him. "They're starting Project Halo up again."

"And producing artificial humans."

"Melody didn't mention androids in her interview. She was vague about artificial intelligence."

Lucas stared at the television. What changed Melody's mind, or had she been lying all along?

The door flew open, and the old man who'd claimed he spotted

Rachel burst into the cantina. He saw them when Lucas waved and hurried to their booth. "Cervesa, por favor."

Lucas scooted over for the man to sit. He held up two fingers. He downed the last inch in his bottle as the waitress brought the bottles.

She set one beer in front of the old man, the other next to Lucas's pretzels. She turned and headed back to the bar.

The old man drank Lucas's beer and opened the bottle in front of him. "Senior Hawk, Senior Nash, Es Raquel."

Rachel. Lucas forced himself to look away from the news. For the moment, Project Halo didn't matter. He'd spent half a year searching for her.

"Ella tiene un bote y una casita." The old man took another gulp.

"What did he say?" Lucas asked Hawk.

"She has a boat and a small house."

Lucas grabbed the bottle to keep the old man from drinking more. "Where? Donde…"

"Donde Esta ella?" Where is she, Hawk asked.

"La aldea."

Hawk looked excited. "She's at the fishing village he told us about."

"Si, village. San Avila."

Lucas handed the man a napkin and a Sharpie. "Map." He made a drawing gesture.

"Mapa. Si." The man sketched a rough draft of San Avila. He drew a square and a boat near the edge of the shoreline. "Chica Bonita."

"Si." Hawk smiled. "Pretty girl."

It was Rachel.

Lucas gave the man his beer and a hundred bucks. "Let's go." He left the pretzels. "Enjoy, Senor."

On the way out, Lucas slipped the waitress a Tubman. "Gracias."

As Lucas drove, Hawk sat in the back seat, making sure their Tasers remained in working order. They hadn't fired them in

231

practice in more than a month. When he finished, he tapped Lucas on the shoulder. "How did you beat me in poker? The rules are simple. I understand the odds. I don't show any emotion, do I?"

Lucas chuckled. "No, but I know how to bluff, and you haven't gotten the hang of that."

"Bluff. It means convincing someone you have a better hand than you do. Isn't that dishonest?"

"No!"

"You should have explained the concept better."

"I was hungry, something you don't experience."

When they reached the village, Lucas glanced in the rearview mirror and barely recognized himself. Rachel wouldn't either. Once Lucas had tracked her to Baja, Mexico, he stopped shaving. A beard would make it more difficult for her to recognize him.

Hawk's appearance hadn't changed. As they'd planned, he served as backup with a long rifle Taser.

The quarter moon provided little light, a definite advantage. Clutching their Tasers in the sleeping village, Lucas and Hawk walked through the quiet hamlet with an occasional dog bark interrupting the silence. An old shack with roses like Bernardi's had to be Rachel's.

Hawk touched a rope tied to a tractor tire with his shoe. "She's taken the boat. See the outline?"

"If you say so." They reached the shoreline and scanned the black water and whitecaps. Lucas pulled his night vision glasses from his pocket and studied the ocean. Neither of them spotted anything until he pointed. "Two o'clock."

"I think that's her."

Hawk took cover behind a cart and rested his Long Rifle on a mound of hay.

Lucas read the map one more time, then stuffed the Taser in his jacket and made his way back to her shack.

With his night vision glasses, he peered in a window—no Rachel or anyone inside. He glanced back at Hawk, hiding behind a cart of hay, and flashed a thumbs up.

He tried the door. It opened without effort. The prospect of intruders didn't frighten Rachel.

Lucas's heart pounded. He hadn't seen friends or Beau for half a year. Would his quest finally end?

He checked the dial set to the maximum, ten. In Melody's limo, it sounded easy to terminate Rachel, but it wouldn't be. He'd spent the past few months wondering whether he could do it. He reminded himself she was not a living entity.

Lucas took off the night vision glasses, allowing his eyes to adjust to the darkness. He wondered what he would say when she entered.

He also considered the Taser. Lieutenant Clark wanted Rachel brought in unharmed. Melody insisted that he terminate the android, and she was paying his bills. But why was she restarting Project Halo in such a public way?

At Hawk's suggestion, Lucas texted her once a week to keep her up to date and tell her how helpful and efficient he'd been—how he followed orders like a good soldier or police officer would be expected to do. Now, she was on the news announcing she'd reactivated Project Halo and showed Hawk running the forty. Son-of-a-bitch. Had he inadvertently given Melody confirmation that an android could follow orders?

Did moving forward with the production of androids mean Melody had voided their agreement? Did he need to get rid of Rachel?

Footsteps crunched the ground outside the front door, shaking his concentration.

When Rachel entered and closed the door, he pointed the Taser at her.

She turned on a battery-powered lantern and noticed his presence but didn't appear to recognize him. "Hombre…"

"Hello, Rachel."

She stood less than ten feet away from the end of his weapon, aimed at the center of her chest. His defensive instincts went on high alert. Remembering her lunge at the rattlesnake at the cabin, he knew how swift and powerful she was.

Rachel surprised him when she smiled. "Lucas? I would never have recognized you, Bulldog. Why did they send *you* after me?"

"I volunteered, entirely my idea."

"You're still mad at me about killing Dr. Beltran and Captain Koenig? I called you, so I could explain why I had to do it. They left me no choice. I had to survive."

The more she talked, the more human she sounded, like the young woman he came to care about before finding out she was an android. Still, this Rachel, the artificial human, was psychotic and dangerous. She'd kill him if given a chance. He'd never give her the opportunity.

She laughed. "You think I'm crazy. I'm not. I had a choice. I could have let them end my existence, but I chose to save myself."

"For twelve years, I've heard every justification for murder you can imagine. Yours doesn't even make the top ten."

In the dim light, he saw the pleading in her artificial eyes. "Can't we put this behind us?" She held out a hand. "You don't need to do this. I have plenty of money. The people here are wonderful. I speak Spanish, of course. We could have a fabulous life, just the two of us."

"You lied to me about everything."

"It broke my heart when I left."

Sure, it did, Patsy.

She stepped toward him.

He took a step back. "Rachel, stop." This had to end.

"I've changed. This village has changed me. I wake every morning and watch the sunrise and feel the wet sand between my toes and a cool breeze. I bought a boat. An old man taught me to

fish, and his wife showed me how to cook! I'm learning to paint."
She pointed to a watercolor of a whale surfacing by the door.

"Very nice."

"I'm teaching English to children. This place is exactly the kind
of place I wanted when I used to dream about living among humans
back at Dakota."

A tear slid down Rachel's face. "Stay with me. Send for Beau.
We can be together always."

Lucas wouldn't let her manipulate him.

Rachel cocked her head. "You're not alone. You brought that
crazy Calvin Hawk. I can't trust you." A flicker of anger swept
across her face. She lunged toward him.

He fired the Taser.

Her face registered surprise as she took the voltage and stumbled
past him. She fell to the floor, jerking and twitching. A moment
later, she grew still. Her eyes stared at the ceiling.

The room smelled of electrical charge. Lucas couldn't take his
eyes off the blonde hair covering half of Rachel's face. I did it, he
told himself.

Hawk kicked in the door. He stepped through the shattered wood
with his long rifle sweeping the room as a dog barked nearby. "You
did it, Hombre. You damn sure did it. Melody thought you'd find
her, but she didn't think you'd actually shoot her."

Lucas slipped the weapon back into his pocket. "That's why she
sent you. And you didn't tell me?"

"We've become friends, but I take my orders from Melody." He
propped his Taser rifle against the wall, grabbed his phone, and
began to take pictures. "On the way back, we're bound to pick up
Wi-Fi, and I'll send these to Dakota."

Hawk was as deceitful and manipulative as Rachel, but Lucas
didn't want him to recognize his anger and sense of betrayal. If he
could reach the Taser rife without Hawk seeing him, he might fire a
jolt at Hawk. Would he earn a double bonus?

Lucas smiled and kicked away shards of wood. "You need to stop doing that to doors. Stand beside Rachel." Lucas waved him closer to Rachel. He took out his phone and snapped a picture of Rachel's unseeing eyes, so he could send the image later to Melody Fleming at Dakota Industries and Lieutenant Clark and Freddy.

Hawk lifted Rachel over his shoulder like a half-empty laundry bag. "Let's get rid of her body."

"That's not a body. It's a machine, a defective piece of equipment."

32

At the border, with Rachel in the trunk, Lucas flashed his police credentials and crossed without incident. During the twenty-four-hour trip from the border to Green Valley, he plotted his revenge against Melody Fleming. While driving, he called Freddy and Lieutenant Clark. Both agreed to his plan.

A day after returning home and the plan in place, he pulled up to the gate at Dakota Industries. He spoke to the now-familiar robot, "Lucas Nash, to see Calvin Hawk and Melody Fleming."

"Welcome to the Dakota team, Mr. Nash. I'll inform Mr. Hawk you're here. Follow the drive…"

"I know the way."

"…will lead you to the lot across from the entrance. Have a pleasant day."

Lucas parked and checked himself in the mirror. He'd shaved off his beard and cleaned up as best he could. He ran a hand through his long hair he'd yet to cut.

Calvin Hawk stood in the lobby and greeted him like an old friend. "You made it. You're looking well, though I liked the beard."

"I'm glad Melody decided against terminating you."

Hawk smiled. "So am I. For that, I have you to thank."

"I'm here to meet with Ms. Fleming."

"She's with Colonel Urias and a few other Washington officials now. I just stepped out of the meeting."

"Did you run the forty for them or snap a tree limb in two?"

"I can tell you're still upset about Rachel." He led Lucas to the conference room. "I'll be down the hall. If you need anything, just speak to the potted plant by the door."

"A joke?"

"I've been working on my sense of humor. How am I doing?"

"Needs a little work."

The wall beside the door displayed promotional materials for Dakota Industries. He sat and watched the promotional video. "Increase volume."

The sound came up on the screen. The narrator was talking about the next generation of robots. The video showed Hawk exercising, firing a weapon, and dunking a basketball. Then came stock footage of police in distress and military in action. "Dakota Industries, making America safer again."

From what he'd learned since he returned from Mexico, Melody had announced the creation of artificial humans to the public. The story was Breaking News on CNN for several days until a hurricane hit Florida.

Although politicians and religious leaders condemned the announcement, a recent poll showed seventy-one percent of Americans approved of the concept of benevolent androids.

Lucas muted the volume when Melody and Hawk entered. Hawk closed the door and remained standing like a doorman while Melody sat across from Lucas. She checked her watch with an impatient glance. "Thank you again for your work over the last six months. The bonus money will be transferred in a few days."

"From all the publicity, I bet you get your picture on the cover of *Time Magazine*."

"I wouldn't be surprised. I'm sure taking care of Rachel was…difficult. I'm aware how much she meant to you." She smiled at Hawk. "I've grown fond of Mr. Hawk, though he's a machine like any other robot wheeling around here."

If her words offended him, the android didn't show it.

Melody folded her hands in front of her. "I'm surprised Hawk didn't help you dispose of the body. I can't say I approve."

"Wi-Fi is unreliable where we were. I thought it best he return to you and confirm what happened in Mexico as soon as possible, so I put him on a bus. He didn't approve either, but he does follow orders, after all. I made sure no one would find Rachel's body."

"Excellent. You not only resolved a major embarrassment and legal liability for the company, but you demonstrated that an android ingrained with human memories is feasible, with the proper guidance you provided. I want to offer you a position in charge of training our artificial humans destined for law enforcement."

"I have other plans."

Melody's mouth opened in surprise. She wasn't the type of person too many people said no to. "I'm sorry to hear that. Dr. Beltran and I were premature in our pessimistic assessment of Hawk's failure. You proved us wrong. I sent you on a quest in one final attempt to determine whether the concept of artificial humans was still feasible. You furnished weekly texts documenting your success with Mr. Hawk."

"Son-of-a-bitch!" Lucas clamped his eyes shut. He'd figured her scheme out long before the meeting but wasn't ready to show his hand.

Melody laughed. "Thanks to you, Project Halo will be a monumental achievement. I just left a meeting where the Pentagon confirmed they are willing to take a second review of the program."

Lucas gazed across the table. "I guess now wouldn't be the best time for adverse publicity."

Melody's eyes narrowed with contempt. "An artificial human, Rachel outsmarted you in a few days. Calvin Hawk did the same things in a few months. My advice is not to try to outmaneuver me."

"You're probably right."

"Nothing will interfere with Project Halo." She smacked the table. The sound alone shook off loose dust trapped on the surface for years. "We've developed plans for expansion and adding to production staff. It turns out, our original estimates were far too low. The military loves the concept, especially since our androids are produced in the United States. America first, as Trump used to say."

Lucas chuckled. "And how did that turn out?"

"Is there anything else? I think you're wasting my time." She slid the chair back and stood.

"About the bonus money, you can keep every dollar. I want to show you one thing before you go."

She sat back down.

Lucas couldn't help but smile. He picked up his phone and called Freddy.

He answered on the first ring and switched to video.

"May I cast the call to the monitor?" He showed the image to Melody.

With a curl in her lip, she gestured to proceed. "Be my guest, but I really have more important things to attend to."

Lucas pointed the phone to the screen, and Freddy's face appeared on the wall. "Hello again, Lucas. Mr. Hawk, Ms. Fleming."

"How's everything there?"

"Under control."

On the monitor, Freddy turned his phone, revealing Rachel sitting on a couch with Hawk's titanium handcuffs that came in so handy in Mexico. Lieutenant Clark sat at the other end, aiming a long rifle Taser at her.

Melody's face reddened with heat one could fry an egg on.

Hawk dropped into a chair.

"She's much more cooperative than this morning." The lieutenant grinned. "Hello, Lucas."

"We had a deal. We paid you handsomely. You double-crossed me, Nash." Melody glared at Hawk. "This is all your fault."

Lucas chuckled. "Don't blame him. He thought we were friends, that he could trust me, you could trust me. Oops."

"Where is she? Is that an abandoned warehouse?"

"It *is* an abandoned warehouse."

"In Green River?"

Lucas laughed and wagged his finger at her.

Melody's eyes narrowed. "I misjudged you, Nash. I thought I made a deal with a man of integrity."

Lucas rose from his chair and raised his voice. "Don't lecture me about ethics!"

He regained his composure and sat. "Your mistake was giving me a weapon that allowed me to dial back the charge. I thought I'd killed…terminated her. I had to make sure. After I put Hawk on a bus, I opened the trunk to check on her, and imagine my surprise when her eyes blinked open. She grabbed my throat, so I shot her again."

"You should have ended my existence when you had the chance, Lucas," Rachel shouted from the monitor. "You'll regret it. I promise you will."

Melody held her forehead in her hand. "I put my trust in you instead of Hawk, but I couldn't be certain an android would terminate another android. I thought a man who'd lost his job, had few friends, and no wife would want something to rebuild his life. I was wrong. You're right, Hawk. I should have sent you alone."

"You realize," Hawk didn't sound convincing. "Ms. Fleming only has to give me the order, and I'll kill you where you sit."

"I taught you poker. You should know whether I'm bluffing." Lucas pulled the handgun Taser from his pocket and aimed the weapon at Hawk's chest. "So convenient that this is made of ceramic, so it didn't set off any alarms when I entered."

Melody's eyes squinted. "We had a deal."

"Let's make another deal. Don't take this personally; call it business."

"I call it blackmail."

"Blackmail is such an ugly word."

She gritted her teeth, then let out a sigh. She leaned back in her chair. "I'm a businesswoman. I'm reasonable. What's on your mind?"

"Once we crossed the border, I pulled over a few miles up the road and opened the trunk. I discussed my plan with her. She was against the idea, and as you can tell, she still is."

At the warehouse, Rachel slammed her fist into her palm. "I'll never cooperate."

Lucas kept his weapon aimed at Hawk. "I don't think that will be necessary, Rachel, or you wouldn't be so upset."

Melody drummed her fingers on the table. "How much?"

"Not everything in life can be solved with money. I want you to find a sweet, non-psychotic woman, preferably one on life support, and transfer her memories and identity to Rachel."

"She'll no longer be Rachel."

"That's the idea. It's why she's against it."

"What about my rights?" Rachel pleaded.

Lucas felt like throwing something at the screen. "What about your friend, mentor, and father figure's rights; Koenig's rights?"

Rachel shouted. "I demand justice!"

"Justice?" Lucas chuckled. "You're a machine."

Melody studied Lucas's face. "What if I say no? You might be bluffing."

Hawk paused for a moment. "He's not bluffing."

"If we can't make a deal," Lucas said, "Lieutenant Clark takes Rachel to jail. The DA calls a press conference to announce the first trial of an artificial human, the kind the Pentagon wants to invest billions in. Rachel gets tried for murder. Every media outlet will report on the court's decision on whether androids can commit murder. Those overwhelming clients won't even return your phone calls."

"I won't cooperate, Lucas!" Rachel shouted.

Clark fired the Taser at Rachel's arm. Her surprised expression faded, and she closed her eyes. "Sorry, the bitch was getting on my nerves."

Melody took out her inhaler and breathed in a gulp of medication. She put it away with a look of defeat.

"You're not considering this?" Hawk asked Melody.

Lucas knew his long-shot idea was about to become a reality. "My plan will preserve Dakota's position as the leader in benevolent androids. You'll continue to reap untold riches."

"Project Halo was never about wealth, Mr. Nash. It was about making a better future for humanity."

Lucas laughed. He didn't believe her newfound empathy.

"I suppose you want to be financially compensated."

"I want my old job back, and the lieutenant said it's mine no matter what you decide."

Melody let out a ragged groan. "Very well, I agree."

Lucas couldn't help noticing a hint of a smile flicker across Hawk's face. "Before I leave, I want our agreement in writing, and I want to be there when the procedure is performed."

"Agreed."

"How long will it take?"

"Assuming we find an appropriate donor, we can begin this week."

Lucas stuffed the Taser in his jacket.

"Just one simple question, Nash. Why give up a sizable amount of money, a future with our company to do this? Love?" Melody let out a hearty laugh. "Once the memories from a donor are downloaded, Rachel, the Rachel you care for, will no longer exist. Her memory of murdering Dr. Beltran and Captain Koenig will vanish, of course, but so will her feelings for you."

"I know that." He didn't have a simple explanation for wanting to resolve the android problem, as Lieutenant Clark called it.

His emotions regarding Rachel remained complicated. Though she ended two innocent lives, Lucas couldn't help concluding that her defects resulted from errors made by Beltran, Melody, and countless others. Those mistakes resulted in her psychosis, but he didn't think justice would be served by terminating her existence. "I think at important times in life, we need to do what's right."

After signing an agreement with Dakota Industries and transferring Rachel to their custody, Lucas anxiously awaited confirmation that they'd found the perfect donor.

The call came a week later.

He sat in the conference room with Melody, watching the procedures on the monitor. Rachel lay strapped to a gurney and appeared lethargic, though he hadn't a clue how one sedated an android. Even sedated, she resisted until the end, when a technician pressed a device to her neck. The electrical charge did the trick—no more resisting.

"How long will this take?"

Melody got up to leave. "The identity transfer procedure will take at least an hour. Then the various databases we download will last about ninety minutes. After that, she'll come out with her memory as Rachel completely erased and her new identity intact."

"Which is?"

Melody checked her phone. "April West. Ms. West was in a boating accident two days ago. She's single, a high school teacher, and twenty-five. She's intelligent, articulate, and likes pets. She'll make a perfect spokesperson for androids. I'll send you her file."

While they waited, Lucas read more about the donor. She seemed like a wonderful person. The photo showed a woman who only slightly resembled Rachel. She had dark hair, a petite nose, and a sweet smile. April had been an honors student from Alabama. She was single with no children but left a fiancé in Birmingham.

Lucas was angry at Beltran and Melody. They'd screwed up an idea that had potential. They broke a promise to humanity and to an artificial human that she could learn and grow and become as honorable as they were. Melody is the one whose mind should be wiped clean.

It crushed him that Rachel wouldn't remember their time together, but at least the android would emerge with a new life as April West.

The young woman had been air evacuated to a Green River hospital. A Dakota team transferred her memories electronically and stored them in a recording device. After that, the doctors took her off life support and shipped her body back to Birmingham for burial.

After the transfer procedures were completed, the robot entered and led Lucas to a room outside a door marked No Admittance. Melody and Hawk were waiting like expectant parents.

"Did you bring cigars?" Lucas found a comfortable chair at the far end of the room. He flipped through a tablet of magazines like a family member waiting to hear how an operation went.

The door opened, and a white-suited technician came out, guiding Rachel by the arm. Her hair was now brunette, but she looked the same. "The electrical current is stabilizing. She'll be her new self in a minute."

Melody took Rachel's hand with a tenderness Lucas would never have imagined. "How do you feel, April?"

April. That would take getting used to. April wouldn't remember sleeping in the same bed at the cabin, or saving Beau from the snake, or escaping Dakota thugs by driving their SUV into a lagoon. She wouldn't recall anything of her experiences as Rachel, and for that, he felt more than a pang of guilt.

The brunette rubbed her forehead. She spoke with a southern drawl. "I was in an accident?"

"Do you remember what happened?" Hawk asked.

She shook her head no. "My cat." Her voice rose in alarm. "Someone needs to feed my cat, Hennessy."

Melody squeezed her hand. "Your cat is fine. Once you're settled in, we can bring him here if you'd like."

"Her. Hennessy's a girl." She studied Melody's face. "My vision's a little blurry."

"Your eyes will clear up shortly," Melody assured her.

"You must be Melody."

"I am. Melody Fleming. You're going to work for me when you're up to it."

Lucas watched the scene unfold with more than a little regret. Rachel was gone.

Her artificial human body was the same, but her mind was replaced by a woman he'd never met. He pictured Rachel's blonde hair the first time he saw her and the baseball cap she wore backward, trying to look like a boy. He remembered the touch of her body as she lay in bed beside him at Bernardi's cabin. He recalled their first and only kiss. She would remember none of it.

The young woman bit her lip and cast an apprehensive look at Hawk. "You're Calvin Hawk, chief of security for Dakota Industries."

He gave her a sweeping bow. "At your service, Ra... April."

She shook his hand. "Can I see myself in a mirror?"

Melody pointed to the wall next to Lucas. "There's a mirror by that gentleman."

April crossed the room on steadier feet and stopped beside the mirror. She blinked several times and studied Lucas. "I don't know you."

"My name's Lucas. Lucas Nash."

She sounded like a southern belle. "Nice to meet you, Mr. Nash."

Lucas swallowed a lump in his throat. He forced himself not to think of this young woman as Rachel, but with Rachel's face staring at him, it was hard. "Are you feeling better, Miss West?"

She nodded with a friendly smile. "Call me April. I feel wonderful. Thank you all for…for saving me."

"The person you need to thank the most is Mr. Nash," Melody said.

"Is that right?" She checked her appearance in the mirror, then stuck her hand in the back of her hair and made an adjustment. Instantly, her hair turned blonde. "I think that looks better, don't you?" she said, sounding like Scarlett O'Hara.

"You look lovely."

She fluffed her hair and smiled at him in the mirror. "They won't believe you; you know."

"What?"

She winked at Lucas and grabbed his hand with a familiar cold touch. She kissed his cheek and whispered without a trace of an accent. "I don't know how I'll ever repay you for saving me, Bulldog."

The End

ABOUT THE AUTHOR

Mystery writer, Michael Murphy, lives in Arizona with his four children, four rescue dogs and a feral cat.

BOOKS BY MICHAEL MURPHY

Goodbye Emily
WOODSTOCK NOVEL

Scorpion Bay
MYSTERY NOVEL

**JAKE AND LAURA HISTORICAL MYSTERY SERIES
SET IN THE 1930'S**

The Yankee Club
BOOK ONE

All That Glitters
BOOK TWO

Wings in the Dark
BOOK THREE

The Big Brush-off
BOOK FOUR